Unzipped
Twenty-One

Hallie Hart

PRAISE FOR THE *UNZIPPED* SERIES

"Hallie Hart is the next E.L. James with this riveting novel of innocence and seduction!"

Caroline McBride, novelist

"The *Unzipped* series by Hallie Hart is an absolute must-read for any discerning female. Juicy, seductive, and completely compelling, you can't put them down. Hart shows insight into her incredible international life through her modeling career, and the lusty males barking at her door. Learning through her alcoholic and drug-addled mother and her life growing up in Manhattan, and on the French Riviera. Prepare to learn a few things!"

Lucia Gillot, Staff Writer SPIN, European Editor WONDERLUST, New York Metropolitan Magazine, Yahoo, AOL

"Brimming with lush detail. A true conversation starter, one that you will have you debating with yourself long after you turned the last page... is this fiction or not?
Celebrities, fashion, sex, drugs, money, love, hate... all the makings of a steamy novel!"

Steven Lyon, Film maker and Editor in Chief, The Indulge Magazine

First published in Great Britain by House of Hart Publishing in 2023

Produced by Softwood Books, Suffolk, UK

Text © Hallie Hart 2023

ISBN: 979-8-9884589-2-0

This book is dedicated to every woman out there fighting to be heard. You'll find your voice, if you just listen. Be strong and focused and don't let anyone speak for you. Just hang on and keep believing in yourself, always.

One of my favourite quotes is, "Figure out who you are separate from your family and the person you're in a relationship with. Find who you are in this world and what you need to feel good alone. I think that's the most important thing in life. Find a sense of self. With that, you can do anything else." – Angelina Jolie

CHAPTER I

Five Years Later… Winter New York City

You're probably wondering who I ended up with… what makes you think it was just one? Men have been running this game of leading multiple girls around for centuries, even having multiple wives. Why should I be any different? Why should I be any different than Tory? When you hear or see it enough, you begin to do it. You mimic the authorities in your life, until you are the only one that you mimic. Make sense? To me it does, but if you continue on this path with me, you'll see everything clearly. Almost like you're living it with me. This fucked up tale is something that goes on for a while. I have many more stories of my life and the unheard of, behind the private, and well-known peoples lives, including myself, that no one, I mean no one knows about. The existence that I've lived is a full pitcher of life's purest indulgence. I hope you find it's as yummy and delicious as hot molten cake at a Jean George restaurant, or as equally as fucked up as putting a hot poker in your eye socket while watching it burn out. I told you I liked Bukowski, *didn't I?*

I was told by a friend today that I have the most fascinating stories. I found that ironically funny. He was one of the men in my life that I met while modeling in Paris. We're still friends, even after we stopped playing around. He knows a bit about me, but not everything, that is for certain. He has no idea how fascinating the river of stories runs. He only knows what I tell him. Here's where I will let it all out, my story. It's also where the truth or at least half-truths will unfold. I have to hide a bit behind embellishments, I couldn't for a second tell the entire truth, I would be in a world of trouble. It's not because the truth isn't just as exciting, it's just that I need to hide a bit, so that I'm not completely revealed, so that I am not completely vulnerable to the gossipy people that want to stick it in my side like a sharp knife through butter. So I don't come off as some fucking monster of a sex addict and or a cold-hearted bitch like my Tory. Sex has become something else for me now, but enough of that, we'll have plenty of time later to talk about this and that.

I'm 21 now and five years have passed. I didn't celebrate my twenty-first because I've been drinking and carrying on for years, so I don't feel, nor do I act my age. I've gained some insight and hold onto my heart closely now. I don't want everyone to get in there with their greedy little hands, I need to keep part of me joyful and exuberant. My life isn't miserable now, it's just seasoned full of sex, love, deceit, money, friends that come and go, success stories, failures in some of all, and what always remains in my life; my mother Tory.

Let's get back to where we were. Ahh yes the night I walked in fashion week NYC and I'd just turned 21 is where I'll pick back up. "Hello Allie, Happy belated birthday", Tory stood tall and ever so beautiful. She wore a white Tom Ford suit with a signature white silk blouse that was unbuttoned down to the third button, very Tory as well. She loved to work masculine in with feminine in her fashion and life for that matter. She had a pair of cut out boots to match. All in a version of one color, she knew how to bring it, I'll give her that. I mean I could see what others did, she was stunning, sexy and knew it. She had the room. I often wondered if I would someday have that power. Maybe I already did a little, but not to this degree, I may have youth, but she had the power I now wanted.

"Hi, thanks, I'm surprised you remembered. What are you doing here, you're the last person I expected to be here." I smirked a smile at her, because I was actually pleasantly surprised to see my mother at one of my runway shows for James John. I always wanted her to be proud of me. I couldn't help but be a bit suspicious as well. *Why is she here? She wants something, Tory doesn't show up for me, who am I kidding, she fucking wants something, so typical.* I began to feel the fuel of anger start to rise up in my mouth. "Why are you here? I know you're not doing this to be my mother all of a sudden!"

"Oh Allie, don't get so upset, your face is beet red, you'll overheat and smear your makeup if you're not careful," she said as she continued. "Just listen, I have something to tell you, your grandmother died and the will is being read next week," Tory said with half a smile. I knew her mother and she hated one another, and that Eve wasn't nice to her, but I happened to love my grandmother, so I wanted to wipe the smile off her damn face, yet I still wanted to hug her, I knew she loved Eve as well, even if she wasn't a good mother to her either.

"Tory, I'm walking in five minutes, thank you for letting me know and I'll ring you tomorrow, ok." I walked away quickly as the tears streamed down my face. I got emotional for a second and then took a deep breath, I had no room for crying right now.

The backstage crew ran over and shoved me towards the

catwalk and into my place in line. I heard a faint string of words in my head from Ella.. *"You are loved, you are loved."* Something I would do when I was a kid, repeating these words made me smile, a memory of days when I needed a friend and didn't have one, so I made her up. Her name was Ella, and she was always there. Don't ask me why, but Ella was half white and half black, with long black curly hair, she had oversized eyes, and a defining slim nose, she had perfect hands for some reason; long and thin, like a pianist, and she was taller than I and had amazing fashion sense. I know it sounds ridiculous, but I was a child with a great imagination. I spoke back to Ella in my head, "Thank you Ella, I knew you would never leave me." I shook my head with sheer joy that I could see her so clearly once again. It was a huge relief, and a comfort to have this *friend* back.

"You're up Allie, go go go!" the stage manager yelled as she tapped me on the butt. I walked fast until I got to the edge of the stage. I was walking yet again for James John. I felt like a queen in his clothes. They oozed sex and bling, it was a different me, the me I secretly wanted to embrace more and more. The crowd was full of Hollywood A-listers and beautiful people. I walked the catwalk like a pro as I did most times. As I was walking the last leg of my third outfit, I saw him as I exited the stage. I didn't know what to do, so I kissed his cheeks.

"Bonjour Dominique! It's so wonderful to see you, but I didn't expect you to be here... does James know you're here?" I was in shock to say the least. I hadn't seen him in a while, but all of the feelings came boiling to the top, as if we had never missed a beat. I felt love for him, but why? My prince was standing in front of me, not looking a day older and even more handsome than I remembered.

"Hello angel… you look so beautiful, I cannot begin to tell you. James doesn't know, and I would prefer to not have it out with him," Dominique said, mostly with happiness, yet a bit of sadness towards the end of his sentence. I think there was a lot of regret I was hearing.

"Of course, mum's the word! Thank you, same… you look great!" I stammered over my words like the girl he first met. I will forever feel like a girl around him. It's his power over me. Dominique was immortalized by that sixteen year old girl. Oh how I thought to myself, "damn he looks fuckable, beyond gorgeous." I also wondered if my face gave it away, just how much I missed him.

"I came as soon as I heard," he explained. I was a little baffled, I'm not going to lie, why was he here?

"Pardon me?" I asked.

"Tory sent me an email, she explained that you might need me, that your grandmother passed." Dominique tenderly cupped my hands. My hands looked so small in his. I felt like the blood was rushing to my vagina at this point, I know I should have been upset that Eve died and I am, but his touch threw me into a spiral of emotions I couldn't stop. Could he see this? I must hold it together. I cannot let him see me like a foolish kid. Pushing my shoulders back to appear composed, "Tory sent you an email? I'm surprised to hear this. I'm also a bit suspicious of why she would." I pulled back my hand to regain composure.

"I know, I know, I too was very thrown back. I didn't think that she had a good relationship with your grandmother... did she? It's neither here nor there, I had to come, I know you loved Eve, even if, well you know." Dominique continued to speak, and his mouth was moving, but I couldn't hear a word, instead I just stared at him, again losing my shit. He was right here after all of these years, so surreal. I think I know that he cared and loved me very much, but to come here now, it was all just a little fucked up, I now became suspicioius over his presence as well. Why the fuck is he here?! What the hell is Tory up to? I knew it was too good to be true.

"I think the cat's out of the bag..." Dominique said.

"Bonjour my old friend!" I could hear James coming from behind me. Dominique, like the gentleman he was, said hello back. "James, it is nice to see you. You look well, and congratulations... congratulations on the show." He replied monotonically. "Allie, I've got to go, I'm a bit tired from my flight, I'll ring you tomorrow if that is ok with you?" Dominique waited for me to answer, but I paused because I was still in the past with the two of them, it felt oddly familiar, almost like deja vu.

"Yes, um yes, that would be fine, I'll be around late morning." He left quickly and then there were two.

"Well that wasn't weird was it... you're not going to call him right?" James just laughed with his coy boyish smirk. I wanted to wipe it off his face, but part of me loved his alpha male behavior, it was who he was. I couldn't help but melt when I saw him, so sexy with his thick dirty blonde hair and piercing dark eyes.

"I have to get down the runway to let the kind people of money applaud me… are you coming queen? After all, you are the star of the show," James grabbed my hand, not asking as he dragged me to the bright lights of the catwalk. I willingly participated with a devilish grin, he knew I loved the attention that the runway gave me, but even more so how he made me feel walking down it with his formidable frame. I like that I was the most important thing in his life. He made me a star, and I loved him for it.

CHAPTER 2

King George

I woke up early in James's place. Well, it was our place by this time, but I also had my own apartment as well, far away from his in Manhattan. He maintained his still ever so beautiful townhouse and I kept a spacious loft in Tribeca. I wrote a quick note and put it on the breakfast table where he liked to sit and have his lattes in the morning. I didn't want to wake him, he looked at peace and he worked tirelessly to put on his show. The NY Post was at our door already, as I knew it would be, so I grabbed it to see what they had written about his show. It read *"Another smashy hit for splashy designer John!"* I was relieved because no one, especially not James, liked rejection. The last time someone wrote a negative review about him was the last time they wrote anything that I've seen or heard of. I put the paper next to the note and kissed the paper with lipstick I just applied. I was proud of him, he was a fighter, loved his work and loved to win and most of all loved me. Even if he got me being underhanded, this I didn't find out till much later. Funny how the universe does these funny little things, one slight deviation and boom your path is forever changed. I think they call that the butterfly effect. Was it a wrong turn in life? No, I don't believe so, I still think I'm exactly where I'm supposed to be.

I went to the garage and asked Burt, the attendant, to grab my car.

"Your new car… is it as fast as they say?" Burt asked while looking for my keys.

"Yes, I think so, I really haven't taken it out of the city yet. I'll let you know next week, because I'll be driving out east!" I finally got a car I really loved and paid all cash. I picked a 911 Porsche in matte black, I thought it was perfect for me. I could drive it, really drive it, not like other exotic cars that you had to be so careful with. I felt like I had made it when I got that car, I even named her Raven.

I walked into my loft, relieved, I had always felt like this coming home. I don't know why, it's not like I was anxious or anything with James. I just really liked my space from him and the world in general. I lit a candle and put on something easy to listen to. *Home sweet home* I mumbled as I undressed all over the place while hopping into the shower. I knew it would take me an hour and a half to get ready to see Dominique. I also knew I couldn't do it alone.

I called my friend Georgie downstairs to come and help me with my hair. At this point I still had long hair, and it was thick as it ever was, so help would be a relief to me. The doorbell rang and I felt so lucky that he answered. Georgie a forty-year-old transgender, and once was a girl, now a beautiful boy and my friend. Georgie worked at a local hot spot in the West Village. He worked so late and rarely answered in the morning.

"Hi Georgie porgy! Do you know how much I love you?!" Jumping into his arms with all of my weight almost knocking him over.

"Alright, I know I know little one. What is the emergency here, talk to me!" George said smugly, because he knew I was up to my eyeballs in something. I would never bother him in the morning unless it was an emergency. Georgie had been my neighbor for four and half years now. Yes I've had this place since I was 17, legal age in New York and the year I emancipated myself from the viper.

"I'm kind of seeing Dominique this morning!" I screamed with panic.

"Whattttt… now sit down and tell me everything young lady," George demanded. Pulling me down to the sofa, he knew I was shaken. I explained everything, Eve, Dominique, the show, and the fact that I may still have feelings for him. George made us tea and shoved me into the shower, he like many other times in my life told me everything was going to be alright. He was always there, I don't know why, he just was. Georgie was the closest thing I had to family.

I went pawing at clothes in my closet, not having a clue as to what to wear to see Dominique.

"Georgie, pleaseee help me, I don't know what to wear… I want to look hot, but not desperate!" I whined like a child.

"Ok Ok, now now, King George has you, now step aside and let me find something that doesn't scream fuck me now!" I did as he ordered and waited patiently for my friend to find the "right" outfit for my former French addiction.

"GOT IT!" Georgie said as he handed me a Vintage Chanel fall 1997 navy blue and red jacket and skirt suit. It belonged to my mother. I nicked it years ago, and now I could finally fit into it perfectly. I had forgotten all about the suit. I had seen my mother walk across the Plaza Hotel in her heyday, she really knew how to wear the best and walk like she owned the room when she entered. She still does. Georgie then pulled a black Chanel bootie and small quilted bag to match, he said I would look proper, yet undeniably stunning. I felt relieved in his words, he had the magic touch when it came to women's clothes. He played with my hair up, but decided in the end to part it on one side and leave it down. I had a nice balance of high fashion with a more rockstar hair and makeup approach. I'm only repeating what he said.

"I absolutely love this, I can't even fucking believe you found this in my closet, I must have taken this from Tory when I was just a kid." My mouth was wide open, I was in awe of just how perfect I looked and also a bit sad because I was wearing a woman's clothes that I really didn't know that well; my mother. "Funny how the universe works." He paused to take me all in. Don't ask me why, but I could see that he saw a little of Tory in me in the mirror as he held me close to him.

"Now listen, I want you to know I will have my ringer on today, if anything happens or you're not sure of what to do, please ring me, I'll talk you off the ledge.. Ok? I've got to go now… come here, give me a smooch!" Embracing me with a quick peck on the forehead.

"Ok, I will. I can't thank you enough Georgie, I don't know what I would do without you… I really don't!" I said while gently kissing his hand as I had done so many times before. It made him smile, and I know it made him feel important. George was very important to me, I loved him.

CHAPTER 3

She Loves Him…. She Loves Him Not

I walked into Sant Ambroeus in Soho, it was always a special spot of mine and I knew all of the people that worked there, I guess that's what happens when you're a regular. I couldn't believe I was going to see Dominique. It had been so long. Why was I so god damn nervous? I mean I was the one that broke it off with him, not that he left me a choice. Part of me actually thinks he wanted me to do it. I had so many questions for years, but did it matter anymore? He ripped my heart out over a kiss. This may not seem like much to anyone else, but to me that kiss brought down the house and also put up a giant wall between me and any other man that got close. The wall is still intact to this day.

Dominique had a corner table near the windows. He stood up greeting me with a big smile.

"Hello Allie, you look stunning!" He moved towards me awkwardly trying to decide whether to kiss or hug me. I had made a plan ahead of time, so I went in for a hug. Maybe a handshake would have been a better idea, because just the smell of his Hermes cologne made my body tingle, bringing me back to our love making immediately. Pheromones really know how to mess you up sometimes. The wave of pure animalistic excitement was almost too much to bear. I wanted this guy and we were only seconds in. Staring at him, my thought was *how the hell will I be able to contain myself through lunch…* When all I could think about was sitting on his cock. I wondered if he felt the same, he had to, we had something beautiful, or at least for me it was, but what did I know, I was only fifteen when we met. I'm a woman all grown up, but with the same crush that I had then.

"How are things? I mean you look amazing Allie, you've really transformed. Not that I haven't followed your very successful career… you're killing it. I mean you're the face of James John and now work as Naeem's muse. I also heard you bought some real estate, is this true?" Dominique rambled on, but suddenly came to a stop, realizing that I just sat down and appeared to be a bit overwhelmed.

"I'm surprised you've followed my career, I didn't… I didn't think you… cared." I couldn't help but stammer, I was floored by his words.

"Of course I care Allie, I still… yes, I care, I've never stopped caring about you. You mean, you meant the world to me." He was also now visibly upset, his words were as broken as our relationship.

"I'm sorry this is a lot for me Dominique, I think we should have a drink. Don't you?" Signaling the server. "I'll take a Clase Azul Reposado on the rocks with a generous wedge of orange please." Not that I had to ask, everyone knew what I drank here.

"I'll have what she's having," Dominique said eagerly. The drinks came quickly and I felt relieved, I needed alcohol, after all I'm my mother's daughter. I took a large gulp as if I were drinking a glass of water. I think Dominique was surprised, but he didn't dare to say anything. After all he was in my place, well not my place, but my hangout.

"Allie, I am sorry about Eve. I know you two were close," Dominique spoke softly as he pulled my hand into his. "I would have come earlier, but I didn't know if you would see me or not." Looking down to avoid my eyes.

"Thank you, I appreciate it. What can I say, she's gone and now there are only two of us, me and Tory. I um, don't know what else there is to say about Eve. I actually would rather not talk about her. Ok?" I felt the lump in my throat grow as I spoke the words, I know my voice cracked a bit towards the end, enough for Dominique to notice and put his arm around me. I needed him to do that, I felt pain in my heart, not just because of Eve, but because of him. I still felt love for him. I didn't know what to do with my mixed emotions. Should I tell him or just hide them away? Impossible situations. I have James now, he loves me and I actually love him too. Could I have love for two men at the same time? Is this even possible? Would sleeping with him make me a bad person? I actually think I have to at this point. I mean why the fuck would I be here otherwise. I think I knew from the moment I heard his voice that this would happen. He had a spell on me. I wanted him inside of me.

I waved the waiter down for another round. After the third round we were laughing about the past. Dominique was teasing me about the first heels I walked in and now look at me stomping down the runway as a supermodel. I didn't feel like anything super, but I did feel pretty goddamn good these days. Life was really special for me, I was living a dream like existence. I had a big ass loft, a famous designer boyfriend, a Porsche, yes I said it a Porsche, and some amazing friends. I was happy, yet there was a small piece of me that was broken, deep down I was more like Tory than I ever cared to admit. I can somehow relate to her now, because she passed on that hole she carries inside of her to me. Maybe it's a genetic defect, I don't know, or maybe we're both mentally ill. After all that runs in the family too, so why the hell would it skip me?

I couldn't help but emulate my mother a tad, even when it came to my now "sexual" power as a woman. I put my index finger in front of my face and moved it, signaling to Dominique to come closer, he listened like a good boy. I took in his smell like a drug, and pulled him by his jacket gently towards me and whispered in his ear, "Kiss me." Turning his mouth towards mine, he softly kissed my mouth. His lips were soft and full, and his face was scruffy as it brushed my chin, it all felt good, I felt alive. We entered one another's mouths lightly kissing for what seemed like a minute, but I knew it was only a sweet ten seconds. Dominique spoke in a low, now sex-filled tone.

"Can we go somewhere to be alone?" I wanted to say yes right away, but what kind of girlfriend would I be if I did? I wondered for a second if James were sleeping around with anyone, but that faded very quickly. I wanted to have sex with Dominique and I had the opportunity to get away with it.

"Yes, let's go to my place." I couldn't say no, there was nothing to me at this point, my brain wasn't working, only my pussy was throbbing, and that was my only guidance system I had at the time. We got the check and headed towards his car where he had a black Escalade waiting to take us wherever we wanted. I look back now and think he must have hoped for this to happen. Eve was most likely an excuse for him to come back into my life and fuck with it.

"Well this is my place," I said while pointing to my sleek warehouse building. "Impressive Allie, very modern, yet has the old-style square windows, but obviously all new," Dominique commented as he helped me out of the car gently brushing my ass. "Yes it is, actually the architect is Zaha, isn't she a friend of yours?" I responded quickly. I guess it was my way to impress him.

"Awe, I thought I recognized her work, yes she's a friend of mine, but we haven't spoken for a while," Dominique said. I knew they weren't friends any longer. They had a falling out a couple of years ago over some real estate deal in London. Word in our circle travels fast.

We took the private locked elevator to my penthouse loft, the doors opened into my grand living space. I had an open floor plan, everything was in one space, except for the master and guest bedroom. I had taken the other two bedrooms and incorporated them into my living space. I wanted to be able to throw parties or paint if I wanted to. I kept a corner of the loft hidden behind book cases where I'd like to paint at night. The corner wasn't small, it was about 800 square feet of pure joy. I also had a mixing station where I would put together cool playlists and a few lounging chairs where I'd like to meditate and read. I wanted it to feel cozy there, if I wanted to break from painting and it did. My living room had big white walls with tons of modern art. I liked buying emerging artists, because they could benefit from my money, not like the dead ones and also they were really talented. I also had a couple of my paintings on the walls. I was really proud of the work I was doing and happy to share it with my friends, which happen to include a lot of artists. I loved having them over to share ideas and make art, or just dinner together. I felt closer to that world than the world that I grew up in. The artists in my life were authentic and didn't want anything but my friendship. The kitchen was also open, but I had a breakfast-bar of poured gray cement built to separate the dining area. I loved to have dinner parties, so the table had to be quite massive and I only ever wanted a round table, so that is what I had; a table for eight, but could fit ten. A beautiful white and gray marble table with chairs made out of clear acrylic by Philippe Starck. I like the look of clean lines with the only real color being my books, art and collection of vinyls.

"I like your taste Allie. It's very inviting. A real home," Dominique complimented me sincerely. He wouldn't have said it unless he meant it, but my dirty mind went to, "I like your taste," something he used to say all the time. I didn't really care if he liked my apartment, I only cared about taking him to see one other room and that was my bedroom, but I had to play it cool, I didn't want him to think I was out of control over his presence. Even though I probably already gave him that impression, after all he was in my loft and I practically begged to be kissed. I offered him the same drink we had at the restaurant and he graciously accepted. I put on some chill tracks and asked him if he would like to sit down pointing in the direction of my sofa. Before I could even sit down, Dominique grabbed my drink abruptly and placed them both on the coffee table.

"What are you doing to me Allie?" He scolded me like a child, "I don't think you're being cute, teasing me, what kind of game is this? You're much better than all of this!" Dominique shouted as he suddenly walked towards the elevator.

"Better than what?" I screamed back, "I don't get it, what the fuck did I do? I only wanted to die when I saw you. Everything just rushed over me and I wanted you… now are you happy? I wanted you!" I returned fire. I wasn't going to let him talk to me like I was a child and then walk away from me, but I was still that girl, because within seconds I was tearing up. I was hurting again, I felt the pain in my heart like a hot knife through butter. I was falling apart. I needed to suck it up. I had to tell myself to not cry, so I held my breath in order to stop it and god willing it worked. I had never done that before, but I felt so much relief because it did. He could still hear the pain and crack in my voice, as he turned around and walked back towards me.

"I'm sorry, I'm so sorry Allie, I came here to make you feel better and all I did was make you feel worse. I didn't know what all of this was, I am fucking French, what can I say, we are stupid." Dominique stood right in front of me, put his hand on the small of my back and the other under my chin, pushing my face up to his.

"I want you angel. I want you right now." I couldn't help what would happen next. "Dominique," I said in a breathy voice as I pulled him towards my bedroom.

As we moved through my vast room of all white, we found ourselves in front of my king size bed. It was low to the ground with white fabric lining the corners that hung from the beams in the high ceilings. I only had candles, books, art and a bed in my room, I didn't think there was much else to do in there. James rarely came over to my place and didn't know the code to my elevator, so that was something I wasn't afraid of. I'd fantasized about this happening, but never thought it would. I never thought I would actually be this insanely drawn to him again, but all of the memories weren't memories anymore, I felt love and a strong desire to be his. I wanted him inside of me, but this time as a woman, not a girl pretending to be a woman.

I began taking my clothes off, and his, going between us, I was in a sexual frenzy and he followed my lead, within seconds we were naked, pressed against one another in my bed. He maneuvered me onto my back and pushed his cock slowly deep inside of me. Every little bit that went in was like pure ecstasy as my wet box throbbed for something harder and faster, but he wasn't going to give me that right away. He was going to make me long for it, like he was. Every push was bringing us closer to it, to one another again. *"I wanted you for years, I thought about you all the time, Allie. Oh, you feel so fucking good, I want to cum so hard right now, but I need to get you off first angel,"* Dominique grunted and then pulled out of me and put his beautiful face between my legs. I was ready for him, I was so ready to be pleased, and he was hungry for it, he wanted my pussy in his mouth. Oh the sounds he made as he ravished my clit, pushing his finger inside of me while playing with my G-spot, swirling his tongue around in tiny circles, everytime just brushing my now pulsating jewel, I was ready to go, I was losing my mind. He grunted making everything vibrate, it felt so good, I was at the top of my threshold.

"*Dominique… oh my, Dominique, I…I…I'm going to, oh my god, I'm going to cum for you darling!*" I screamed out as the warm juices flooded his face, he kept going taking me to another and another. I fucking lost myself in the bliss, it was the most euphoric feeling, my body involuntary jumped as I tried to catch my breath. Dominique crawled back on me and with one forcely push he went inside, pounding away like a barbarian while screaming my name.

"*Allie, Allie, fuck Allie! I love your pussy angel… oh fuck Allie! You make me crazy, I'm cumming for you angel, I'm cumming!*" Dominique collapsed on me with all of his weight. I could feel his cock throbbing inside of me, and I liked it. I immediately thought to myself, *I want this man again.*

He repositioned me on his chest. It felt like old times, when he would hold me after sex and we would fall asleep. I would always wake alone. I had hoped that wouldn't happen this time. I wanted him to stay the night, but I didn't know how to ask him. I mean for all I know, he had a girlfriend or someone in his life. I wanted to believe that his words were true, that he didn't forget about me, and that he might still love me, but why? I had James now, I should be thinking about him, not this man from my past and yet he was here and I just had the best orgasm.

My thoughts quickly turned to James, he will be calling, he'll want to see me for dinner. I have to get to him first and let him know I'm not around. I never lied to him before, I never had to, because I never wanted anyone else except for him. He had trust in me and I in him. Even though he was one of the most sought out bachelors in town, I knew he was not looking at other women. I decided to just speak up and tell him what I wanted to happen tonight and see where the chips would fall.

"I don't know if you have any plans, but I would like to have dinner with you, if you like you can shower and get dressed here. We can pop into Nobu and eat at the sushi bar. I know everyone there and they'll take really good care of us.

"Look at you little boss! Yes, I would absolutely love to eat with you. I'll have my driver go to my hotel and get some of my things and bring them here... I assume I can stay here this evening?" Dominique was waiting for me to respond to his question with that cute smirk of his. Oh how I missed that sexy smirk, he really was a beautiful specimen of a man. Tall, strong jaw, the bluest eyes, the kind of eyes that just made you want to do anything for. He had me, again.

"I'm going to run around the corner to the wine store, they have a great rosé Champagne that I love," I said as I pulled on a pair of jeans.

"No no I will go, I think I should remember what you like to drink angel. Stay here, take a shower. Just tell me where it is and I'll be back soon," Dominique insisted like the gentleman he was. I explained to him where it was, I knew that he would want to go and that it would take him around fifteen minutes to walk there, so that left me with around thirty-five minutes to call

James and chat, explain I wouldn't be around and hopefully that would stick and he wouldn't find anything odd. Dominique leaned over me, lifting my chin up and kissed me. The rush of emotions I felt, one would never believe I had a boyfriend. I felt slightly desperate, he was in my apartment and at this moment I never wanted him to leave. I had hoped this would pass, because I had something really special with James.

"Alright angel, I'll be back soon, if the door buzzes it's either me or my clothes." He said as the doors of the elevator closed.

Now I can turn to the task at hand, my very hot-blooded boyfriend James. I felt bad, knowing that Sundays were our day to be together alone without any distractions. Sometimes we would take romantic walks in Central Park followed up by a candlelight dinner at home and you know the rest. We never spoke about work on Sundays, it was just us. So what was my excuse going to be?

I rang him and he quickly picked up. "Hello there, I was wondering when I'd hear from you!" He was so excited to hear my voice. "Hi babe, I'm sorry I had a drink at lunch and I passed out cold. I still feel a bit tired. I found out that Eve, my grandmother passed away, so it's been a really tough day." My voice cracked a bit, I don't think it was because she died, I think it was because I was lying to the man I loved for the first time. "Oh Allie, I'm so sorry. Do you want me to come over or would you prefer to be alone? I don't want to crowd you, but I'll do whatever you need me to do," James saying the perfect thing to me. I had my out, and I felt like hell because of it, but not enough to stop the insanity I was about to do with Dominique again. I felt badly on the phone, but that didn't last long before I would be back in the throws with another man I might also still love. "I love you so much James, thank you for saying exactly what I needed to hear. I'm going to take a bath and just be alone to rest. I have to see Tory tomorrow and I would really like it if you could meet us for lunch, you always make it easier with her." I explained where we were meeting tomorrow and he graciously agreed to come.

"I love you Allie… call me if you need me," James said softly.

"I love you too, you know that right?" I asked him if he knew I loved him…why?

"Of course, you chose me, I always know. Are you sure you're okay Allie?" James was now worried and questioning my state of mind.

"Yes…yes of course…I'm fine, I'm fine honestly. It's just Eve, you know, I loved her." I again used my grandmother for the guilt I was feeling.

"Ok love, rest and I'll pick you up at noon." The phone went silent. I couldn't believe just how easily I lied. What the fuck is wrong with me? I'm more like Tory by the minute. I now couldn't help but think about Dominique, he was on his way back with fucking Champagne and his sexy body. I couldn't help but want him again. Am I that bad of a person, or am I just living like we are meant to… satisfied? I'm beginning to think the latter of the two.

CHAPTER 4

Sex and Sushi

Dominique returned announcing his great taste in Champagne.

"I've got it angel, your favorite rosé all day… remember how you used to say that when you first started drinking it?" Looking back, we loved those days, but I know now we did for completely different reasons. I fell in love with an older man and became a woman and he fell in love with the idea of molding into his perfect woman and that is exactly what happened. We both got what we wanted back then, but what did we want now? Did we just want sex and passion? I wasn't sure and I'm still not completely sure of what he was thinking. After all, telling someone what you feel or think is really only half true, would you agree? The facts were this, he and I were in the same space together and wanted nothing more than to just fuck one another like animals in the wild. My head was spinning from my moral dilemma, but that didn't stop me in the end, that's for certain. I didn't want to ask myself if he loved me anymore, I just didn't, I only wanted to know how much he needed to be inside of me. We made our way to the bathroom.

"Would you like to take a shower first or..?" I asked sweetly knowing he would definitely want to join me.

"Don't be silly angel, you first," pulling at me as he removed my robe. I knew damn well he would be in the shower in 3.2 seconds.

"Why thank you kind sir, I shalt be long!" Smiling from ear

to ear Dominique removed his clothes and tossed them on the floor.

"Now who's going to clean all of those parts you can't get to?" He said, pressing his hard throbbing piece into my stomach. Oh how I loved his swimmer body; tall, broad shoulders, strong legs and arms. He was like a mythological god, or at least what I had read about them. Just pure perfection.

He looked at me with hunger in his blue eyes, as he whispered in my ear. "Let's get dirtier before we shower." Just his breath on my ear made me squirm.

"Yes please." I gasped. He picked me up as I straddled him, walking me to the bed. He was a little rough as he threw me down, then went for a pillow. Turning me over with my face down, he placed it under my vagina propping my ass into the air. I was openly exposed, what would he do next to me? I didn't care, I wanted anything he did. He put his face in my ass and privates, swirling his tongue around my little box, working it with soft licks and circular moves. It felt so good, I was vulnerable with my ass up and he knew exactly what to do to me. I could feel a finger go inside of my wet pussy and then another finger start to work on the outside of my ass. I had never had this before and it felt wrong, but oh so right. Dominique was delivering another first for me and I loved him for it.

Methodically he moved to my back, carefully caressing my clit with his fingers, keeping me fired up for what was next. Sliding another wet finger into my ass simultaneously he began to fuck it and my pussy. He took his time, keeping me eager for more. Firing me up even more as he talked about how good it looked from behind. He wanted me, all of me. He wasn't selfish, he kept going, pushing into me as he increased the pressure on my hard clit, I felt it all over, I was tingling, I wanted to cum. It was suppressing it, but now I was over the breaking point. I couldn't hold on for a second longer as the rush of warmth filled my privates and entire body with pure ecstasy.

"Baby what are you doing to me...don't stop... please don't stop... I'm there, oh my god, you're making me cum... ahhhhh!" I screamed out like I had never done before, the sensation was overwhelming as my body shook involuntarily.

"Fuck Allie, that was so hot to see! I have to be inside of you now!" Grabbing onto my ass cheeks he entered me slowly and methodically pushing back and forth to gain his rhythm. I was weak from my orgasm, my face falling to the bed, but he was full of strength as he lifted my hips up in the air to meet his throbbing cock. It felt primal the way he handled me face down. I love the feeling of being taken. I was a little thrown back as he screamed out over and over.

"*I love you, you're mine, you'll always be mine angel... do you understand, do you fucking understand?!*" I had to respond to him, I was his right now and wanted him to know. I wanted him to cum hard, to love it more than anything he ever experienced, so I called out over and over.

"*Yes, yes I'm yours! Yes, I'm yours!*" Dominique screamed out one last time.

"Angel, I'm going to explode inside of you, right now... right now!" Digging his fingers into my skin he came, then collapsed on my back. My body was vibrating with his, we were both drained. "Ahh Allie!" Dominique in awe of what just happened. Our connection just grew by leaps and bounds or so I thought at that moment. It's so strange thinking so clearly one thought and then later on laughing at just how ridiculous you were... or is this just me? How could we feel that much passion for one another after not seeing each other in years? We laid together for ten minutes without talking. I couldn't help but think about food, I was suddenly famished, so I shot to the shower first announcing my departure.

"I'm first, be out in ten minutes!" I insisted that he not come with me or we would never get out the door. Saved by the bell, his phone rang and he ran down to his driver outside to retrieve his clothes.

We both dressed. He had a cool pair of Tom Ford dark blue jeans, a white button down, a black blazer, black belt and a pair of DG calfskin loafers, paired with a silver and black Audemar watch. Moving his thick dirty-blonde hair back a bit with product, not enough as it fell quickly, a look that I believe was purposeful, because it looked so damn hot. All of this man, from head to toe was perfection, he was very fashion oriented and loved to make an entrance. Every woman would be looking at him this evening, including me. I went for a dress, men and especially this one loved dresses on me. So I pulled out all the stops.

"I've yet to wear this, I hope you like it!" I yelled out from my walk-in closet, well more of a room that resembled a designer showroom, thanks to my designer boyfriend, who filled half of it with his clothes and the other various designers that gave him whatever he wanted. I felt proud and beautiful as I walked into my bedroom in a one-shoulder bow back ruched mini dress by Oscar de la Renta with matching 4-inch heels by the same designer. I kept the jewelry simply with just a gold and diamond bangle and diamond studs. I didn't think it would be appropriate to wear Phillip's designs, that just felt wrong, not that fucking Dominique isn't. I didn't feel great about everything at this point, I felt kind of like Miley Cyrus on the wrecking ball in her video.

We walked into Nobu, it was buzzing, and of course I recognized a girl I knew when I walked by her table. I had hoped she didn't recognize me, but she did. Her name was Dandelion, yes you heard it right, Dandelion, my guess is her mom really likes the flower or she just wanted to be as strange as some of the celebs out there naming their kids after planetary stars and bullshit. It is the thing to do after all, stranger the better! It might have been all of five minutes and Dandelion approached our table. I was just happy that we ordered our drink before she got there, because I certainly didn't want to invite her to sit down and have one with us. She had on a red leather mini and a Bolero jacket to match, too short is all I can say and her hair was two toned; yellow and orange. It was something to see. Dominique was cordial and stood up to introduce himself and I followed suit.

"Hello Dandelion, how are you, long time, you look great," I said as sincerely as I could. "Don't be a bitch, you know I look horrible with this hair, better not to say anything if you're going to lie," she laughed, which made everyone a bit more comfortable. She continued chatting about her dinner this evening, which was a bit much considering I had just had a bunch of sex and was now ready to eat off someone else's table if I didn't get food soon. I kindly explained to her that we were starving and that was it, she split and we finally got to order.

"Darling, can I order a bunch of things to share?" Dominique asked.

"Yes, of course that sounds amazing… oh but you order two orders of crispy rice?" I smiled back at him.

"Yes angel, I was already going to do that, I know what you like," looking at me with his hauntingly sexy grin. I smiled at him and then slyly scouted the room for anyone that might know me as "James' girlfriend." I was after all James' girlfriend and he makes that very clear to anyone in the room. He doesn't like men thinking they have a chance in hell with me. My thoughts went to James, I did love him, I didn't want him to find out this happened, for me I felt love when I was with Dominique, but I know now that it was because he was my first and I felt like a girl with him. I don't know how to explain it exactly, he had just had this "thing" that I was attracted to. James on the other hand was like a bull, manly and raged a bit over work and scared me a little. He reminded me of a hot soccer star; intense, built and would run anyone over if they got in his way. You didn't want to get on James John's bad side, he had a reputation of getting whatever he wanted. I'd always wondered if he set Dominique up that night in the restaurant, so that he could come in and swoop me up. Except for the off and on of the first two years, which part of that I spent with Raph, I had been with James for most of the five years after that night. Everyone seemed to disappear when James was around. Little did I know what he was capable of.

We shared the dinner like old times, catching up on all of his jaunts around the globe and my successful career in modeling.

"I didn't tell you much about the art though, I really love it and have decided to take some time off of modeling after my next show and study with a really well known British artist." I gushed. Art brought out another side of me, something internal I could share with the world. I felt like myself when I was painting.

"Congratulations, this would be amazing. You'll be in London I assume?" Dominique was happy knowing that I would be on his side of the globe.

"Yes I'll be looking for a spot in London," I explained the position, responsibilities and that I wanted to live in Chelsea.

"Who is this well known artist?" Dominique asked.

"You're not going to believe it! It's David Lurst!" I gushed, this was a big deal. No one gets to just walk into Lurst's studio, but I wasn't just anyone, I was James John's girl. Dominique knew as soon as I told him who I would be studying under that James was the one responsible for it. He didn't have to say anything, I could see it on his face. Everyone, including Dominique knew they were good friends and James collected his work. I guess the shark in the James new showroom was a dead give away. James liked to show off, so he made sure the press had full access to write about what he paid for it. I couldn't deny that I loved the way he flaunted his money, there was something bigger than life about him. He didn't see walls, he saw what he wanted.

Dominique ordered us a beautiful bottle of Montrachet, I had grown fond of it because he introduced it to me.

"You know you might have the best taste in wine." I was a little tipsy and feeling really good.

"You might be right and I may have gotten you a little drunk angel, but I'll take care of you." Dominique brushed my hair back from my shoulder and touched me softly. I must have lost myself a bit because I completely forgot that I had a boyfriend and had become the biggest flirt out in public. I even leaned in and kissed him briefly at the table, not knowing that Dandelion and her friends were still in the wings. We finished up the bottle and decided to head back to my place. The night air was crisp and I was shivering a bit, Dominique noticed and put his jacket and arm around me.

"I miss you Allie. I've missed you the entire time." I didn't say anything, I just listened. How could I have known, he never called or wrote to me. I didn't know if he was telling the truth, but I could hear sincerity in his tone. It was him and I here in the chilly autumn night with five years that passed us by. I was beside myself, but I wasn't going to let it take over the night. I had bigger plans for us. I was only going to see this man for one night and I wanted it to be memorable.

I kicked off my heels as we entered the loft and before I could move further into my loft, his hands began to unzip my dress. I suddenly only thought about what was right in front of me currently, not my beautiful, fierce James. Pulling it down, he asked me softly to step out of it. I was there exposed and undressed like so many times before when he was seducing a young girl. I felt really young once again, I think that is what I liked most, feeling vulnerable with him, like no wasn't an option, I wanted to please this man. He picked me up into his arms and carried me into the bedroom.

"I have something for you, a gift." As he sat me down on the bed and went to his luggage. I felt like this was another moment that I remembered quite clearly as well; the gifts he gave to a teenager pretending to be an adult woman. Dominique pulled out a small black box with a red ribbon tied neatly on it. I opened it slowly and methodically, so as not to destroy the ribbon or the box, again something I used to do with him, because his gifts were the first I had ever received. Inside I found a long, low cut silk red number with a slit up the side. It was so elegant and just the right amount of sexy. I asked him if he wanted me in heels or barefoot, he said barefoot and I left for my master bath to change into it.

"What do you think?" I asked as I spun around for him.

"Tu es la plus belle femme du monde entier. Je t'aime, mon

ange." Dominique told me in French that I was the most beautiful woman in the world and that he loved me. My French was up to date, as a matter of fact, I was fluent by this time. I spoke back to him in French, explaining to him that he was just flattering me.

"Tu me tues avec cette flatterie." I felt beautiful and he did have this power to make me feel special, like his little angel. I stood waiting for him to tell me what to do, for what seemed like an eternity, but maybe only seconds, I was beginning to get past fired up and heated from my desire to be with him.

Dominique sat down on the bed and pulled me in front of him. He ran his hands across the silk and my breasts, then down my legs and around to my buttocks. I loved how slow and deliberate he was, it was building anticipation for both of us. For a split second I thought about James as I turned my head, I could see he knew it too, but he didn't care, he kept going at me. Slightly moving me away from him, he dropped to his knees and began to move his hands up inside the lingerie.

"Open your legs angel," he said as he pushed lightly to spread them. I did what he asked. There he made his way to my exposed womanly parts, rubbing lightly around my pussy, just barely brushing it with his fingers as I let out a faint moan. I could hardly stand it… but why? I wanted more, I was so hot for him. I moved my hips a little to indicate how ready I was, this made him react. "Now I'm going to take this off you ok angel." As he slid the silk number off me and once again I was standing in front of him naked. Exposed is how I will always be and feel with him.

"Oh my god Allie, my sweet little angel, you are so soft and beautiful, I love the way you feel and look. I still remember the first time with you, never have I felt that good with anyone," Dominique said as he kissed my stomach and caressed my bottom. I felt like a girl, but I wasn't anymore, I wanted this man and had to have him. I moved down to him and started to unbutton his shirt quickly. I felt like enough was enough, I wanted to have him inside of me and I couldn't wait anymore.

"Please take your pants off, I want you," I begged.

"All grown up little one?" He did as I asked and laid down on his back, signaling that he was ready. I could clearly see a huge, hard cock in his hand just asking for me to sit on it and I did just that. I slithered up on his body with my legs on both sides of him and slid down onto his cock. I went slow in the beginning to get situated, but after a short time I rode him furiously. I wanted it to hurt me, it did and I loved it. I went fast, I didn't care if he came, I just wanted all of it deep inside of me, so that I could feel the pain tomorrow. He went crazy with me on him, he had no control over when he would cum, but I did. I got up on my feet and lingered on the tip of his dick with my pussy sucking on him hard with my muscle control. It drove him to the edge. Dropping back down on him, I bucked like I was riding a horse until he couldn't hold on any longer.

"Allie, I'm going to cum so hard inside of you, I'm going to fill you up angel, hold on it's coming now, hold on angel!" Dominique screamed out like I had never heard from him. I was pleased with myself, I had taken control and fucked him well. I wanted him to remember this night, I didn't want to be forgotten, for

some reason I still had these deep issues with myself and his approval was important to me. I fell to the side and laid with him for a few minutes. Tired, and ready to collapse, yet I didn't want to sleep with my makeup on, so I excused myself and went to the bathroom to remove it. He had slipped into the shower for a quick rinse and then went to the bed, I followed shortly behind. I felt like we both had a lot to say, but we were exhausted and fell asleep entwined. How long will this moment last? I'll tell you, five seconds and I was out without a care in the world. Maybe I was more like Tory than I cared to admit, after all I was in love with another man, but for some reason I was able to compartmentalize all of a sudden, just like dear ole mom.

I woke up in the morning to the playlist "Paris is for Lovers." He used to play it for me in the morning in France. It brought a big smile to my face, but that soon ended with me panicking because James was arriving at noon. I knew I needed time to decompress from this night, but also to get glammed up for my guy. I was relieved to see it was only 7 am. I went into the kitchen and Dominique was showered, packed up and had his shoes on.

"I'm sorry angel, I've got a flight to catch, something happened with one of my companies and I have to head back to Paris right now. I'm hopping on a friend's plane, but unfortunately I must leave now or I'll miss my ride." Dominique was saying exactly what I wanted to hear, more than anything I desperately wanted him to go. I was in full mode girlfriend now and this, whatever it was, it had to stop and now. I needed to get my head out of whatever cloud I was in and get back to my reality.

"I understand, no worries, I'm completely fine. Let's catch up when I get to London, ok, maybe it's not such a good idea to call me," I said as I walked him to the elevator, we hugged for all of a few seconds. Dominique leaned in kissing my forehead.

"I understand. I hope we see one another there," pausing while he gazed deep into my eyes. "You know I still..." I placed my finger over his lips and shook my head.

"Please don't say it, please just don't." He graciously agreed not to and poof he was gone. I know the words *I love you* would have destroyed the thing that just happened, and I wanted to try to remember it as an affair and not a mistake.

CHAPTER 5

James the Punisher

I ran around my loft looking for anything that might resemble traces of Dominique, but there was nothing. I was so relieved, I thanked god that he was gone and promised to never see him again as I jumped into the shower. My chest started to feel tight, I felt the panic begin to spin me out because now I wasn't sure if I did anything last night that anyone would have seen and told him about. James had so many friends and my carelessness may have tripped me up. I didn't feel remorse for what happened between Dominique and I, but I sure as fuck didn't want to get caught. I knew just how angry my hothead James could get. He had been mad at me before and to be honest scared the shit out of me. This was something that he would completely lose his mind over. I wasn't sure what he was capable of and was forfeiting anything that resembled reality. So, I did what every sane girl would do and grabbed the Clase Azul and took a swig. It relaxed me a tad so I could slow my breathing down.

James was such a man and no one would ever have me, he'd made sure to tell me this often. I kind of liked how masculine and dangerous he came off. James was known for hitting a couple of different guys in public and that got him a reputation of being a badass, and also a few big lawsuits. It didn't hurt his career, on the contrary, it actually helped it, and the girls flocked to him even more after that, metaphorically throwing their panties like he was Elvis or something. I think he wanted me because I was naive and he, like Dominique, wanted to teach me to be their perfect little girl. They did for a while, but that didn't last. You can't keep a bird in a cage forever, it's gonna want to fly, especially when that bird was born from a vulture-like Tory.

I got dressed in a Balmain double-breasted blue blazer, adorned with gold buttons and a white vintage Rolling Stones t-shirt and a pair of Rag & Bone black skinnies, I paired it with a pair of black patent leather pumps that he designed. His heels were sexy, so it finished the outfit off perfectly. I also accessorized with a gold Daytona watch that he gave me for my twenty-first birthday. My hair had to be perfect, so I made an appointment at Drybar downstairs and had Veronica do it like she had done a thousand times before. She knew what I needed when Phillip was showing up, big beachy waves. He liked my hair very feminine, as if I were walking the catwalk in his clothes or in a Victoria Secret runway show. Forever sexy hair is what he called it. I finished up with a dark smokey eye and a natural lip color gloss. I had to look completely ready for his arrival and I did. Standing in my flat I could feel my heart beating out of my jacket. I suddenly felt like I had made the biggest fucking mistake in my entire existence. I'm not sure how I feel right now. Look, everything is the butterfly effect, you should just accept it and move on… easier than it sounds right?

It was at 11:30 when he called and told me to let him up. He was early, but I didn't think much about it… God knows why, I should have. For some reason I gave him the code to my elevator, I had never done that before, so subconsciously maybe I was feeling guilty and was already trying to make it up to him, who knows.

"Hi babe!" I yelled across the room from my art and music room that was perfectly placed behind a bookcase. I waited for him to speak, but I didn't hear anything but the elevator door slam closed. I turned around and there he was behind me looking possessed.

"Oh, you scared me!" I jumped pretty high, not expecting him to be so close, so fast. "Kiss me!" Grabbing my hair in his strong hands he pulled me close to him. I was in pain quickly and in a bit of shock, he had never done anything like this before.

"What are you doing James, *please stop* that hurts." He slowly released my long hair from his fingers. I could clearly see he was beyond fuming, this was something I had never witnessed before. I was in deep trouble, how much was the question?

My thought was he knew something, my second thought was just how much he thought he knew. I didn't want to ask, I was scared, but I had to. Stepping back behind a fairly substantial chair to get protection I asked the question.

"What's happening…tell me why you are obviously mad at me? I mean James, come on, you hurt me! Whatever is going on doesn't excuse your manhandling me." I tried to sympathize with him, but I don't think it actually helped my case.

"You know why! You know fucking why, you embarrassing little fucking… ugh!" James yelled at me with such disdain, I had never seen anything like this from him before. I'm not going to lie, it was pretty demonic. He then stopped abruptly to pause for a few seconds. Even he knew he needed to calm down. I wasn't

one of the guys that pissed him off and got written up by the press.

"Allie I love you... you know that right? And, I really think you love me too. *So, why the FUCK are you out and about shaking your ass with Dominique? You're supposed to be mourning your fucking grandmother's death! What is wrong with you?... You're acting like your fucking mother, crazy and slutty!*" I wasn't prepared for him to know all of that and furthermore to say such hurtful things. I was in shock, and I must have looked like it, because I couldn't say anything for a few seconds, then I stammered out a few words.

"How... how... did you, how do you know this?" I'd seen James angry with other people to this degree, but not me, I was his life. What had I done? I was completely consumed with fear, the fear of losing his love and everything else he offered. I didn't know what he would do, hurt me, take my work from me, I wasn't sure what he was capable of if he made me an enemy. Thinking back, I was more scared that I would lose him. I wasn't good with people leaving me, at least not back then. As fucked up as it all sounds, he looked so goddamn hot. Oh how his manly 6'1" frame and all of his tattoos made me want him. Not to mention his glorious blonde mane and angry, yet seductive dark eyes beaming at me like a hot white light. Snap out of it Allie I thought, this man is not here to make love to you. He was way too sexy for me to bare, but this wasn't the time to go there in my head, I quickly came back to reality.

"I found out because of that little cunt *Dandie fucking lion*! Her brother works in my office Allie! Did you really think you could go out with him? Haven't I given you everything?! I got rid of all of the other girls, I haven't been with anyone else except for you! Do you know why Allie? *Because I only want you! I would fucking kill for you!*" James wailed out with emotion as he continued for what seemed like an eternity. I couldn't speak and even if I could, It would have sounded condescending. I do recall thinking that this was the first time I had witnessed him in a vulnerable state. He was losing it, he really did love me and I didn't know what to do. Should I go to him and try to embrace him? No, I thought. Should I cry to prove that I too am hurting? No, that didn't seem to be a good idea either. I was trying to figure out what to do, I must have looked crazy myself.

"Come here now Allie! Come over here." He pointed in front of his feet. *"NOW! Get your ass over here RIGHT FUCKING NOW!"* He demanded and I complied. Walking over to him swiftly like a child, I stood in front of him waiting to know what would be next for me. Grabbing my face, *"Come here right fucking now Allie!"* James wasn't asking as he pulled me into him forcefully. I was a bit confused, but everything in my body wanted to kiss him, so I stood on my toes and went in for his mouth. James returned my kiss with an overwhelming animalistic fire in his mouth. He was ravenous. I could feel his rock hard cock pushing through his pants. Did he want me to touch him? I wasn't sure if I should or not, but I did anyway. I placed my hand on his manhood and rubbed it lightly. Grabbing my hand he dragged me into the bedroom while continuing to kiss me. He was furious as he ripped off all of my clothes. I loved his anger, it began to make me feel submissive, I wanted to please him. I wanted him to control me. I didn't know this side of him or

myself, but it was feeding my desire and his beyond any words that could not be spoken. I fucked up, thinking back, but did I? This seemed to make him want me even more, but there was definitely a line drawn in the sand that night.

We were in the throes of something beyond sex. Bending me over the bed he told me to not move, I didn't. I could hear him unbuttoning his pants and pulling them down, but he didn't take off his clothes. He then spit on his hand and wiped it on my pussy, shoving his cock deep inside me. I don't know what it was, but all of that testosterone made him wildly jealous and I got seriously turned on by it. My pussy hurt from Dominique, so it made it even more painful, but I liked it, no I loved it. James didn't stop there, grabbing my hair with one hand and smacking my ass wildly over and over. The pain was more intense than I imagined, but I stayed in it to please him, to please me. My cheeks were burning from the smacks, each time he pulled back I anticipated the next hit, almost relieved when it touched me. My body was hot with the desire to please him, to belong to him. Letting go of my hair, he grabbed onto my ass and dug into my skin with both hands, riding me hard till he couldn't hold on anymore.

"I OWN YOU, DO YOU UNDERSTAND, I FUCKING OWN YOU ALLIE! YOU'RE MINE! … OH FUCK WHAT ARE YOU DOING TO ME! OH FUCK I'M CUMMING!" James screamed wildly while he pushed his hips deep into my stinging ass cheeks. I had forgotten all about Dominique from the moment I saw James, that said a lot to me. All I wanted to do was make it all better, make James love me again. How could I?

I wasn't sure, but he was going to tell me and I was going to fucking listen. This was just the beginning of his punishment, we both knew that to be true. I would long for more and he would give it to me gladly.

James didn't speak to me afterward, he dressed not looking into my eyes, which in turn made me feel absolutely horrible. Not knowing what he knew was also killing me. I wanted to run after him as he left, but I didn't, and I didn't cry either. I knew I made a huge error in judgment by letting Dominique in but was it really a huge mistake, or am I just upset because I got caught? I wasn't sure, but my stomach was telling me something. I knew that I loved James, he's my protector, how could I not? I sent him a text and waited to see what he said. *"I love you James, please talk to me, I want to make this right."* Minutes later he responded. *"Let's talk after the wake, you know the wake for your Grandmother. I will pick you up in the morning."* The funny thing is, I almost forgot my Grandmother died, and that I had to be in Bridgehampton in the morning. Could I feel any worse?

CHAPTER 6

The Wake

James arrived downstairs at my place at 8:30 am, he was driving a black G5 Mercedes. I was relieved that he didn't pull up in a sports car, my mother would have flipped seeing an exotic car pull up at a wake. I got in, tried to kiss him and he pulled a little out of my range, so I tried again. "Please James, let me," I said quietly and leaned in to kiss him on his cheek. This time he turned to me, and grabbed my face with both hands and kissed me passionately, like he loved me, then he slowly pulled away.

"We need to talk, you know that," he said, pulling away from my street.

"I know… James can I say something?" I asked sweetly.

"Yea, go ahead," replying with no emotion.

"I don't know what happened with Dominique, but it will never happen again. I am in love with you. I made a mistake, people make mistakes. I was so young when he met me… you know this… I still felt like a kid to him and I guess I wanted to prove I wasn't, I know this sounds strange… but, I have nothing to prove to anyone. I realized that right after he left. I don't have any more unresolved feelings for him. I have nothing for him, no feelings, no love. I'm so sorry I hurt you, that I hurt us. I will do whatever you need me to do to make this better. *I can't lose you!*" I choked up my last words and began to cry. James didn't console me, he just drove as if he didn't hear a word I said. He was just so tough all of the time, blocking me out seemed easy to him.

We arrived at my grandmother's gated home in the Hamptons. It was a beautiful house that I was barely seen at, one I didn't want to be around Tory who seemed to be there all the time towards the end of Eve's life and two, oh and there is no two.

"This oughta be good, how long has it been since you've spoken to Tory?" James asked. "It's been at least 6 months," I said with so much dread in my voice. My thoughts were radical; childhood, him, Eve, but mostly her; Tory. I can't fully understand it all, this thing …our mother and daughter "so-called" bond. The relationship is oh so fucked up, it's hard to breath sometimes, I love her so much, yet she destroys that love with a mere sentence. I'm destroyed to the point that I can't function, nor have feelings at all, almost to the point of feeling like a zombie… whatever that means? I received a valuable gift from her, and that is called detachment.

The last time we had a real conversation was when I emancipated myself from her. I threatened her in a big way, telling her that I would embarrass her in the newspapers unless she gave me my freedom. It would be the first of many times I would get to shut her down. I was quicker on my feet than her. Eve was a bad mother, but a good grandmother and teacher, so I think she actually enjoyed seeing me take my mother down and move out on my own. Some fucked up family, no?

There she was in all of her glory in head-to-toe emerald green. I have to say my mother always knew how to make an entrance.

"Hello James!... Allie." You would have thought James was her kid, I was an afterthought.

"Hello, I'm sorry for your loss, I really liked your mother," James leaned in, kissing my mother on the cheek.

"Yes Tory, so sorry for your loss. You must be so devastated." I said sarcastically.

"Now now little one, show your mother just a tiny bit of fucking respect, you're here for your grandmother's wake, let us not forget," smiling like the beautiful viper that she was. "Now, now ladies, that's enough, we're here for Eve. Let's table this for another day on the battlefield... ok." James grabbed my arm, dragging me into the house to a room full of people that all overheard our spat. Not that I cared too much, I only knew half the people there and I didn't like that half too much. Tory didn't even invite Eve's friends, just her own, you would have thought it was a cocktail party the way people were laughing and carrying on. So strange, so fucking strange.

We moved through the people quickly finding a bar in the corner of the great room. We ordered some Clase Azul Tequilas on the rocks and moved to the beautiful mahogany rich library where I closed the door and locked it behind us.

"You're right we need to talk, this can't go on any longer, I can't take it. I need to know what you're thinking... *please talk to me damn it.*" I said while slamming the entire glass of Tequila for courage. James followed suit, he drank the glass in one giant gulp.

"Ok Allie, you want to do this here... fine. You fucked Dominique and I found out. Now what? What am I supposed to do with you? What Allie?! What the fuck am I supposed to do with you?! What? Fire you as the face of my company or fire you as a girlfriend or both? Or should I just let it go and move on like it never fucking happened? Please enlighten me, what do you want me to say... tell me... go ahead now, fucking tell me!" He demanded.

"Marry me!" I yelled at him. I couldn't believe what I just said and neither could he. *"What?"* James was in utter confusion.

"I want to be with you. Marry me and we will be together. Maybe a part of me always feels insecure, like you're going to leave me at any moment, that's why I wanted Dominique to want me.... someone to really want me. I don't know... I'm all sorts of fucked up because of Tory and you know this more than anyone. I desperately need a commitment from you. It's been almost five years you've been telling me that *I'm yours and you're mine!* If you want me, then marry me." Explaining the best I could until the tears flooded my eyes. I was a wreck at this point and found a bar behind my grandmother's desk, opening a bottle of vodka I chugged it. James, concerned, pulled it from my hands.

"What the fuck are you doing? Come here." He grabbed me by the waist and kissed me deeply. I knew I finally tore down the wall he had put up, because of his actions. James didn't stop there, I made him want me. I guess he needed to hear my words of affirmation. He picked me up and positioned me on Eve's desk, pushing up my dress with one hand and ripping off my panties with the other. He pulled me to the edge, dropped down to his knees and began to lick me. It seemed so wrong, this is where my grandmother used to write in her journals, but I couldn't stop him, it just felt so good to feel his love again. I needed James in so many ways, I couldn't lose him, I felt desperate and relieved all in one breath. He was ravenous, his anger was gone and all he wanted to do was taste me, to have it in his mouth. James couldn't contain himself, he stood up and unbuttoned his pants exposing his gloriously large cock.

"You are still mine, Allie, I fucking love you. You can't do this bullshit again, I won't be here next time." He slid in slowly, moving methodically. He told me to touch myself, I did as he asked. He could clearly see how turned on I was.

"You're so wet babe. You know how much I love you, don't you Allie? *You make me so fucking crazy.*" He moaned loudly.

"I love you James… please give me everything… give me all of you." I cried out.

"Oh yesss, I'm going to give you everything, right now!" James roared as he came. I knew it wasn't over, there was no way this man would stop loving me. He couldn't, we couldn't, we were addicted to one another. This was obvious.

"We definitely belong together." He laughed, joining in, I knew that he was right. We had something powerful, and there was no denying it, even if there was a codependency thing attached. For some reason, I think Dominique may have brought us closer, but would there be any trust left to keep us there, that was the question. We put ourselves together and moved back to the main room which was now filled up. James excused himself to go to the bathroom as I looked around the room till I found a familiar face.

"Kathryn, is that you? Wow, it's so nice to see you." Reaching out to one of Eve's friends by the arm.

"Oh there you are, come here sweet girl," Kathryn said while embracing me. Kathryn was a beautiful 70 something year old woman, a few years younger than Eve. They knew one another only the last ten years of my grandmother's life, but It seemed like they were friends for a lifetime. Kathryn was a jovial, large redhead with big blue eyes, she had so much kindness in her heart. I think she brought out the best in Eve. They were really close and did everything together.

"I cannot tell you how much I needed to see you right now Kathryn. I hope you know how much you meant to my grandmother," I said with tears in my eyes.

"Oh honey, no crying. *Do you know how much you meant to your grandmother?*" She continued, "I don't want to speak out of turn, but Eve was a smart cookie, and let's just put it this way... she left it all to you." Blurting it out, Kathryn could never keep a secret, even Eve used to say that. Maybe she wanted her to tell me before I found out for the attorneys and Tory.

"Are you sure?" I asked while the uncontrollable tears streamed down my face.

"Yes I'm sure, I saw the papers, I was actually the witness with her attorney Mr. Roberts." She answered as a matter of fact.

"Can you excuse me please Kathryn, I need to speak to my mother." Hugging her quickly, as I turned towards Tory.

"Tory, can I talk to you?" Now standing in front of her.

"Yes, meet me outside in the garden in ten minutes." She said as she walked away. I was confused, I needed to know what she knew, if what Kathryn said true. Was I to inherit my grandmother's estate? If Tory knew, she wasn't acting like it. I was beginning to wonder if this was the appropriate time to even ask her. What if she didn't know? Would I be the culprit in making her lose her head at her mother's wake? I thought to myself, it might be better to go fishing for answers, rather than to expose it all right here.

James approached me with a glass of wine.

"Hey, you ok? You look like you just saw a ghost." Funny wording, my grandmother is dead and he's using the word ghost I thought.

"Almost… Eve left me everything, or at least that was what I was told by her best friend. Which means we are standing in my house." Whispering close to his ear as not to be heard.

"I'm not surprised, are you?" James huddled close to me.

"I guess not. Some part of me wanted her to leave something to her only daughter. I kind of feel sorry for Tory." I sympathized. God knows why, she would never wish this for me.

"Don't feel sorry for her, she has enough money for three lifetimes. Plus Eve really loved you. Promise me you will keep the money and the house," James said as he pulled me to him.

"Yes, yes I promise" I replied.

"This doesn't mean you're off the hook young lady, we are going to sit down tonight at my place, understood. I'll leave you to Tory, see you in a few minutes." James said as he walked away to say hello to someone he knew.

I turned myself to the dreaded conversation I was about to have with Tory. I didn't even know how to start it. We had such an estranged relationship now, I didn't know if we could even be civil to one another for more than a hot second. I approached her on her cell phone in the garden, she saw me and signaled her index finger. It sounded like she was having a disagreement with a lover. Ironic, don't you think? That we were both doing this today. Pulling the phone from her face and into her pocket she approached me.

"How are you kiddo?" How does one respond to this I thought to myself. Kiddo really? "I'm not a kid anymore Tory, in case you didn't notice." Digging my nails into my hands. She knew how to get under my skin with just four words.

"Well you'll always be my little girl Allie," Tory said it like she meant it, but I doubt that very much. I smiled involuntarily, why I'll never know. I felt like she tricked the smile out of me. Tory was hell on wheels, but sometimes could be quite endearing, even if she never meant to.

"Well we might as well talk about the elephant in the garden," I said firmly.

"I assume you are talking about the estate and the fact that my mother left it all to you?" Tory asked coldly.

"You knew, why didn't you tell me?" Confused now beyond my comprehension. Tory was keeping it quiet, but why? There had to be something else she was hiding.

"Of course I knew, as soon as the old bag wrote it up, she sent me a copy. *Didn't your boyfriend tell you?*" Tory maintained her composure, yet she now carried a wicked smile on her face as she continued. "Listen, the reading is tomorrow at the attorneys on Park in the 80's, I'll send you the address, if you could please unblock me from your phone now, it's only been however many years. Let's try to play grown-ups, ok Allie." Tory walked away without even letting me respond. So typical of her. My only thought now was there was more to this than she was letting on. What was it? What was she keeping from me? What did James know and why didn't he tell me about the will? I needed to find out, but I knew it would be best to wait till after we got back to his place. There was already enough drama this afternoon, even for a wake in my family.

I moved back inside and found James, the service was beautiful and loads of people spoke about Eve. I did as well for fifteen minutes, but I didn't want to take all of the glory away from Tory. She on the other hand spoke for thirty minutes about their close relationship growing up. Why didn't I know they had a tight bond before me? What was that about? Was she lying? I felt like I didn't know anyone at this point, not even myself. We said our goodbyes and headed back to the city. I must have passed out from drinking so much, when I woke we were in the city in Jameses garage.

"Why didn't you wake me, I would have kept you company on the ride back," I asked sheepishly.

"You seemed pretty out of it, I thought better to let you sleep it off... but look, now you're up, we can go eat something!" James was in a good mood, but I was wondering when that might change, I knew we still had a big talk tonight and I suddenly felt nervous again. His temper was explosive and I was on the end of it for the first time, I had never thought in a million years he would be this way with me.

"Ok, can I freshen up for a minute? I think I need a quick rinse after our little playtime in the library," I joked trying to keep him in a good mood and it seemed to be working... for now. I had been having sex with two men in the last couple of days, and now I'm going to have to talk to him about it. I had never been in this kind of position, no pun intended. I would in the future many times, but we'll get to that later.

"Sure, I'll make a reservation for us," James said as he opened his grand townhouse doors. This place was exciting, it screams luxury, sex and masculinity.

I ran to the elevator and took myself up to the top floor

which was our bedroom. I may have had my own loft, but I lived an equal amount of time with him and had a designer closet here to die for as well. After all he was at the top and so were all of his friends in the fashion world.

We had a beautiful marble bar in our master, so I went and made another Clase Azul, put it back quickly, shaking my head back and forth not realizing how big of a gulp that was, but that didn't stop me, I did it again. I headed to the shower while throwing my clothes off in different directions, thinking about what to wear. After my much needed rinse I went to my closet and grabbed a hot little white pantsuit with silver bling skull heels that my love designed for his latest collection. I opted to keep the jacket buttoned up with nothing underneath it, instead I layered multiple gold and diamond necklaces, various lengths. I looked very rockstar chic, I knew my sweetheart or at least he used to be, would love it, even if he was still angry.

I walked into our kitchen where he was having a glass of Champagne and chatting with someone on the phone. He had his back to me, so he didn't know I had walked in.

"Yes, I understand what you are saying… Listen, I don't take orders from you, ok! I'll do whatever I fucking please. You may be her mother, but you're not her boss and you're sure as hell are not mine… understood. I already agreed that it is best for her!"

I cleared my throat loudly, I wanted him to know I was standing in the room. James hung up quickly on whomever he was talking to. I didn't put it together because I was a little out of it. I actually don't think I wanted to know, even though a piece of me already knew, if that makes any sense. To me the drama filled day was just too much, I needed my guy to just be one on one like before.

"Hi… I'm sorry that was a business call," James apologized. It seemed strange to me, he never apologized for work stuff ever, but I brushed it off. I suggested he take a shower as well and he complied.

While I waited I had a couple of glasses of the bubbly he popped and at this point I was visibly drunk once again. This was not a good thing, he didn't like it if I drank more than a few drinks, he said I got too flirty, so I went to my stash of Adderall and popped it in my mouth quickly. They were prescribed to me as a child, but James forbade me from taking them, so I did what all good all-girl private schools did… hid it. This would keep me alert enough to fake a buzz and not too off my ass. I knew all the little tricks and the tricks would get bigger by the day.

My guy met me at the front of the house wearing his designs, the opposite of me, he was wearing black fitted trousers and a black fitted jacket that had the entire skull of bling on his back. He also had a black fitted crew neck t-shirt and black bling kicks. He looked so cool and hot as fuck, every girl wanted to be with him and he was mine, or at least I had hoped. He had grown his blonde hair in and now had a wavy shoulder-length cut, that he pushed behind his ears and those ever so mischievous steel dark eyes were just too much to take, he was the entire package.

I mean this man was a catch, any girl would've dropped their clothes for him. I felt very lucky at this moment in time.

Would I always feel like this, I'm not too sure about that. It felt pretty amazing to be on his arm, the way people stared at us made me feel very important. Something I never felt growing up. I actually still don't most of the time, but at that time, the glimpse of that feeling was enough for me. I was a queen that night and he was definitely my king. I loved him madly.

CHAPTER 7

The Charmer and The Punisher

We walked into the high society Upper East Side haunt of Le Bilboquet at 9:00, the lounge music played out throughout the well-appointed, loungy restaurant by a cute female DJ in the corner. The music was buzzing and so was the crowd of beautiful people. The restaurant white, with accents of black, very dim with lots of candles. We were immediately seated by the maitre d', Laurent, a middle-aged gentleman that worked there for as long as it had been open, which was over a decade. Our table was in the center of the room, no one would dare put James John in a corner, not unless he asked for it. He loved to have people watch us. I also knew that he loved the way I looked, after all I was the center of his campaign and had been for years. No matter how much he might have loved me, he loved to make money more, so he would have replaced me if the numbers weren't astronomical, or at least that is how I felt at the time. Maybe I was wrong.

"You look beautiful," James pulled me closer to him.

"Thank you baby, so do you," I smiled and planted my mouth gently on his soft pillowy lips and kissed him tenderly for a minute. He didn't mind, he loved the adornment by me. He ordered me a Clase Azul on the rocks with an orange slice and a bottle of Montrachet for us to share. He didn't like hard liquor, because he never wanted to be drunk and out of control, plus his penis would never have a chance of disappointing. This I do know to be facts. Little did he know I had already had four drinks, but he would soon find out and be none too happy with me.

We drank the wine and I had another Tequila. He and I spoke with loads of people that presented themselves to our table like we were royalty, it was quite amusing. I excused myself to the ladies room while he was talking shop with another gentleman that works in his industry. He squeezed my hand pulling me towards him and slightly turned his head so as not to be rude to the man and said, "Don't be long, understood, you have five minutes?" I thought to myself, *now he's timing me... what the hell,* but I agreed "Yes...I'll be quick." I didn't want to rock the boat anymore than I did, but trouble seemed to love to follow me around from city to city.

I had to walk upstairs to use the bathroom and could feel Jameses eyes on me the entire time. I turned a corner and was escorted by an attendant to a private bathroom. She had known me for a long time and knew our status, so the five minutes wasn't going to be an issue. I used the toilet and then grabbed another Adderall. I knew I needed to stay alert and awake because we were going to have "our talk" later and I needed to be present, also I was starting to sway from the drinks and I didn't want to appear to be drunk. I touched up my lipstick, washed my hands and left the room exiting into a private hall that led to the public bathroom.

I didn't expect to see anyone in the tiny hall, but there he was my *"charmer"* Raph. He must be thirty by now and even more handsome than ever. His thick black hair and eyebrows, dare I say sexy, especially against his piercing green eyes. Oh and that bronzed skin and striking frame was almost too much to take in visually. I felt like a kid that was looking at the fancy desserts that they brought around at restaurants. I was so excited and in awe.

"Allie baby!" Raph stood in front of me with his blazing white smile.

My feelings quickly turned from excitement to hurt. "Oh my god, I can't believe you're right here in front of me! Why didn't you return my calls or emails? I wanted so badly to explain. You just... you just shut me out!" I cried out.

"I know Allie... I wanted to reach out, *so many times,* but I didn't know how to, you know the story. I needed to get space from all of it." He stopped smiling and became a bit sullen.

"I know, me too, but I gave us six months before I reached out and nothing." Grabbing his hand was a reaction, but a bad one because he pulled me close to his chest, "I didn't know how to talk to you, I just thought I should leave it alone, the situation was bad Allie." I didn't pull back from Raph even though I knew I should have, I felt calm again just like before, he was always so gentle and kind to me. Suddenly I was filled with panic, my mind became fearful, so I glided my hands down and gently released myself from his touch. It was a good thing I did, because I heard footsteps approaching quickly.

"What are you doing? I'm at the table by myself." It was James and he looked pissed. "Hi, I'm sorry, yes." I apologized and was turned to both of them at this point in the hall. "Hey I know you," James said while pushing Raph. "What the fuck Allie! Why is he here?" James was becoming explosive.

I had to diffuse this situation quickly. "Listen to me, he's here with his family celebrating, stop being so weird... ok?" I spoke in a stern tone in hopes of making him feel ridiculous.

I then turned to Raph, "Tell your family I said hello. I have to go, nice seeing you." I said while grabbing James by the hand and tugging him in hopes that he would follow. He did thank god. Raph didn't say anything, but I turned to see his face as James was dragging me down the hall, he was smiling and then I knew. Raph might not be going anywhere anytime soon.

We returned to our seats without conflict, which in all seriousness surprised me. James waved down our server and ordered two double Tequilas for us, and told me to drink. I did what he wanted, I actually did what I wanted as well, which was drink more. He then ordered a bottle of Champagne and an entire bottle of Clase Azul, and began to invite random women and men to our table. They were all happy to oblige, who didn't want to be near the fantastic James John right? It was overwhelming to say the least, I felt like the girls were ready to kill for him, I could feel their dagger eyes all over me. He was playing with me and I wanted no part of it.

"If you keep this up I'm leaving, I swear to you James," I whispered in his ear.

"You'll leave when I fucking tell you to, understood hot shot?" James pushed down on my leg, warning me to stay put. I did stick around for a while for what seemed like an eternity, pretending to have a good time.

I could still see Raph in the corner with some people, James didn't, which was good for everyone. We locked eyes, and it was as if I could feel his heat from across the room. I quickly turned away, the last thing I needed was my boyfriend to lose it while drinking. He must be so angry with me, because I had never seen him drink like this. What was next? I wasn't fearful, because I was drunk, I was just fed up. So I made a move. I secretly gave the waiter one of James's credit cards and closed out our enormous bill. I then got my bag in hand, stood up and walked out. He watched me for a while before he realized I was actually out the door. I was met with his fury on the street.

"Where the fuck are you going you little bitch?!" He screamed at me. I was over it, I didn't care what I did to deserve this, I was leaving.

"Shut up! Go back to your whores." I opened my mouth to a suitably retorted remark, again another first. I didn't speak to anyone like this and especially not him.

"Oh funny, now look who's talking." Tittering from amusement, he grabbed my waist pulling me into him. I didn't want to love him, but I did, flaws and all, so I gave him a cute smirk while shaking my head. "You are impossible James."

He was like a tornado and I was the tiny house in the wake, I could move if I wanted to. "Kiss me now." Grinning, he pulled me harder to his body. How could I say no to this man? I couldn't, and so this is where it began to get dysfunctional. This was only the beginning of what the "punisher" would do to us, but more so to me. I leaned into him, barely brushing his lips, but he returned with hunger in his tongue and mouth, grabbing my hair in his hands, pulling me deeper into his kiss. I didn't care at the time if anyone saw us, but unfortunately someone did. James wanted me, even more so than before, and I knew it. This would be his downfall.

We went home and straight to our bedroom. James was tipsy, but not too much that he couldn't have sex before sleeping. He actually had to, he needed to have me until he felt better about what I did, but not before we sat down to talk. I didn't get how this could be a serious conversation, after all I was buzzed too, but this was his game, I had to play it or else. I certainly didn't want to know the alternative to not listening.

"Have a seat." Taking my shoulders he pushed me to the large velvet bench that was in front of our bed, then walked to our bar and poured two shots of Clase Azul, came back and handed me one, we toasted because he wanted to and then it began. Like a good girl I drank it down and prepared for what was next.

"I don't even know where to begin with you. Ahhh… Dominique… that's where I'll start. I don't know all of the facts, but from what you told me earlier I have somewhat of an idea why you felt obligated to that guy. Allie… he isn't who you think he is! He lied to you so many times! *Do you really think you were the only one he was sleeping with?! NO ALLIE YOU WEREN'T!"* James stopped and grabbed onto his composure. "Now what are we going to do about all of this… huh Allie? No, don't answer, it wasn't a question." He paced like a lion in a cage as he ranted. "I need to know now if this is what you want?! Do you want to be with him? NOW YOU CAN ANSWER!" Firing at me with spit coming out of his mouth. He was now visibly beyond upset. He was a little scary, but for some reason I laughed, I guess because of my nervousness. James was not having this, not even for a second. He ran at me like a charging bull, tearing at my pants like a mad man in search of the buttons. I didn't know what to think, my first thought was that he was going to rip my suit and the second one was he wanted to revenge fuck me.

"Ok ok ok stop, stop pulling! *Please baby*, don't rip my clothes!" I yelled at him, slapping his hands repeatedly away from my clothes as I began to undress myself at light speed, as not to irritate him anymore than he was. Removing everything from head to toe as I stood before him naked, I felt exposed, in more ways than one. I couldn't help but like the way he ran his dark eyes over my body. Like Jekyll and Hyde, his face softened and again he was back to being *"my James"*. He didn't say anything to me after that, he just moved towards me, picking me up while I straddled him and laid me gently on the bed. *"You're mine, do you understand, you're mine Allie"*. Looking directly into my eyes, while pushing his fingers in my mouth and partially down into my throat. He was possessed. I quickly realized then that he would go mad if I did that again. I couldn't risk it ever, he was my future or at least at that moment I felt like the world just dropped away and we were the only humans left on this planet. His possessiveness brought with it his heat, making us both ravenous. I needed James and he needed me. We were completely entwined in our fuckedupness.

Slowly I pushed his fingers out of my mouth, "Yes baby I'm yours and you're mine, I don't want anyone else but you. *It's always been you.* I'm so sorry I hurt what we have, I'll never do it again, *I swear to you.*" Kissing his hands softly. He looked at me with love at first, but I could see the doubt and anger behind his eyes. James got up shortly after, undressed and returned to bed. He didn't fuck me that night, this night he made love to me. Just the way he looked at me when we first started dating, with love in his eyes. I felt like we had some sort of breakthrough, he needed to be heard, but also needed to be reassured I was his forever. I think I was the first real love for him, someone that he was afraid of losing, he had never met someone like me before, or had been this crazy about.

James laid upon me, both of us naked and vulnerable, *"I want to marry you Allie. Were you serious when you said that earlier?"* James whispered in my ear.

Smiling with delight I replied. *"Yes, I want that too!"* That night solidified our commitment, but would it last and could I keep the promise I'd made.

Soon I would leave for London to work the next runway shows and it wasn't with The James John Collection. We would be apart for a couple of weeks, a lot could happen in two weeks, but that didn't matter right now. Tonight was special, we were making love for the first time. His touch was even different, just the way his hand held the small of my back made me insane. His beautiful hands were so strong and he was so very powerful. I wanted to submit to him however he wanted, and he would want plenty of that in the future.

James kissed my nipples, pulling at them, knowing that this got me aroused. I ran my hands through his hair longing for more. I desperately wanted him to go down on me, so I begged for it.

"Please my love… lick me." Licking his lips he moved slowly down to my tight stomach, kissing it all over on his way down between my legs. He put his manly hands under my ass to prop me up and then began making love to my pink pearl using his tongue. It was different, he used his whole mouth to engulf me, it felt wonderful, I squirmed in delight. I wanted more, so he pulled back and put what felt like two fingers inside of me, while simultaneously playing with my clit, his combined efforts were pushing me quickly to the edge. This man knew my body.

I moaned loudly, "I love that, I love you James… don't stop my love." He didn't, he kept going methodically working his tongue like a pro, over and over brushing my clit, simultaneously pushing his finger up and around onto my G-spot. I couldn't take it anymore, I was losing my mind. *"Oh my god James, Oh my god my love. You're making me cum… baby…baby I'm there!"* I felt like the entire day was released with my orgasm. A rebirth of a new day for us. Just like heaven. James was once again fully mine, I had no doubt now. He wasn't going anywhere.

I wanted desperately to please him the way he did me,

moving slowly after a minute I ordered him on his back, he smiled moving to my request. "I want to suck *everything* out of you my love." Looking into his eyes I moved towards his already shiny, humongous cock. "*AHHHH.*" He moaned loudly as I took him in my mouth. I could taste his pre-cum already, it was warm and salty. I kept at it, licking it and then working the tip lightly, while I stroked his shaft softly repeatedly. I knew exactly how to please him, this I learned from him years ago and I loved making him scream while he came. It made me feel empowered for some reason.

I wanted nothing more than to serve him, I needed his cum in my mouth. I felt animalistic. The idea of it turned me on beyond words. I knew it would bring us close again. Licking, stroking, faster and faster, simultaneously bringing my man to the edge. I could feel his balls tighten in my other hand, I knew I had him. He was close, so I kept at him until he could take no more. I felt the blood fully engorged his manhood.

"*ALLIE, DON'T STOP I'M ALMOST THERE! FUCK… MY FUCKING GOD, I'M GOING TO CUM! THIS IS ALL FOR YOU, HERE IT IS… ALLIE… FUCK ALLIEEE!*" His hot juices filled my mouth as I swallowed, while some of it spilled out of the sides of my mouth. I stayed there and let him release it all while his body convulsed. I loved it, he was mine again. We were entangled in love, we owned one another.

CHAPTER 8

Green with Envy

The weekend came and we decided to escape to my new Hamptons house, to have a look around, and confer with a decorator about upgrading. It was cold, but I really wanted to get away from the noise of the backlash. The staff was there getting wood for the fires and preparing for dinner. I still kept everyone that Eve loved at the house as per her request. I would have regardless, they were like extended family. Haru was an old Asian man, probably late 70's, from Japan and was with my grandmother most of his life in this country, he had no one else. Haru greeted us at the door with a rose in his hand for me. I almost cried on the spot.

"Ru Ru" I called out as I gave him a big hug and received his rose. When I was little I couldn't pronounce Haru, so Ru Ru is what I called him and still do to this day. There was also Tate, Eve's chef, a jovial 50 something year old man, he had been cooking for Eve for over a decade. He was from South Dakota, originally a farmer, but lost his crop to a beetle colony that ate everything. His wife was Anna, a slim, tall redhead from Dublin who was a little younger and always full of energy. Her job and a job she did well was to manage the estate, the grounds and the companies that cleaned it. They had two 16 year old twin boys, Nathan and Nick, they both were in high school and lived on the property as well. Soon they would be off to college and so I would never put any of them out. On the contrary, I was going to give them something this weekend, so I was very excited about the trip.

"Hello Tate! Hi Anna!" Giving them both a hug. James said his hellos as well, shaking Tate's hand, but kissing Anna on the cheek, turning her a bright cherry red from embarrassment. She gushed over James, I mean even Ru Ru did, I knew why, he was a major rockstar designer and definitely a celebrity and boy oh boy did he *ever* look like one. I had only started bringing James out to Eve's two years ago, and he was the only man I had ever brought home, so everyone knew he was extremely important to me.   We all caught up for a minute, then James and I headed upstairs to our room.

"Hey you love birds I'm preparing a special meal for the two of you in the solarium garden, we have it all heated and ready to go!" Tate called from behind. You could tell he missed the cooking, so I was happy to oblige.

"How long have you two been planning this little soiree? You're both hopeless romantics, you know that right." I had missed them more than the cooking. They were my grandmother's loyal friends and companions. I had a lot of love for them, and they I.

I had a sprawling 800 square foot boudoir on the east side of the house. My grandmother wanted me to have the largest bedroom in her home, she also always wanted me to have a childhood. This was a special place for me to play and actually be a kid when I could, which wasn't very often. It's kind of funny, she skipped a generation with her love. I never questioned it, I just took what I could get. Maybe Tory will do the same with my children. The room had been redecorated last year by James and I. We wanted a space for us to be comfortable in. I let him do most of it except for the bathroom. He made it rich in wood, keeping with the theme of the house, but added his masculine flair; dark blue-grays and rich wine burgundies were splattered around the room. He replaced the fireplace facade with gray, black and white marble. Architecture, fashion and art books lined the table in the sitting room, perfectly placed in front of the stoked fire. It was something out of A & D magazine. He had such an eye for detail. Even the drapes were perfect in their richness, and of course blacked out. He liked to sleep in complete darkness, it took me a few bumps and bruises on the way to the bathroom to get used to. We had a lovely assortment of summer things in our massive closet, but not much for the winter, so I came prepared knowing this, as I unpacked both small travel bags for us while he showered. Looking outside of the massive twelve foot windows, I wondered what it would be like here in five years. Would he and I have children or even be together? At the time I really hoped for both.

I made my way to our master bathroom. I had made it completely white with a beautiful clawfoot tub in the large windows off to the side overlooking the gardens and the pool, and an all-glass shower that could fit six people. Also a perfectly placed vanity area for me in the middle of the room next to a white velvet chaise longue. Double sinks for us, but not separate from each other. I liked brushing my teeth with him, I don't know why... I just liked it.

"Hey gorgeous, come in with me!" James stood all soaped

up with the door open wearing nothing but a devilish grin. I walked over to him thinking how lucky am I and gave him a light peck on the lips.

"I cannot my love, I have to go arrange a few things for us, I'll be back and then we can pick this back up... ok?" All the while teasing him while I touched his manhood.

"Oh is that right young lady, not so fast!" Pulling me into the shower fully clothed, I squealed.

"Babyyyy... I didn't want to get my hair wet!" As my full face of makeup ran down my cheeks.

"Look at my little racoon," teasing me, as James began kissing me playfully. *"Get over here woman, take these off,"* as he lifted my arms up and began to strip away my soaked clothes. What else could I do, I was in a shower with a man I was falling in love with all over again, he was everything you could ask for and more.

I had forgotten all about his crazy temper and he forgot all about my misgivings. He would later in my life surprise me with some even bigger lies than I told, but that didn't come till much later. For now we were perfect.

"Now what boss?" I joked.

"Get over here wifey and kiss me." Manhandling me, pulling me in by my waist like he did so many times before. I loved just how virile he was, there was nothing feminine about him, he was all man. It was so fucking hot to just look at him. James picked me up and slid me down on his cock while pushing my body onto the shower wall to gain footing. His strong frame moved me up and down with ease. My eyes closed in rapture as he pushed further inside of me. I moaned the sweet sound of bliss, I pushed myself through his hands and took all of his eight inches deep inside of me. I felt everything and so did he.

"I don't want to cum yet baby, let's go to the bed." Groaning, he moved me off him, placing me on the floor. Quickly we showered and moved to our lush California king.

"What do you want me to do to you my love?" I asked innocently.

"Nothing, I want you to lay there and let me take care of you first." He loved to eat my honeypot. I happily complied. I longed for his beautiful face between my quivering thighs. I felt submissive even when he was going down on me. It was just the way he held my body with his masculine hands and his demeanor that made me feel like a possession, I absolutely loved it.

"*Ohhh James, my love...* how do you know me so well, that feels so good." I was on a cloud of pleasure. Working my pussy was an art for him, he moved around it like a hunter looking for his prey and the prey was my clit. Making it large by teasing it with the flip of his tongue and then sucking it softly made my body move to try to get more. He then put a finger inside of me, then two and began to push inside and out rapidly while he continued to tease my every growing thirst for an orgasm.

Faster and with slightly more pressure on my clitoris, I was at my threshold. I let myself feel it all and until I could no longer hold on, I was there in all of its glory cumming on his beautiful face. *"MY LOVE... I'M THERE, I'M THERE BABY, DON'T STOP, OH MY GOD DON'T STOP MY LOVE!"* The rush of warm like water ran out of me like a flood. It was the first time I had cum like that, it was different than the other times.

"What just happened to me?" Peeking up from my pillow I asked sheepishly.

"You squirted Allie... wow that was fucking hot, so fucking hot babe!" Smiling from his accomplishment.

"I did? That was so amazing. I could die right now and be happy." Laying back on my pillow. I felt like I melted into the bed. I heard my lover get up, but I didn't stop him, I was exhausted and wanted to rest. He never came back, or if he did he didn't wake me.

I slept for an hour and then got up, finished showering and dressed for dinner. I opted for a Loro Piana camel cashmere sweater and some comfy vintage Levi Boyfriend jeans and a pair of furry LV slippers and went to meet him downstairs. I must have walked into something because everyone got silent as I approached.

"Hey you three, what are you talking about?... I assume it's me, no secrets!" Teasing Tate, Anna and James while wrapping my arms around my sweet boyfriend's waist. "Nothing you, don't be so nosey." Picking me up he carried me away on his shoulder while spanking my butt.

"I guess I'm going this way!" Joking while I waved back at them. They just shook their heads in amusement. We were pretty damn cute. He had a way of just being relaxed and himself around anyone. Unlike me, I was still awkward around almost everyone, but not him, I could really be me or at least this current version of me.

"Where are you taking me you brute?" Hitting him lightly on his shoulder. Placing me down, he grabbed my face and kissed me deeply. Pausing for a second, "I am fucking crazy about you Allie." He was no longer joking, I felt his desperation and sincerity come through his words.

"I know you are... What's wrong baby?" Concerned because he appeared to be physically upset with a tear making its way out of his eye.

"Nothing's wrong, everything's fucking right!" Picking me up and spinning me in a circle, he held me up over him and then gently brought me down so that we were eye level with my feet dangling he said, *"I can never share you with anyone, Allie."* James looked at me so intensely. I knew at this moment just how much he really loved me, or at least I thought it was love. I started to cry as he placed me on the floor. Kissing my tears and then my lips, we both felt it, all of it... we were crazy in love with one another. The crazy part would become more apparent as time went on with us.

I looked around not realizing he had us in the solarium where Tate and Anna had set up the entire vast space with tiny white lights and beautiful arrays of white candles all over. My grandmother's potted plants and roses were overgrown, transforming the room into a movie set. In the center of the room there was a beautiful round table dressed in white with candles on it and my favorite Rosé Champagne. James pulled a chair out and asked me to sit, I obliged. He sat quickly appearing to be anxious or excitable. Magically, our song Turning Page came on, it was the most romantic night I could have imagined or so I thought, little did I know there was more.

"I didn't know where to do this, but I couldn't think of a better place than the only place you considered home. I would also like to make this a home for us and our future. I love you Allie, and I want to make you happy. I want to spend my life with you. I couldn't imagine wanting this with anyone else." James continued as he stepped out of his chair and onto the floor in front of me. He had one knee on the ground.

I sat with a goofy smile. I couldn't believe what was happening.

"Alllie, will you marry me?" As James presented me with an 8 carat emerald cut Emerald. He remembered the engagement ring I described to him years ago when he first met me. I had told him I wanted the stone as close to my eye color as possible. *"Yes... Yes! Yes James of course I'll marry you!"* Jumping into his arms I screamed like a little girl. I was marrying James John! I felt like the luckiest woman in the world. He chose me, it felt unreal, maybe it was unreal. Maybe it's all too good to be true. Would our fairytale life unravel? That was the question. I wasn't sure, and I didn't want to know, I had seen too many bad endings and it was my turn for just a little piece of happiness. Looking back

through the good and the bad, this was probably one of the best days of my life.

We dined all night and laughed, enjoying the memories of our last five years together. We weren't exclusive in the first two years, but when he saw me out with someone else he went ballistic, sometimes even pushing the guy around. He's lucky the press didn't catch him on tape like they did us last time. To the best of my knowledge he paid the boys off, I say boys because they were all around twenty, not his age. He met me when I was just sixteen and he was thirty. Now our age gap didn't seem like that big of a deal like before. James was a walking contradiction back then, he was a playboy out with hot girls nightly, and then boom, he'd see me at a club or something and act like a jealous boyfriend, sometimes even leaving the woman he was with to scold me or throw me into his car forcing me leave with him. I didn't want a relationship at first, but his passion and fury got to me somehow in a good way.

Towards the end of our glorious evening my new fiancé laid another box in front of me on the table, but this one was an odd shape..

"What is this?" I asked, a little confused about what was going on. Anytime someone handed me an envelope it was some sort of contract. It made me a little nervous. I'm not going to lie.

"You look scared… don't be, it's a gift." James teased and immediately my fear subsided. I took a deep breath, "You know me so well, don't you." I opened the box and inside I found a long black envelope with his initials in gold lettering. I found this to be odd, but I happily proceeded, now very curious. To my surprise it was a set of keys.

"Ok you, are you going to tell me what's going on, you're killing me with the suspense!" I grew very excited about the surprise and leapt into his lap straddling him.

"Ok, ok, let me pull out my phone and it'll make more sense then." He pulled up his album titled *real estate* and showed me a loft that was a stripped bare, but it looked vaguely familiar, and then it hit me.

"Oh my god James! Is this what I think it is?" He looked like a cat that swallowed the canary.

"Yes, it's the loft below yours." The vast gutted space below was something I had dreamt of buying. I had the grandiose idea of making it a gallery slash art studio, so that I could paint and hang all of my work.

"But... someone bought it, I know I asked many times if I could. So, how did you?" I was floored.

"Allie, I bought it five months ago and waited for the perfect time to give it to you." Grinning from ear to ear. All I wanted to do was just make love to him now. I thought I knew everything about this man, but now I felt like I knew nothing. I kissed him passionately, thanking him.

"I love you so much... thank you... thank you." I babbled about the plans I would make for the loft, while he sat watching me in full animation. I think he was as happy as I was. Afterwards, we were quite exhausted and headed to our room. We shared the bathroom while getting ready for bed.

"I love brushing my teeth with you." While smiling with toothpaste on the corners of my mouth.

"Why are you so damn cute?" Shaking his head he left. I got into bed only moments later naked hoping to fool around, but that was not the case, because James was passed out cold. I laid there my mind stirring. Thoughts of when we would make it official with the press or my mother, but I knew I had to talk to her first or I would never live it down. I may have freed myself from her legally, but emotionally we were still very much bonded, as much as I'd like to think we weren't, we definitely were. I thought it best to get ahead of the curve and sent her a text, *Hi Tory, It's happening… I'm engaged! Dinner, Monday night?* Then snuggled into James and fell asleep.

CHAPTER 9

The Engagement Party

The night was utter bliss. I couldn't have guessed in a million years that he would propose to me, not after what I did. Maybe it was an ownership thing. Looking back on it all, I'm sure it was. We would have many more surprises between the two of us. This thing of ours was special and oh so dysfunctional at times. I think the special outweighed the dysfunctional, but I'll let you decide. It seems this could be a running theme in my life… fantastical though, don't you think?

We sat in the formal dining room to eat a feast of a deliciously gourmet breakfast Tate had prepared. The dining room was rich in mahogany; the table and the wood beams on the sixteen-foot ceilings. Four floor to ceiling windows bowed out, overlooking the lawn. The drapes and the ten velvet chairs were off white. Lastly, above the table was one massive crystal chandelier. I wasn't planning on changing the house entirely, but I did want some modern aspects to it, such as the art. I wasn't fond of fruit paintings and women walking in lawns with parasols, just not my style. I was more of a Jackson Pollock and Helen Frankenthaler connoisseur.

"I want to clear something with you first, but I got nervous and texted Tory last night." Explaining that I didn't want her to find out we were engaged from the press. I told him I had arranged for dinner alone with her on Monday and he agreed that it was better if he wasn't there for the initial talk. I invited him to come after dinner and he agreed. That was a relief, I knew they would overtalk me, and nothing would get accomplished. I could at least have a civil one on one conversation with her beforehand.

"It'll be alright, just promise me you won't let her take over. This is our wedding, not hers, ok?" I knew he was right, that was the very first thing that she would attempt. I had to shut her down, but that was easier said than done. I had moments of strength, but other times I was utterly pathetic. I felt like a yoyo, just slipping down into my chair if she said something mean. I would never actually outgrow this.

I walked into Le Bernardin, one of my mother's favorite French Michelin Star restaurants in the Upper East Side. When the definitive history of NYC's dining scene is written, Le Bernardin will have a chapter all to itself. The chef Eric Ripert's an icon and has been entertaining the city's movers and shakers for over 20 years. I knew when meeting my mother she would dress to the nines, so I opted for something special. I wore a Naeem Khan red, embroidered, backless, mini dress with a classic pair of black Manolo pumps. Tory was waiting at the bar chatting it up with someone. All I could think about when I approached her was *wow she is beautiful.* Wearing a black Giorgio Armani Metallic Rafia Motif Blazer with a flat black trouser, under it she had her signature button-down silk, this time it was a soft pink. Her red bottom heel was high to the sky and a brighter pink. I had to hand it to her, she was a baller when it came to clothes. I'd like to think that I was too, after all I was my mother's daughter in some aspects.

As I approached my mother we locked eyes and she tapped a man that was standing next to her. He turned around, "Hello little miss, your mother has been filling me in. I hear congratulations are in order." Not to my surprise it was Chef Ripert.

"Hi Chef, it's so nice to see you… I'm dying to know what she's been telling you." I leaned in to kiss his cheeks, he had been someone I knew since I was in my late teens.

"Well that you might need me to recommend a place to have the venue," replaying the conversation and adding his own expertise into the mix. I listened for a while, and jumped in as soon as I had an opportunity.

"Yes, all advice would be greatly appreciated," looking over his shoulder I glared at her. "Of course, I'll have my assistant call you with a list. Now with that said, I bid you farewell lovely ladies, I must get back to it or I might lose a star!" Chef Ripert laughed, said his goodbyes and left.

"Thank you Tory!" I barked.

"What, what did I do?" Shrugging her shoulders she presented me with her wicked smile. "No offense, I don't want you involved in my wedding. That is what planners are for." Handing her a list that I'd compiled.

"We don't need a list young lady, I am the list!" Tory noticeably angry. I didn't get why. "What is this really about? Are you upset over something I should know about?" Questioning my mother. She denied anything was, and asked me if I wanted a drink. Of course I needed a drink to get through this.

"Yes, but don't worry I'll grab the guy." Putting my hand up I very quickly caught the attention of the bartender. I ordered my Clase Azul Reposado on the rocks with a wedge of orange, a Dirty Martini for her and sunk into the bar stool. The cocktails came and I drank mine down quickly.

"Problems at home already?" Tory smiled sarcastically. My first thought was to say something unkind, but that wasn't me.

"No not at all, on the contrary as you know things couldn't be better." Smiling, I held up my emerald with pride.

"Wow Allie, now that is absolutely beautiful. James did well! Let me see." Pulling my hand close to her face. This was probably the first time I'd experience a joyous moment with her in a very long time. It was a real moment, how long this would last, one never knows, but I'll take it whenever I can. That moment was as rare as my emerald.

Tory was examining it as she complimented me. I was happy, actually very happy for the first time in a long while with her. I felt like I was with my mother and not just Tory. But then my head snapped out of it, and suspicion set in. What was next, kumbaya? Pulling my hand away from Tory, "Shall we get our table, I'm starving." I was excited to eat here, James never liked it, he felt that the crowd was too diverse for him, he liked to know his audience.

"Yes, it's already set, follow me." I trailed behind, curious to know where she would have us this evening, I thought for sure it would be in the middle of the restaurant, she and James had this in common, being the center of attention. To my surprise it wasn't.

We passed the entire room and went through a single, swinging, black door and into a room that was entirely dark. I couldn't see anything, I was just about to yell and then it happened. The entire room lit up and there were at least forty people, including James in front of me, yelling "surprise!" I couldn't for the life of me understand what was going on.

"Allie, you just got engaged. You are my daughter. You didn't think I would let you go without the best party?" Grabbing me, my mother hugged me. I returned the embrace as tears flooded my eyes. I was floored and a bit overwhelmed that she did this for me, for us. Like I said before *"it was a real moment"* and those were rare. James joined in the circle, "Hey I'll get in on that." Wrapping his arms around us, I could smell his Hermes cologne, it made me a bit mad in a good way, screaming sex in every delicious note of fragrance. The funny thing is, it was the same cologne that Dominique wore, but this was the man I loved and he was here now. I inhaled his smell and pulled away with a smile. I was in love.

"Hello my husband to be!" Pulling out of Tory's arms, I was now fully immersed.

"Hi wifey, you look absolutely stunning." As he spun me around to get a good look at me. "Awe you're wearing Khan tonight. Good!" Turning to the crowd he pointed. There he was, one of my favorite designers, besides my fiancé of course. I had modeled for him, but why was he here?

"Oh my gosh… babe, what is this about?" I stood there with the goofiest smile. James waved to Naeem and he walked towards us.

"Allie, I have a surprise for you. Naeem has agreed in his busy schedule to design your wedding dress." My mother was behind us and popped in to grab my hand, I think she could see I was speechless. It was actually perfect timing, for once.

"Such a pleasure, I am the bride's mother. May I just say we are all in awe of your dresses, as you can see Allie's wearing one tonight." She gave me just enough time to compose myself, I was relieved to say the least. Naeem formally introduced himself to my mother and I said hello.

"I am honestly beyond words Naeem. I love your clothes and my dream wedding dress is something that you would make for me." I gushed over the details and he was kind of enough to listen. He was in high demand, so kudos to my love for moving mountains to get him.

The night was filled with a celebration; amazing food, live jazz and a final toast made by James.

"I want to first thank my future mother in law Tory for putting this amazing evening on for us, this lady knows how to throw a party! Can you all please raise your glasses…To Tory!" I was grateful and raised my glass. What can I say the night was utterly picture perfect. I couldn't have asked for anything more magical. Tory did this for me? I didn't know at the time, but the snake was slithering and I was going to be her feast.

The car ride to his place was short and we were in bed within a half an hour. I was excited, I felt like I was on a cloud and couldn't think of anything else I wanted more than to be with him.

"I've been dying to do this all night young lady, come here." Pulling me softly by the nape of my neck, as we laid facing one another, he began to slowly kiss me.

"How did I get so lucky to have you?" I asked.

"How did we get so lucky?" James kissed me deeper pulling me even closer to him, our bodies now pressed tightly. Methodically maneuvering my body onto his, he grabbed my bottom and began to move me back and forth on his manhood. I could feel it growing as he rocked my body. I could feel my heat turning up as my clit lightly rubbed against his cock.

"I want you James." That is all it took, he moved me onto my back and slid his cock slowly inside. I whimpered softly from his touch. He knew I needed him and he needed me more than ever. Looking into his eyes, I could see the longing for us. James was showing me something vulnerable and I loved him for it, beyond what words could convey. I wanted to be this man's wife.

I felt everything as he pushed my legs up and got deeper. I welcomed all of his eight inches into my already wet pussy, as he pounded away at me, his body hitting my ass. I felt like a sub to this man, I wanted him to own me. *That was all I wanted was for him to own me.*

"Take me James, it's all yours!" I screamed.

"Yes Allie, yes I am… fuck Allie, can I come babe? I don't think I can hold on!" Holding still on top of me for a second to hear my response.

"Yes my love!" I whispered. James pushed as hard as he could, again and again until he couldn't, *"Allie, I'm cumming, it's all for you… Fuckkkk, oh fuck!"* James' sweaty chest hit mine as he gently let my legs fall to the bed. He had a lot of strength, I felt depleted of mine. I laid on him, so small, cuddling in his muscular arm and chest.

"Let's make one another a promise," I said sweetly.

"Ok, what is it?" Squeezing me with his manly arms.

"Let's promise no more secrets between us." I was sincere when I said it.

"Yes, I promise, no more secrets between us." He paused. "Now turn over!" Pushing me lightly so that he could scoop me up with his body. I smiled, I felt safe spooning, and quickly fell into a deep sleep. I couldn't have dreamt of a better way to end the most incredible evening of my very youthful existence.

CHAPTER 10

Parting of Ways

Time flew and I was now packing in my loft for my journey to London. It was beyond my wildest dreams to study with David Lurst. James had arranged it all, including my new spy, I meant assistant that would be traveling with me. I wasn't sure the young girl was much of a spy, after all she went to bed at 9 o'clock every night. I agreed to take her, I knew that it would ease his mind. Her name was Jenny. She was from Westport, Connecticut and rarely came to NYC, she had been working for him out there in a satellite office doing some spreadsheets and other boring things. She was kind of a bookworm, so I'm not sure why he sent her. I don't think I'll ever know, but oh well. She was coming regardless, so I arranged that she have a studio apartment below mine in a basement flat, while I on the other hand had the first and second floor on Tite Street in Chelsea. I insisted on using my savings from modeling, so I would control my choice of housing and it would be all mine, no one else's. Tite street was one of the most exclusive streets in London.

It was an early Sunday morning and James was still sleeping in my bed. My flight wasn't until after dinner. I wanted to spend one last day and evening with him. I took a pause and went to the kitchen to make a matcha latte and to send Tory a message. We had been getting along and I knew she was actually pleased I was getting out of New York to do something other than model. I wrote, *I wanted to say goodbye, are you around later… say 5?* Seconds later I received one back from her, it read *Yes, five o'clock King Cole Bar.*

I was flying private at 10 pm, so this was perfect. I could have a drink with her, meet James for dinner, then jump on a plane. It was all falling into place. I felt really secure in my life right now, so the separation from my new fiancé didn't seem like a big deal. Famous last words right.

I went to my DJ mixing board in my loft and played a mix I made of chill classical music and put it on low. I went back to my books and looked around for something to take on the plane, I was old school. I love the feel of a hardcover in my hands, I never did grasp the kindles, no pun intended. I found a great book that Raph had given me before he ghosted on me. It was called *The Secret*. I absolutely loved this book and in turn it made me believe I had the power to make anything happen. I still believe this.

I heard footsteps come up behind me and turned, there was my sleepy, hot man.

"Babe, why are you up so early?" Looking at me through half-closed eyes.

"I'm not sure, I guess I'm excited about London, but not so much about leaving you," I replied while wrapping my arms around his waist.

"I know you are, and everything will be fine, I'll be over to see you as much as I can, ok… you know I can't go that long without getting my Allie fix," James smiled with a bit of sadness in his eyes.

"You know how much I love you right?" I asked.

"Yes, I do," he answered. "You're mine Mrs. John," pulling me in gently for a sweet kiss. We were in such a good place, I questioned whether I should be leaving multiple times, but this opportunity was too big to pass up. So, I took it. I made him a French Press and some avocado toast for us while we sat to make plans for his first visit. After mapping out our calendar, I went back to pack and he went to the gym in my building. I finished before he got back and headed to take a rinse. When I got out he was back.

"Perfect timing, you're naked," he joked.

"Later mister, shower please I have a little surprise lunch for us," I teased, smacking his tight butt.

"A surprise lunch sounds like fun, I'm in," he agreed.

I had planned on restaurant hopping with him, so that we could go to a few of our favorite places downtown. I spoke with all of the maitre d's to make sure we could have corner tables, I wanted to be able to sit right next to him. First taking him to Balthazar in Soho for oysters and Dirty Martini to start, we'd had so many late night conversations there and this was the first place he told me that he loved me. The second place was Locanda Verde for their scampi and grits, my all-time favorite brunch item.

The third and last place was the Soho House art club in the meatpacking neighborhood for a drink on the rooftop. It was cold, but we had coats and part of the roof was enclosed, plus they had heat lamps to keep you warm. Since we were both members, I had arranged with management to bring six of his friends in to celebrate our engagement that couldn't make it to Tory's surprise event. I don't even know if they were invited.

We did the first two and he was beyond pleasantly surprised. Then I had the driver take us to the club.

"Babe, what are we doing here?" He asked.

"Never you mind mister, wait and you'll see," I giggled as we jumped out of the car. We shot up the elevator to the roof and there they all were, his two best friends from the city and their wives, and two of his guy friends from childhood. We immediately caught their eyes as we entered and the group jumped to their feet and yelled surprise. He was confused and elated, "What are you all doing here?" They all started talking at once, so Ben, his best friend since they were in grade school, interjected, "Excuse me, excuse me everyone. First, please someone hand these two a glass of Champagne….. Ok, now that we all have a drink. I would like to make a toast to my best friend and brother, and his bride to be, I wish you both all the happiness in the world. I love you brother, and Allie he loves you, so I know you're the one." Choking up Ben pulled us all in for a group hug. It was one of the best days I think we had ever had. I heard funny little stories about James from all of his friends, things I didn't know, we laughed for hours.

James would occasionally look across from me and lip the words I love you and I would return the words. I knew he was happy and proud of us.

The party was over and it was now time to stop and see Tory for a quick hello and goodbye. I explained to James that I would prefer to see her alone and he couldn't have agreed more. I took our driver and he took an Uber to my loft in Tribeca. I did a quick makeup refresher, spray of perfume, hair brush, sweater to blazer and changed my flats to heels. As a NYC girl you always have to come prepared, because there would be times I would have to go from jeans and kicks to a cocktail dress, so I always had something black and chic in my car to pop into.

We pulled up to the St. Regis where I could see Tory talking on the phone. I waved from the door and scooped up my bag walking towards her. She quickly got off the phone and addressed me.

"Allie, you're on time, actually you're early kiddo." I really didn't like her calling me kiddo, but it had been going on for so long that it was hard to stop her from doing it, but I was determined to try.

"Mom, please stop calling me kiddo. I'm twenty one years old." I think we were both surprised by what I said, but even more so her.

"You haven't called me mom since you were ten years old." I don't know, but if I weren't mistaken she had a tear in her eye. God knows why, she was the one that told me not to call her mom, I never wanted to stop.

"Sorry, it was a slip." Trying to brush it off, it felt awkward between us. We stayed in silence until she broke it at the bar.

"Let's get some of that pink bubbly stuff you like!" We laughed for a good minute. "Champagne it is Tory!" Smiling back at her.

"Sounds good *Allie*… see I can learn," she teased. I like that she actually made an effort not to call me kiddo, maybe you can teach a not so old dog new tricks. We spoke about London, she wanted to make sure I had her list of all of her haunts and contacts, she didn't want her daughter to ever stand in line for a reservation or a private club. God forbid. It was endearing, so I enjoyed her rattling. After two glasses I had to excuse myself, it was six-thirty and I wanted to get home to James. I would only have a couple of hours before I had to leave. We said our goodbyes. As I was walking away from her in front of the hotel she called out to me, "Allie!" I turned back to her. "I love you." Quickly she jumped into her car as I watched her pull out. Confused, but it put an immediate smile on my face. I whispered to myself as I got in my car, *I love you too mom.* My first thought was, is she dying? Then I laughed to myself. No that isn't it, but she was acting so freaking odd. I wondered what was going on, she never acted like this; nice.

Walking in the loft was exciting, I could hear the music and smell a delicious sauce cooking. "Honey, I'm home!" I yelled.

"There you are, you made it without any battle wounds," James teased.

"Very funny, it was actually quite nice seeing Tory." Sharing my visit with my mother, I told him all the strange, but wonderful things she said to me. He seemed genuinely happy for me, he knew how much she hurt me growing up and still continued to do on occasion. We didn't dwell on it too long.

"Are you making us dinner Mr. John?" I asked sweetly.

"Yes my angel," he replied. The word angel threw me into a meltdown.

"Don't you ever call me angel again, ever!" Walking away I needed to compose myself, I couldn't grasp why he would call me that. He didn't know what the hell I was doing, so he followed me to find out.

"Babe, what did I do?" Turning me around he could see I was upset.

"I'm sorry, but please don't call me that. It was the pet name Dominique gave to me."

He could clearly see I was upset.

"Ok, ok baby, I understand, never again… now please get your fine ass over here and kiss me bitch," he joked.

"That's better!" Jumping on him I straddled his waist and gave him the longest kiss.

"I'm sorry James." Holding on to his neck, he carried me back to the kitchen, placing me on the counter he handed me a big glass of Chablis.

I overreacted and I'm not sure why. I think it was because I almost ruined everything by sleeping with Dominique and now felt that *angel* was almost perverse to me. Everytime I heard it my stomach turned. We sat down with a candle-lit dinner and made plans for his part of the flat in London, he wanted me to arrange to have a desk and a drafting table that he ordered to be placed just so in a window there. James needed light, he was like a flower during the day, but a vampire at night.

"I have to get to the airport soon my love, so maybe we should fool around a little?" Lowering my voice to make it sound sexy. It must have worked because he responded like a wild man. He needed to dominate me and I absolutely loved it. He was just so strong and oh so masculine, I could be all woman with him and he was definitely all man.

"Let's go girl!" Dragging me to the bedroom, he tossed me on the bed, then crawled on me slowly, as not to hurt me. Most of his brut was for show, he was actually quite tender with me. I always knew he was coming from a good place and he made me feel safe.

"James... babe, I'm going to miss this and you... just seeing you everyday." I kissed him. He felt my love in the kiss and responded quickly.

"Me too, but this is only temporary. I'll be there as much as I can, besides who's going to take care of you if I'm not there?!" He teased making his way to the buttons on my pants.

"Well then... you had better do a good job now, so I have

something to remember you by." Oh and he always did. He slid my pants down, but kept everything else of mine on. Placing my legs on his shoulders he began to tenderly lick my wet box. Working his fingers lightly, teasing me so that I wanted more. He knew my body, it was melting into his face and I could feel my excitement building. James was also building, I could see he was grinding his body, which meant he was hard and ready to go.

"Please baby, put your fingers inside of me, do that thing you do." I wanted to cum, no I needed to cum. He slipped one inside of me, pushing it slowly in and out.

"Please James!" Begging him for more. I needed to feel like I was being sexed inside and out. James groaned while he ate me, the vibration from it was divine. Placing two more fingers in me while pushing his hand down on my stomach ignited something in me. James had me, I was under his control, he could make me involuntarily cum at any time. Again, a first for me.

"James, what are you doing to me? Baby! Oh my god! More please, more baby please!" Crying out with a strong desire to release. He continued to lick me simultaneously, wildly fingering me.

"I'm cumming James, oh my God, oh my God my love!" I completely lost it, without my participation, the fucking from inside made my pussy gush out a watery liquid everywhere covering his face, then another clitoral orgasm, completely different. It engulfed my entire body.

It was magnificent. I was in awe, collapsing. I was drained from it. I felt euphoric beyond words. *My god I thought, I love this man.* James pulled his face out of my lady parts, his face wet, he looked like a tiger that just had a drink of water and was now ready to hunt his prey.

"Don't move, I am not going to be here long. I need to cum as fast as I can, *I'm fucking dying Allie.*" Pushing his rock hard rod into my dripping pussy, he moved fast and deep into my tight little cave. *"Fuck, I want to cum so fucking bad right now, I need to fill your pussy up..... I have so much cum for you! You're fucking mine... I'm cumming for you Allie, FUCK I'M CUMMING!" Collapsing on me from his mind-blowing orgasm, he laid there for a while. I was still vibrating and we were in complete mind-bending bliss.*

I had to get right up and shower, or else I would miss my plane.

"I love you," pecking him on the lips.

"I'll drive you to the airport, ok?" He asked.

"No, I don't want you to, I'll just get emotional." Arnie, his driver, was coming to pick me up in twenty minutes, so I ran off to rinse and grab my bags. When I returned James was waiting in the kitchen with a card. He knew me, I love written words of affirmation, I guess it's because my mother never gave them to me, actually no one ever did. So, I constantly reminded him and he always remembered.

"What is this?" I asked with a big grin.

"It's something for you, please read it after you're on the plane, not before." Smiling like a boy, he was very proud of himself. It was romantic and it had become a habit, which for me was everything. I even liked it when my friends sent or gave me cards for my birthday, holidays or just because. It says a lot about a person, this is just one girl's opinion.

"Thank you my sexy, beautiful, romantic fiancé." Pressing my lips on his as I wrapped my arms around his neck. He returned my kisses softly while he whispered to me.

"I'm so proud of you Allie." It was the very first time anyone had ever said that. My eyes began to fill up, but I held onto my tears.

"You are?" Asking bashfully.

"Of course I am, don't be ridiculous, have you seen yourself lately? You are an accomplished woman already and you're just getting started." Surprised by my lack of confidence. I guess he was right. I did have confidence, but sometimes I would feel this hole of darkness under my feet and it would drag me in, not always, but it did happen, and still does periodically. Less now, but still it lurks in the shadows waiting to take me down. I think everyone can relate to wanting to be better or not feeling good enough to yourself or someone in your life. I think?

The buzzer rang, it was time to go. I felt a lump in my throat, I was extremely attached to this man, he really took care of me, always watching over me like a superhero protector. This would actually be the first time I would be in a major city alone, well without a man keeping an eye on me. I suddenly felt a burst of excitement.

"Love you baby!" Kissing him one last time as I headed to the elevator with Arnie and all of my eight bags.

"Love you too Al. Do you think you have enough to wear?" He teased. Laughing, I blew him a kiss and the doors shut. I got to Teterboro airport and the jet was waiting to take me and all of my luggage to my new life in London. I suddenly felt sad and happy in the same breath.

When I got settled in my seat I reached for my handbag and pulled out James' card. On the card was a single, red rose hand painted on the front and the inside read, "You will always be mine and I yours. Please don't forget. Love, James." It made me smile, because I was the only one he wanted, no one else, but was he the only one I wanted? I didn't know at the time, but there was a lot more in store for me than I could ever imagine. I was about to step into a whole new pair of shoes.

CHAPTER 11

Party Crashers

I got to my townhouse where Jenny, my new assistant, was eagerly waiting. Jenny was just twenty, even though she was just one year my junior, she appeared to be much younger. My grandmother used to say that I was wise beyond my years, I didn't see it, but today I felt like a real grown-up.

"Hello! It's so nice to meet you. I am excited to be here, working with you and want to thank you!" Excitedly nervous Jenny rattled on.

"Jenny, Jenny, I appreciate it. It's nice to meet you." Kindly interrupting her.

"Sorry, I talk too much!" She laughed and snorted loudly. Jenny was a nerdy, maybe 5'4", black girl with bright pink cat eye frames. She wore a one-piece black jumpsuit with white polka dots, I could tell it was a Betsey Johnson original. I liked her quirky style right off the get-go and her for that matter. She smiled a dazzling white smile and waited for me to speak.

"I slept the entire way, so I am thinking of staying up, so that I can stay with London time." I continued. "Can you help me get all of this luggage to my master and start to unpack it for me Jenny?" She jumped at me like an eager cheerleader at a pep rally, and began grabbing multiple cases at the same time.

Jenny got my walk-in closet ready with the hangers I requested, color-coded them and organized my entire wardrobe on her computer before I even arrived with the clothes. I mean come on, Jenny was a dream assistant.

"Wow Jenny, I can't believe how efficient you are. I really appreciate this." Excusing myself to the sound of my phone ringing. I wondered who could possibly be calling on the very first day of my arrival. I answered and to my surprise it was the one and only David Lurst. He welcomed me and asked if I could attend a party tomorrow evening at his home in London. I was beyond elated. David Lurst was calling me! Of course I agreed, this was the man I would get to know personally and watch create some of his masterpieces here in London. My head was spinning from the possibilities.

I went upstairs with a few bags to unpack while I got to know Jenny. Turns out Jenny was somewhat of a fashion designer. She made clothes growing up, because they didn't have any money to spare in their house, reinventing herself through sewing oversized thrift store clothes into cool outfits. I was really impressed and also thought she could be a real asset in my life. She was grateful and modest, I liked her. I didn't like the fact she might be reporting back to James, but it wasn't like Jenny lived with me 24/7, I had her downstairs below ground in a studio flat. It was important for me to live alone, I got used to it, I had been alone most of my life, so it's something I treasured. I wasn't sure exactly how James would feel about me keeping my loft downtown, because I really didn't want to sell it after we were married. It was my home or at least the only home I really knew, the one I created for myself. I loved staying with him half the week, but man did I ever love my own space; my books, music, food, style, art, just everything, I loved it all.

"Hey, maybe you could help me find something for tomorrow night's soiree!" Tapping my shoulder to Jenny's. She smiled a goofy grin, "Hell yes... oops sorry, I meant yes I would love to!" We giggled like two kids, after all we were close in age, even though we weren't in some ways. She grew up with two parents that really were normal.

"Jenny, please don't stop yourself from being you. Swearing is encouraged amongst us girls." I joked.

"Thanks Allie, I'm really stoked to be here with you!" Heading into the closet Jenny was gone. I stopped to grab a bite from the kitchen that she had stocked with all of my favorites. I noshed on some salads and rye crackers in the living room. I took a deep breath in and realized for the first time, I was exactly where I was supposed to be. There was a certainess about the feeling I had in my heart. What tomorrow would bring, well that's another story.

Who's the Shark Now?

After I made my call to James to let him know I was safe and sound in my new place. I went to bed with a couple of sleeping pills, I desperately wanted to feel good for the party. I woke spritely in the morning to a new home and somewhat of a new life. I couldn't wait to see what options for this evening that Jenny had put aside in my closet. To my surprise she had only pulled one dress and one pair of heels.

A Retrofete long-sleeved metallic silver and black dress. It had some flash because of the metallic, but the conservative cut balanced it out. She had paired it with a black four inch, with a silver heel, a pair from James's winter collection. It was quite elegant, yet I would look my age. I couldn't have picked a better outfit for this evening, but I would have been in the closet for a half of a day destroying the organizing she had done if it were up to me.

I heard a buzz at the door and ran down a flight to see who it was. It was Jenny with a humongous arrangement of flowers. I invited her in and looked through the flowers. I couldn't imagine who would be sending me flowers today. No one knows I'm here. There was nothing amongst the exotic arrangement, I was bewildered to say the least. "Hmm. I wonder who sent these. Did you see a card?" I asked Jenny. She had said no, so I asked her to call the florist and find out who the mystery sender was. Jenny returned shortly and told me the person that came by paid with pounds and that they didn't remember if it were a man or woman. So odd I thought, but then went about my business at hand. Jenny and I worked out a loose schedule for the next few days.

"Oh Allie, you have nails and hair in two hours. Can I make you lunch before you go?" Jenny asked me sweetly.

"Wow, look at you! You have me all sorts of organized don't you and no, I will take you out to lunch today. You worked so hard on my closet. My treat, go grab a jacket and I'll meet you here in ten minutes," explaining while running up the stairs.

I remembered this great little place on Sloane Square called Coberts. Tory had taken me there for lunch and of course drinks, they had a great lunch and it wasn't far from my place. I got to know Jenny a little more, and I began to feel great about having her around. She no longer resembled a spy, more like a friend. Which for a second brought me back to my two besties, neither spoke with me any longer, I was all alone and for a second I felt sad, I thought maybe it was time to reach out and see how they were doing. I went back into conversation with Jenny, realizing that I had it good and stayed focused on what was happening in my life right now. How lucky am I.

Lunch was fun, but then the panic of just having three hours till countdown began, but that was short-lived when Jenny guided me to a posh salon on the square, just minutes away from the restaurant, where I could have my hair, nails and makeup done. All of my anxiety went right out the window as I sunk into a chair. Jenny was already invaluable. The only thing left was to slip into my dress and be on my way. Walking in my house I realized everything was under control and that I shouldn't get frazzled, but then reality sunk in, I was only on my way to see one of the greatest living artists and then I was flipping out again in my head, which in turn became vocal, "Holy shit, I'm so nervous all of the sudden. Jenny, can you get me a drink please?" I waited for her response.

"Yes, what would you like?" I told her Clase Azul and explained how to make my drink, which she would continue to do for me the entire time we were in London. Hey, might as well get her up to speed I thought. I felt more relaxed, took a deep breath, and told myself *you got this Allie you got this Allie.* I knew I had it all under control but I thought it better to be safe than sorry and told Jenny she was coming with me. I didn't have a plus one, but decided to apologize, rather than ask permission. I handed her a beautiful Valentino dress and she went to change. Jenny looked very elegant, yet still had an eccentric twist with her ever so revolving door of eyeglasses.

David Lurst lived in London's prestigious Regent's Park in a massive mansion. He was the richest living artist in the UK, possibly in the world. David made his name and fortune by selling a shark preserved in formaldehyde and also a diamond-encrusted crystal skull. The man was an eccentric genius in my eyes.

I had watched a documentary on George Condo when I was quite young, after that I desperately wanted to become an artist. I felt like I knew him, or at least pieces of him as an artist. Now here I am, in London, getting ready to walk into David Lurst's house. I wasn't nervous any longer, now I was just overly thrilled to be a part of this evening, like a child in a giant candy factory. The doors were pulled open by *two men in black,* no pun intended, there were two extremely large men wearing all black, it was almost comical.

His house was decorated British-style and was loved because of its austere elegance, classic luxury, with the highest quality materials. The presence of many beautiful decorative elements, and of course art made it the most valuable home in north London. This was living at its finest. There were people everywhere, but it looked like we were being directed to a private area in which I assume the party was to be given. I had Jenny count after we got in the room and there were thirty people invited. I like this number, it felt lively enough, but yet attainable in the way of speaking to all of them for a few minutes. Tory always said you never know who you could be standing next to, so you'd better make an impression and that is exactly what I wanted to do. Starting with the host.

Walking across the vast room as I grabbed a rosé Champagne from a waiter, I could clearly see David in a corner speaking to a much older gentleman. I decided to get it out of the way and approached him.

"Hello gentleman, I'm sorry to intrude. I wanted to introduce myself." I sweetly addressed them both, but waited for him to respond.

"I know who you are, and you're not interrupting, Mr. Roberts and I were just ending our chat. Weren't we Mr. Roberts?" David now directed his question at the other gentleman. "Yes we were, now if you will excuse me." Mr. Roberts nodded.

"So, where was I, yes… you are Allie Hart, I recognize you from your photograph that James sent from his last show. I don't know the rules of engagement, but I'll say it regardless, you are even more beautiful in person. It's very nice to meet you." Extending his hand to shake mine, I quickly returned mine. I was in a bit of a trance, our hands stayed locked for a few too many seconds, but when I realized what I was doing, I quickly pulled away.

"I'm sorry, that wasn't me, I mean it was me, it's just I'm just a bit of an admirer." Stammering over my words like the rookie I was. He realized that I wasn't as mature as I might have had him believe. Surely I was flattering him, considering the big smile that he wore.

"This is the second apology in ten minutes. No need, I mean it." We laughed for a moment. Moments later, someone he knew walked in and he politely excused himself while he chuckled. He asked me to enjoy the night, and asked if I could stick around after the party, so we can talk about tomorrow's schedule in the studio. David Lurst wanted to speak to me in private, I couldn't believe my ears. I was walking on a cloud all night. I would soon have a "chat" with him in his home in London! Could it get any better than this I thought? Again I felt like I was a kid. The flip flop between grown-up and child seemed to be my biggest feat and still is. I always maintain a little "Peter Pan" in me, something that just won't leave me.

The night was festive, there were a bunch of blues musicians in the corner, two bars and passed hors d'oeuvres. There was no formal seating, but there were beautiful tables sprinkled around the room to add privacy to conversations. If only I could have been a fly on the wall, to know what they were all confiding in one another over, I bet it was delicious. Well, I sort of did have a fly on the wall and that was Jenny. She stood around the room barely chatting to anyone, but like a smart spy, listened. It was more than halfway over, so I told Jenny she could go home, she graciously left, but not before telling me she had a lot of gossip to share. This definitely peaked my interest and I knew breakfast with her would be the highlight of my morning. Afterwards, I spoke to a woman named Suki. She owned a prominent art gallery and from what I could understand was arranging his next private show in London. I had wondered if there was going to be a private bidding war amongst the elitists. Most likely, they lived for this type of spending and I was here to witness it all.

I was fading towards the end of the party as everyone was leaving the house, but got a sudden burst of energy knowing that I would be with David alone and soon. I could feel him looking at me from across the room and locked eyes with him, I didn't move them from him, instead I imagined what he would be like to kiss. I'm only human, how can you not wonder, this was a living piece of history, I found him utterly intriguing and dare I say handsome. Suki was the last person to leave, I could see her saying something close to David's ear, then she waved in my direction, then was gone. I returned the wave, but she didn't wait to notice. Now I was alone in the monstrosity of a house with him. What would he want from me?

I walked to meet him on the other side of the room where he roamed near the bar.

"Now it's time for that much needed drink, what's your poison Allie?" He asked while pouring a large Scotch.

"I will have that please, and double as well." Pointing to my go-to, Clase Azul.

"Oh you thought that was a double?" We laughed. He was a funny guy amongst all of his other noticeably amazing traits. David pushed the drink back, so I followed suit and did the same, he poured us another drink and told me to follow him, I did as he requested without hesitation. We walked to the elevator and took it down. Below us was a spa with a pool on one side and then the other side through a large steel door was where part of his madness came to meet; his art. I was beyond impressed, words couldn't describe what I was looking at. The shark in the tank, paintings everywhere.

"So, what do you think?" David said in his cute British accent.

"I don't know what to say, I couldn't imagine a more visually stimulating scene in all of my life." I drooled. We spoke about some of the larger works, he explained his take on the art world for all of two minutes, but what he shared was the most insightful bit of advice that I could have imagined. I was in awe of him, his brain was on a different level than any other human being out there. I guess that is why he is who he is right. Kind of like Steve Jobs to what he is to technology, this man was the equivalent in art. He asked me about my life and why I wanted to paint and create. I told him the truth, that it was something I always just knew. He really appreciated that response and agreed that he'd always known that this was going to be his path, that of an artist. To say I was professionally crushing on him was an understatement, I wanted to live inside of his brain, to know what he did.

He took me back out the doors to the other side of the vast basement, where there was a very large hammam pool.

"It's beautiful David." Placing my hand in the water I scooped it up and let it fall away from my fingers. "Wow, it feels so nice, the perfect temperature." Smiling at it, I wondered what the water would feel like on my entire body. I loved water and spent hours in pools and bathtubs. Eve would always say I was a water baby.

"Go in if you'd like," he replied.

"Only if you come in with me." Responding quickly. I surprised him with my words, but it now made him feel a bit more at ease with what he chose to say moving forward.

"With or without?" David pulled at his shirt, exposing part of his chest. I didn't answer until after I slipped my dress off and onto the floor. I had a black, lace panty and bra set "Without." Smiling in delight.

"You are stunning, absolutely brilliant." As he walked to me, I was thinking about anything except for the moment at hand. Seemed to be my future response to everything, which was to go with my intuition, it mostly served me well, I said mostly. I think I was testing him, but I knew for sure that I wanted his skilled, artistic hands on my body, so I moved closer to him to see what he would do. Staring in my eyes intensely as he ran his fingers lightly over my stomach, then my breast and lastly my face. I stood there confident that he would kiss, but I was wrong though.

"Allie, I would like nothing more than to ravish you, but then I might fall in love with you." He joked, but was he really joking? You could clearly see his hard-on protruding through his black pants, but we all know that isn't love. Like a naughty girl, I wanted to touch it, but I knew I was already throwing myself at him and began to feel embarrassed.

"I should go, but I'm not going to apologize." Pulling my dress off the floor, I excused myself to the bathroom without putting the dress back on till I got inside. I wanted him to watch me walk away from him. I could hear him say 'my god woman' which made me smile from ear to ear. I think I knew at this moment it would only be a matter of time before I had him. How dare I forget about my engagement, as I looked down at my emerald in the mirror. I did love James. Tory used to say to compartmentalize my feelings, and so that is what I was determined to teach myself how to do. I must have her DNA, because it worked. As long as I didn't get caught, no one would be hurt. Right?

CHAPTER 13

The Tease

I got up early, grabbed my matcha and went back upstairs to shower, and pick out something amazing for my first day of work. Jenny was already in the kitchen when I returned dressed, ready to go. We said our good mornings, she then proceeded to kindly explain that I was overdressed for the studio.

"I went through your work emails, and I got Mr. Lurst's studio address as well as his assistant Jasmine's specific dress code. You're supposed to wear old jeans and a t-shirt, and sneakers that you no longer care about. She explained you would get very messy and said to bring clothes to change out of after work. Oh, and lastly Mr. Lurst would like you to join him for a bite after at his local pub." Jenny spoke loudly enough as I blended a shake in my Vitamix.

"Oh ok, I'll run up and change quickly."

Pouring us both a shake I exited. I loved the idea of getting dirty in some paint and materials at work. I knew it would be everything to me. I could feel it inside of my stomach, the butterflies, the excitement was growing. I gave Jenny a list of duties and out the door I went.

I walked into his studio, which was at a different location in Battersea. I was surprised, no I was actually stunned to see that he owned an enormous warehouse, it was 20,000 square feet beyond big. The massive paintings that lined the walls, made my head swirl with my own ideas immediately. David approached

116

from behind as I wandered around the space.

"Which is your favorite?" He asked. I turned to him and grinned.

"Hmm… well I think the one that evoked the most emotion was this one." I pointed at a large pink flower that was absolutely beautiful.

"Interesting, my favorite as well." Pleasantly surprised he asked me to join him in a tour of the space as he explained how he worked. I was beginning to realize that there was a certain way he conducted his daily life here, very organized and chaotic I thought. I would later in life become very familiar with all this in my own studio and life.

I knew David had a lot to share as a mentor and I wanted nothing more than to be a sponge. Well there was one other thing I thought about as we walked around the space, what David would be like in bed. Would he be as creative? Would he be uninhibited as his work was? What was his kiss like? I could tell he was a little curious about me, almost like the look on a child's face when they receive a new shiny toy. I started to feel myself do something that became a habit later in my life and that was to see him as a conquest. He wasn't the most handsome man I had seen, actually he was quite average looking, plus he had a receding hairline. His face was kind of round, eyes were blue as ice, nose was strong and his lips were not small, but they weren't large either. His body was stocky, maybe around 5'11". All of that said, he had a sparkling personality, very magnetic, people were drawn to him, and in this moment in time I was too. I was beginning to learn that beauty was something more than your outward appearance, it's internal that comes to the surface, an energy you exude.

We worked on several different concepts throughout the day. What I began to understand is that he appreciated my honesty and valued my eye for art and symmetry. I felt validated, so why would I jeopardize this with a silly girl crush? Yes, I was crushing on him, he was a powerful artist and his voice mattered historically, also the fact that he was a genius. I didn't think I would ever be like him, that successful or powerful, but I knew I could get close to some of his greatness, by learning and growing as an artist myself. We were close to being finished with the day at hand when David turned to me to ask, "Are you hungry?"

I realized I hadn't eaten all day. "Actually I'm famished!" I replied.

"Alright then, can I take you to grab a bite at my local spot, it's just around the corner next to Battersea Park." You could tell he was now finished working and just wanted to leave. I knew that feeling in so many different scenarios.

"Yes, I'd love to join you. Let me switch out of my clothes first." Excited, I hopped up and grabbed my tote bag.

"Ok, I'll do the same and meet you at the exit in twenty minutes. Oh and there is a shower back there, so feel free to jump in." He grinned. Did he want me to get naked or was that a nice gesture? I caught myself being ridiculous and decided I did smell like all kinds of chemicals and paints, so a shower would be a great idea. I went to the back, there was a small locker area, not very nice, but clean and so I slipped on some flip flops that were in a basket, kicked off my pants while pulling my hair into a ponytail. I kept the curtain open. I had a thing about small, confining spaces. A shower curtain always gave me the strangest feeling, like I was locked up or something.

I got all lathered up and was singing a bit in the shower when I heard a noise on the other side of the wall.

"Allie don't be alarmed, I am leaving you a cocktail on the stand, I didn't see anything, promise!" David yelled in.

"Thank you, but you know you're welcome to use the other shower, I won't look," teasing him.

My relaxed reassurance must have been exactly what he needed, because moments later I heard David jump into the other shower. I was excited to hear it, not knowing exactly how I would keep my eyes forward and not have a peak. Would he leave the curtain open like myself? I guess there was only one way to find out, right? I had to. I turned quickly and like I thought, there he was naked soaping up his front, which included his semi-hard penis. Now that was something to see, and he was definitely above average in length and thick, really thick. Something shot through my body like a lightning bolt, I wanted to run over and start stroking his manhood, but I didn't. I had to contain myself. How, well I'm not sure exactly. He didn't look in my direction, I think he was actually ignoring me. Which made me want him more now. How dare he ignore me I thought. For me it was game on.

I waited for him to leave, then got out grabbing my drink and bag heading to the small mirror above a sink. I had just enough light to freshen up for ten minutes as I downed my drink and rummaged through my makeup case for an Adderall. Lucky for me I found one, at this time they needed to be had when I wanted one or I would flip out in my head. I felt very ADD without them or maybe I was just addicted, who knows but I didn't feel like I was abusing them, at least not yet. I looked pretty cool wearing a simple black tank, under a vintage, Gucci leather jacket that once belonged to Tory. A pair of dark denim, Paige skinnies with my slide distressed, studded, Golden Goose kicks.

David met me at the entrance wearing all non-descript black, which in my opinion was pretty cool also. He just oozes a certain amount of "fuck you" confidence. I guess it came with years of being on top of his craft.

I couldn't help it, yet again I got a bit excited, but then my mind shot to the realization that I was his understudy, and I had a fiercely fine and very jealous fiancé. I didn't want to piss James off and knew I had to speak to him tomorrow about his future trip across the pond to see me. I also thought about the conversations he and David might have about my recent engagement. As of now he knew nothing of it. I didn't wear my ring in front of anyone right now. I didn't want to feel owned by him when he wasn't even in the same city, for some reason it seemed wrong. How does he get to run around NYC, and doesn't have a ring to say he belongs to me like I do? Yet myself as a woman, has to wear a big diamond ring that screams unavailable. Fuck that I thought, I mean mind you I love the guy, but still this felt like the scale was tipping in his favor, not mine, am I wrong? I didn't think so at the time, nor do I now.

We walked into a small pub that had around a dozen tables and ten bar stools. A petite older woman named Rose came over to greet us, she knew him for what seemed like a lifetime. Rose brought us to David's favorite table that she held for him. I assumed that was his "permanent" spot when visiting the pub, which appeared to be often. I thought that was nice, down to earth. David was beginning to surprise me. He appeared to be just a cool guy that made it from rags to riches, it made me admire him even more so now. We chatted for a while about his life growing up in the not so great places in London, he described himself as a scrapper and told me he was teased a lot for being the kid with the sketch pad.

"Yes, my brother and I got into fights at least twice a week for the longest time. I finally left school in the eleventh grade and said fuck it, and became the artist you see." He explained his life as hard. It made me realize that I wasn't the only one with a fucked up childhood. I liked the commonality. We felt like kindred spirits.

We drank for a couple of hours, eating some local meat pies and laughed about his years of trying to make it in the art world. You always think when you meet someone that they just had overnight success, but this is never the case, you just happen to finally hear about them one day after years of them struggling. I could see from David that his story and journey was part of what made him this successful and inventive type of person.

I was buzzed from the alcohol and conversation, and found my desire growing. My thoughts now overshadowed all of what he was saying. I couldn't hear him for the next few minutes as my mind began imagining us kissing naked.

"Hey… so, what do you think?" David asked while snapping his fingers in front of my eyes. I must have been staring, oh fuck.

"I'm sorry, I'm so embarrassed," I replied.

"You didn't hear a word I said, did you?" David laughed. I think at this moment he knew I was fantasizing about him and really got a kick out of it. I don't know if it was the alcohol, or I was just beginning to grow in confidence, but the words escaped my lips, "I was thinking about you and me, and if there was a possibility of something more going on here." He wasn't surprised by my words. David smiled with his mischievous eyes and said nothing, as I sat awkwardly. Finally after what seemed like an eternity, but was in reality a few minutes he responded.

"You are a wonderful woman, I like your company… and yes, I, like any man that has a dick would be attracted to you. I however have a partner, and you have someone in your life and this could make everyone's lives very complicated." Explaining with honesty, so that there was zero confusion. David continued to tell me how Becca was there when he had nothing, and that he could never hurt her.

"I don't want to hurt her, nor do I want to hurt James. This can be our secret, just ours." Grinning, I placed my hand on his thigh. David grinned as he shook his head and then asked for the check. To me, this meant yes, and I was ready for it, but did it? We exited the pub and he hailed a taxi.

"Here is where we say goodnight pretty lady." Opening the door for me, I followed his lead and got in. I can't say I was happy, but how could I be upset? I told the driver my address and then I was gone and so was he. I could have sworn he was feeling me, but I guess not. I thought what a tease and my second thought was I needed to get off.

CHAPTER 14

Painting the Countryside

I went into the studio bright and early, excited to see David. I was hoping that he would be going a bit crazy like I was from last night, but there was no David. His assistant Jasmine came to me and gave me a list of what he wanted me to do, explaining that David went to his country estate to be completely alone and create. She told me that he would do this from time to time for no reason and without any warning. I asked her if Becca or other staff would be there, and she without hesitation explained "absolutely no one." I wondered if he was doing this because of me. I went about my work assignments but was obsessed with my stirring thoughts all day. It wasn't any fun without him here, it just felt like a mundane job. I couldn't be his understudy and not work with him. Everyone had left for the day, except for me. I stayed behind. I needed to know where he was, so I did the unthinkable and went through Jasmine's desk. I found David's countryside address. Without thinking, or showering I got into my car and drove to his house.

I was in the car when I realized that this must look insane and stopped the car on the side of the road. *I couldn't really be doing this, could I? He's going to think I'm mad. Fuck! What should I do?* I wanted to see him, this was not logical, but I couldn't stop myself from what I was about to do. I drove up to a lovely farmhouse, but it was dark and had no lights on inside. I could see that there was a small rocky road that went around the back side, so I parked my car, turned on my iPhone light, and walked around the house. To my surprise, there was a large barn with a light shining through the door. I had a feeling this is where I would find David.

Opening the door was a bit scary, I didn't know if my intrusion would be greeted with a smile or you're fired. I had hoped for the best and without hesitation, I opened a small entry door off to the side and entered. *Wow, is what I thought,* it was spectacular. There was only one large painting amongst a village of paint cans and David on a high stool looking onward at it. It must have been at least thirty feet long and fourteen feet high. I could tell it was a work in progress or else why would he come here? Not being much of a sneak, I bumped into a table and fell to the ground. Of course, he heard the echoing of it and my voice in the large barn. I felt his hand on my arm, and as I looked up at him, he extended his other hand. Following his lead I placed mine in his as he pulled me to my feet.

"What took you so long?" Smirking, David tugged me into the inside of his sanctuary. *Had he known I would come?* It appeared so.

"How did you know I would come?" I asked.

"I didn't, I just hoped," he said as he walked away leaving me in the center of the room.

"I guess you want me to wait here?" I laughed. David returned from behind a small wall and had a bottle of red. He poured two glasses and proceeded to tell me all about the art that had been his biggest mind-bending challenge to finish. I loved hearing him talk about his work. He was so passionate and cerebral in his explanation of the process. I fell in love with his voice immediately, everything he said was like poetry. He was utterly fascinating. David popped another bottle of red and asked me to grab a brush.

"No, I couldn't! This is your baby! I would just mess it up, I can't be held accountable." While stepping back, I dropped the brush on a small table.

"There are no mistakes in art love, just take the brush and pick the color, I want to feel what you feel," he insisted. I felt his trust in me, so I did what he asked and picked up the brush. I immediately mixed a few blues together to create something softer, almost a vintage blue jean blue and tossed it on the canvas with the brush. Turning to him I smiled, "That felt good!" He gave me my first feeling of freedom on the canvas and for that I would forever be grateful.

"I know sweet lady, I know," he smiled. I couldn't contain my feelings anymore, without hesitation, I walked over to him and placed my hands around his waist. Looking into his forever-blue eyes of mystery, I softly laid my lips on his and kissed him. David returned my kiss, exploring my mouth lightly, methodically taking his time, as to study our rhythm. I liked it very much, and I could feel something building between us. It was more than attraction, we shared something artistically, and he was my tribe.

Everything else in the world faded, all I could see was him. Would he want me? I didn't know, and I couldn't wait to find out. For the first time, I didn't feel crazy to be me, I just felt relaxed in my own skin. I explained to David that I had come from his studio in the city without a shower or change of clothes. You could tell he liked that I was impulsive. He asked me to follow him to the house. David brought me to a room upstairs and opened a closet, there were some smaller sizes of flannels and jeans, overhauls and shoes.

"These belonged to my mother, she passed away a few years ago. You were around her size. Grab something to wear and I'll show you to your bathroom." You could see how much he missed her as he softly touched the clothes. This must have been her home. Now I understood why he liked to come here alone.

"Thank you, David." I was honored by his gesture.

I finished showering and decided on a pair of old Levi's, a green and tan flannel shirt with a pair of wool slippers. I found David in a living room standing in front of a roaring fire having a Bourbon.

"That was her favorite shirt, it looks good on you. Your eyes, wow they are so green now," he said while extending his hand to me. I walked up to the fire to stand by him. David offered me a drink and I asked for a Tequila, he left to get it. The room was full of photographs of him as a child with her, but no dad, no siblings, just them. He was a mystery to me. I didn't want to ask him a million questions the first night alone with him, so I kept it to myself. David returned with a healthy glass of Tequila on the rocks and the bottle. He smiled and made a toast to his mom. I know the shirt pleased him as we drank.

The night was full of conversation. David let me in on his family, or lack of. His mother was a single parent and worked two jobs to support him in school. That is until he started making a bit of money and then the two of them purchased the house and barn, alongside ten acres of land around it. He explained after that, it started to get better and better for him in his career, until he was able to just create and support his mother. His only dream was to make it big in the art world, so that he could make her comfortable, to want for nothing.

David wasn't like any other man. He was a true artist and one of the most fascinating men that I had ever met. His genius was unlike most, he had a way of delivering his thoughts that transcended into visions. I was attracted to his brain and everything else that stood before me. My thirst was building, how long I could contain myself, while he seemingly looked at me like a friend. The friend that wanted nothing more than to be in bed with him, a friend that couldn't stop seeing what she thought she wanted and that was him. *I can't push, he's beginning to confide in me.* Deciding in the end to do the right thing and not appear to be desperate for his touch, I excused myself.

"Well it's getting late, I think I'm going to call it a night." Kissing his cheek we said our goodbyes for the evening.

I got into my room and undressed, the whole time thinking about him touching me as I slowly caressed my breasts. I desperately needed to get off. If he wasn't available, the fantasy of him was. I laid on the bed with my eyes closed, spreading my legs, pushing my fingers in my mouth to wet them, then placed them on my throbbing pussy. I began to fuck myself with one hand, as I gripped my nipple. Pulling and twisting as I fingered myself furiously. Moaning lightly while I imagined myself making love with him. Only to stop abruptly, because I heard a noise outside my door.

It was him, oh my fucking god, he heard me. I waited eagerly to see if he would knock or just leave, but I could hear him walk away. I was disappointed and sexually frustrated as I returned to myself, I needed relief, I was in agony. I went back to my pulsating clit and began rubbing it, squeezing my nipple till the pleasure and pain shot through it, as ecstasy shot through my entire body. My eyes closed tightly as I fanaticized. I wanted to feel him inside of me, but I could only see it in my dream now. When I got close to cumming I backed away and lightly teased my wet flower. I wanted it to last a little longer. Whimpering softly as I thought of his rejection. I was there, at the very top of my threshold. Everything released from my loin, I could feel the warm, slippery liquid fall from my lips as I came hard. *Fuck fuck fuck that felt so amazing.* Smiling at the thought of making this a reality soon, I sunk into my pillow and fell asleep.

It was early morning when I walked into the kitchen. David had laid out a typical English breakfast of eggs, beans, stewed tomatoes, and of course bangers. I wasn't much of a breakfast eater, but I gladly sat to enjoy the feast that he proudly made for us. I don't know why, but everything he did seemed authentic and pure, and I liked it. It was refreshing from what I was accustomed to. He wasn't going after me, and for the first time I was enjoying a man without sleeping with him. Part of me absolutely loved this, but the other part still longed for him. It was very romantic in its nature. David opened up to me, sharing his most intimate thoughts. I felt honored to be in his very presence. We sat laughing about his childhood memories, him blowing up his mother's kitchen while cooking her a birthday breakfast similar to the one he prepared. I must have looked at him like a starry-eyed kid, but I didn't care, I just giggled at his jokes and let go of my fear of impressing him. We were bonding, and fast. I didn't want the day to end and it had just begun.

"Let me show you around the town and countryside," David said while pulling me to my feet.

"What about the mess?" I asked.

"Not to worry, I have someone coming in. Now let's go!" David insisted. He brought us to a small carport where he had a car enclosed under a cover, removing it was magical. It was a DB5 Aston Martin, baby-blue convertible with a black leather interior in mint condition. It was absolutely gorgeous, so sexy, yet sophisticated, and blue to match his eyes... just perfect. David opened my door and presented me with a hand to get into the car. I gladly popped into the seat, again wearing the very casual clothes of his mothers. This time a soft white dress that looked like it belonged in the sixties, over the knee and buttoned up the middle. I wore it with some ballerina flats, hair down and wavy, and just a tad of makeup on my face. David wore some faded jeans, a white t-shirt, a khaki jacket, and a worn-out pair of Chelsea ankle boots. We looked perfectly vintage Ralph Lauren. I think back to him and this memory and it still serves me as one of the most romantic days of my life, but not all the days would be so lovely.

We drove around for the day, not stopping for lunch, there was so much to see of the green, lush countryside. For a moment I wondered what it would be like to live here with him. I found myself taking my thoughts further away from just sex and to a more substantial life here with him. I knew deep down that it could never happen. I couldn't just forget my other life and disappear. Besides, I didn't even know if he wanted to be with me romantically anyway. We returned back to his home, he apologized, and went to make a call outside. I took the opportunity to do the same and dialed James. I told him I loved him, and that work was going great. He was so thrilled for me and happy to be visiting soon but didn't know when he could leave New York. Explaining that work was too busy and that most likely it would have to be a week and a half from today. Disguising my happiness, I told him I would wait and not to worry. Hanging up the phone was a relief as I walked to the kitchen to look for an alcoholic beverage. I found the Tequila from last night and poured a big glass gulping it down like water.

"Wow, you must be thirsty!" David startled me with his comment.

"Stop, I almost spit it out," holding my mouth I laughed.

"Pour me one just like that but double and yourself another," he smiled. I did so happily. We drank a few more and got tipsy. *So now what I thought.*

Without thinking I stepped into his space and put my hands around his neck, pressing my lips onto his mouth lightly. This time he didn't hold back, pulling me in by my waist, he returned fire with a passionate kiss. His tongue in my mouth, dancing around mine. I loved how slow and deliberate it was. It was softer than I had experienced. David slowly pulled me back to look at me while caressing my face. He stared into my eyes, wounded, he was affected by me somehow. I felt like I had just met my soulmate and I knew he could feel it too. We began kissing again as we lightly touched one another. Brushing my breasts as he cautiously unbuttoned my dress. He opened it, staring at my exposed body, then slipped it off my shoulders and onto the floor. Bravely standing before him I unfastened his pants as he removed his shirt. There we were, finally, the moment I had longed for. Standing completely vulnerable while embracing each other's fully naked bodies. It felt so right.

Looking into David's eyes I softly spoke the words I had longed to say all night and day. *"Please make love to me David."* Grabbing my hand he slowly guided me to his bedroom and his king-size dark wood-framed bed. It was all adorned with blue vintage silk. It fit the house perfectly. Carefully he laid down with me and began kissing me all around my face.

"I love looking at your profile, your lips, your eyes. You're an artist's dream to paint." David whispered in my ear as he moved his kiss to my breast. Patiently taking his time, maintaining his softness. He never rushed, even his lovemaking was art. I had never experienced such tenderness with any man. They looked at me like conquest or something. I was overwhelmed with excitement and appreciation for the revelation that was happening to me. This was making love, not fucking. David moved softly onto my stomach, kissing it like it was my mouth with his tongue, and then lightly onto my thighs. I was elated, I felt like I could have an orgasm without him even touching my vagina. Moving onto the outside of my receptive pussy lips, he licked in a circular motion around my clit, just barely touching the inside.

"Oh David, I waited for you to touch me, it felt like an eternity," whimpering from the utter bliss, as I got louder. *"Oh David! Please don't stop, I love this so much. I love you David!"* Moaning loudly as he put a finger inside of me while he graciously licked me. I was on the edge and knew I had only seconds before the best orgasm would pour out of me. I felt everything in my body become electrified, the heavens were opening up for me. Pushing slightly harder with his tongue, as he played with my breasts skillfully pulling me closer to ecstasy. *"David, I'm losing my mind."* Pushing slightly harder on my wetness with his tongue, he brought me to the floodgates. *"I'm going to… I'm cumming baby, I'm cumming for you now…. now David now!"* I screamed as I lost all of my body to his mouth, exploding as I had never done before, but he didn't stop as my body released again and again and again for him. He loved that I cried out.

I laid weak as I gently pulled him away from me and up to my mouth. I still longed for him inside of me as much as he did. Our bodies were all-consuming and our connection was in that moment, love. He entered methodically, pressing slowly in and out of me, I kept my legs down and open wide for him. He continued, but didn't push my legs above my head or any other rough position that I experienced in the past, but instead close to him as he pushed again and again while cupping my ass with his strong worker hands. Passionately deeper with each thrust, as he kissed me softly with warmth and tenderness.

"Ohh, I can't believe how good this feels, oh Allie!" He cried out. I felt it too, it was something more than just sex. David penetrated harder and harder as we moaned emotionally together like animals in the wild. Pulling his body off my chest to look at my face he pushed his cock into me a few more times till he had no will to hold back. *"Look at me, please look at me. I want to see your eyes as I cum inside of you. You're so beautiful, so...very beautiful. I love looking at you. I'm letting go, Allie... I love you!"* His body shook as he collapsed on me. David buried his face in my thick hair, took a deep breath, and said, "you're intoxicating, so bloody intoxicating." He gently moved off me, as I snuggled into his body. We lay for a while, not speaking, just being in the moment of it all. It was sublime. We both felt it. I didn't know if we had meant what we said, and I wasn't going to bring it up. All would reveal itself in time, but for now, nothing else mattered. It was a small piece of perfection in my life.

CHAPTER 15

Playing House

We stopped at his local country market owned by a nearby family down the road and got some groceries. Walking into his house he turned to me to ask, "Would you like to cook together tonight?" I taught myself to cook, because I was alone half the time while growing up, and I was quite good or at least I thought I was. So, I was all too happy to finally get to cook with someone.

"I would love to," I eagerly replied. David put on one of my favorite composer musicians; Alexis Ffrench and popped open a nice Cabernet. "I love his work David!" Surprised by what he chose.

"Seems we have a lot in common," he smiled. I didn't know about that, I thought to myself, my life has not been as romantic as his. Yes, he struggled in his life, but he had this saint of a mother and I was damaged goods. No one like David could ever really love me. It was James who really resembled me, we made sense, and we were both functioning on codependency. I quickly drowned the negative thoughts and went back to living in the moment.

The night was pure bliss, we enjoyed preparing our feast; roasted duck, red potatoes, and some sauteed spinach. We spoke some more about his art career and my aspirations of being an artist. David promised that he would guide me, not tell me what to do, but to help me make the right choices for my career. Explaining that being a good artist is allowing the art to talk back to you, taking your time was the hardest part, but you had to let it breathe life. He spoke so eloquently about it, it was like a dance of words as he conveyed the process of good art. I felt as if I learned more from one night about art, than I ever did in my entire life. I would never forget it, not ever.

The night got late fast, we began to wind down. David turned to me, "Allie would you like to sleep in my room with me?" I did want to but was it a good idea, probably not, I was already feeling attached to him. I couldn't say no, I wanted to wake up with him.

"Yes, I would very much like that." Walking over to him, I wrapped my arms around his waist and laid my head on his chest. David kissed my forehead, like he had done it a thousand times with such ease. I loved this feeling, I was falling fast for him. Was he falling for me was my biggest question. I was playing house with this man and he was not the one I promised to marry, nor was I his longtime partner Becca that had dedicated her life to him. I suddenly felt conflicted. I pulled away from him slowly. "David, I think…" I began to say as he put his finger on my lips.

"I know what you're going to say, but don't, let's just think of us this last night, then we can worry about the rest tomorrow." He spoke while his eyes welled up with water. I agreed, and planted myself back in his arms. We said nothing while we embraced. I felt safe with David.

I met him in his bed wearing a short, black, lace, slip that had a plunging neckline and slits up the sides. It was very sexy, and I could see by the look on his face that he was in awe. He was wearing nothing, but was covered partly by a sheet. He had the room lined with pillar candles and set the strange with some soft classical music, and a bottle of Montrachet.

"You look so stunning in this light, please may I sketch you?" David asked, reaching for a pad and some charcoal out of his nightstand. I felt celebrated like I had never felt before in my life.

"I would be honored to sit for you," I replied. He asked me to lay on a chaise longue in the middle of the room, where the light of the moon shone through the window perfectly. I did as he asked as I drank some wine. Not only was I intoxicated by the wine, but by this man who was one of the greatest artists of all time was drawing me in his bedroom. I felt immortalized, he was making me his muse.

The night went on as he continued to create, but at some point, I must have fallen asleep. I woke up next to him in his bed. Sitting up slowly I looked around the room to at least thirty sketches of me, even some of me sleeping. It was all too much for me, they were beautiful, so much that I began to cry quietly into my hands. David woke up and pulled me down to him.

"Why the tears?" He said while kissing my wet cheek.

"I'm overwhelmed David, they're me, by you... I don't know, I'm just overwhelmed in a good way," trying to explain to him the best I could. He understood what was happening. Holding my face with his hands, "it's all you. I've never been inspired to do this with anyone. I swear to you." He whispered while softly kissing my lips. Returning his kiss with a deeper one, I wanted to make love with him again more than anything. It was surreal for me, and I had believed it was for him too.

Pushing my hair away from my neck, he began to lick and kiss me, taking my nightgown down and exposing my breasts. He looked at me, no through me, like he was really seeing me. I felt like a different person when I was with him, a different type of beautiful. I felt as if this all had meaning in the grand scheme of things in my youthful life.

"My muse, my beautiful Allie," David said as he laid me softly back onto the pillows. I said nothing, I think the way I looked at him was enough for him. The feeling was so intense and pure. I never wanted it to stop, it was like a dream. *I am falling hard for this man, I don't want to, but I cannot help myself.* My desire for him was at an all high, I needed him.

"Please David.. give it to me, I want to feel you inside of me. I'm dying," I whimpered. He gave us both the pleasure of entering my dripping wet flower. Sliding repeatedly back and forth in perfect harmony with my hips while I gently played with myself. I wanted nothing more than to cum with this man. I wanted to release all of our desires in harmony. I knew the build-up was already there. I was turned on from the night before. *"My little muse... oh you are so breathtaking, sensual, and passionate. Oh my fucking god! Please cum with me soon... my muse!"* He screamed out. I was ready to let go the moment he called me his muse.

"Yes David, I will! I am David, I am!" Moaning wildly as I

kissed him. Rubbing harder on my clit as he pushed deeper inside of me. We were at the point of no return and I was releasing all of my pent-up feelings and pleasures onto him.

"Yes… Yes, my muse…. I'm cumming inside of you now!" David pushed one last thrust as we met one another in our orgasms. It was fucking mind-blowing. I felt his inhale accepting my exhale, we were in sync in so many ways. Pure rapture, and ultimately lovemaking. Looking back on this night, I believed he was feeling exactly the same thing I was, but this would never last. I didn't believe that I deserved something this good and I never would.

We spent the night talking in front of the fireplace about life, art, love of art, books, music, and travel. David was an artist, everything he loved had to do with it. I was drunk off his words, he was completely intoxicating. The romanticism of it all was something out of a fairy tale, or at least that's what it felt like. But, with all romances, there comes tragedy, and this was no different. There was a hint of sadness for the not knowing, the not knowing of what tomorrow would bring for us. He had his Becca, a special woman that stood by him for over a decade and I had James who was in love with me and I was with him. My thoughts raced; what I have with James is so rare, but wildly unpredictable and not always in a good way. We were crazy together, but alive and electrified all of the time. Two different worlds, which did I prefer? This too would unfold and not in a delicate way.

The night went by fast and sleeping was on the horizon. I had planned on going back to my flat in the city allowing David to do whatever he was going to do there. You just know when it's time to go. I felt it in my stomach. Changing the atmosphere and my perspective was a must, so I could get a handle on what the hell I was doing here. Little did I know he was feeling a bit displaced now too.

"Allie… I think you should pack and go to the city tomorrow. I could use you in the studio in my place. I have clients coming in. It'll be good for you to interact. And hey, you might even sell," David explained graciously so as not to hurt me. I was stronger than he gave me credit for. Did I want him to tell me not to leave? Probably not, but I didn't ask to stay either.

"Ok, yes, of course. I'll see you in the morning then. Goodnight David." Kissing him lightly on the cheek, I exited without looking into his eyes. I don't know what I was thinking, that exit seems so dramatic. *Didn't it?* "Well, what is done is done," in the words of my mother. I went off and packed tiredly for an early start.

The next morning I came into the kitchen where I could smell food cooking, but there was no David. An older man with a long beard turned around with a big smile and asked if I was hungry. I said yes and then asked where Mr. Lurst was.

"Oh Mr. David, he told me to tell you that he had to run to a business meeting. He didn't tell me where, but he did say he would be back at the house later," the man explained. Was he avoiding my exit? I wasn't sure, but I knew it made me feel bad about everything. I had, what I thought to be, two epic days with him and then he can't even say goodbye? It felt cheap all of a sudden. But, maybe I was overreacting. Who knows, but I was determined to let the ill feelings go and not let anything bother me. I would just remember the days as they were; amazing.

CHAPTER 16

London Nights

I returned back to an apartment full of music and the smell of baking in my kitchen. I knew it could only be one person; Jenny.

"Hi, Allie! You're back!" Jenny called out.

"Yes…I am. What is all of this?" Smiling, I pointed at the cacao powder everywhere.

"I know you love chocolate, so I'm baking you some vegan brownies." Jenny was so proud, and she had a point, I loved brownies, so what's not to like?

"Thank you Jenny, so nice of you. I'm going to shower and change, I'll see you in thirty minutes, be ready to work ok." Calling out as I exited. I walked away thinking how sweet she was, my second thought was how rude of her to be in my place without asking. I had to explain to her that some ground rules needed to be enforced. *What if David were with me?* This could have been very bad.

I returned shortly to now a perfectly tidy kitchen. Proudly Jenny presented me with a delicious stack of brownies. Smiling as I grabbed one, I sat down at the kitchen table. Explaining nicely to my assistant that she needed to keep my key for emergency purposes only and this wasn't one of them. I even hesitated to allow her to keep it, but I thought if I lost my keys, at least I would be able to get into my flat.

"So, what are my messages?" I asked.

"Well, not much… David's assistant called and she left a list of things for you to do tomorrow, and also James left a message," Jenny answered quickly.

"Wait, James, my James left a message… huh, that's funny, why didn't he just call me? When did he call?" Freaking out a bit as I questioned her like a detective.

"Oh, umm, he said he wanted to surprise his fiancé, but I thought I should tell you instead, as soon as I could. You told me that I should, it's ok right?" Asking frantically, Jenny looked confused.

"Oh no, I meant yes, thank you… yes best to come to me for everything, especially surprises from James! I don't like surprises Jenny… ever." I nervously laughed.

"Ok, whew, you scared me Allie." Jenny paused for a second, then explained that he would be in by twelve tomorrow and was planning on coming to David's studio to see me. I gave her work to do outside of the flat and grabbed my phone. Wait… should I call him? Or should I let him think he's blindsiding me? I decided on the latter of the two. I didn't want James to become suspicious and not think he couldn't trust Jenny to keep a secret. I needed him to believe she could.

James is coming to London tomorrow… James is coming to London, my mind raced. *Shut up Allie!* I yelled out loud. I needed to calm myself down, so I grabbed a bottle of Clase Azul and put it on the rocks, threw it back, and poured another. I was still in love with James, this doesn't fade overnight, I knew that. I also knew the "thing" that happened with David was still fresh, and I could still smell him on me. I needed to compartmentalize and put David away in a tiny box in my mind. It's go-time and James would be here soon. It was a blessing in disguise that David wasn't in the studio and I had zero idea of when he would return. He had a reputation of disappearing from time to time when he needed to be creative and process. I totally understood that, I only wished at this moment I could disappear as well.

The next morning I was busy trying to put myself together for James' arrival, even if it was supposed to be a surprise, I needed to look amazing for him. I worked out, showered, blew out my hair, and applied some smokey eyes and gloss. Jenny did my nails in the Uber, as we headed to the studio. I was greeted by Becca of all people. I'd recognized her from some press photos I had seen.

"Hello Allie, I'm Becca, David's partner." She smiled warmly. I'll never forget how sweet she was, such a kind and pretty lady. Becca had blonde shoulder-length hair, a cute high-pitched voice, and was petite only standing around 5'3". She was dressed eccentrically, wearing red pants and a yellow top, black Doc Martens, and a large cuff with studs on it. It didn't all go together, but who am I the fashion police?

"Hi Becca. So nice to meet you, I've heard wonderful things about you!" I replied. We had some small talk about the studio. She was nice enough, but I didn't like her, just because. *Why would I like her, that could get in the way of David and me right?* There was chatter in my head again. *No! I would like her, because*

I'm a good person and so is she! Chiming back in as Becca explained the selling process, and all of the logistics of the studio, she was actually quite informative. I got it quickly, so she went off to do her own work. She ran a PR company in London and from what I could see was quite good at doing it. So that gave me some relief.

I got started on some of my assigned projects. One of them was to paint the background for David's latest works. It was mundane at best, but therapeutic as well. I didn't really have to think about what I was doing, so I zoned out to some really great music. There wasn't anyone else there, so I played some of Emmit Fenn's mixes as loud as I could, which in this case was close to a dance club. I always like to paint to music, that never changed. Then I heard a voice over the music yelling my name, I turned to see who it was and there he was, my sexy rockstar James. Smiling ear to ear, standing before me was my gorgeous, manful fiancé.

"Baby you're here!" I shrieked. Running I jumped into his arms, as he picked me up and swung me around. Seeing his face made me immediately forget about David… David who?

"Allie… There's my girl!" James kissed me over and over again. Kissing him back as I popped myself up to straddle his waist.

"James, James, I missed you babe!" I giggled.

"Well don't you have a lunch break?" Grabbing my ass firmly as he spun around.

"I do, but let's take it back to my flat?" I pleaded. The last thing I needed was one of his galleries or collectors to walk into the studio and see a naked intern. I don't think my position, no pun intended, would last here.

We got back to the apartment and began kissing again. I pulled back from James while holding my hands on his sculpted face.

"I missed you James… so much." I needed him to know this. He was my fiancé and I did love him, even if I had a fling and terrible crush on my idol.

"I missed you too," he paused. "Have you been a good girl?" He teased me. But was he really teasing me? He must have been, James had a temper like no one I had ever met. I was his love interest, and also his obsession and possession to some degree. I liked it to be honest, actually I loved his fire. It made me want to fuck him all the more.

"Don't be ridiculous, tough guy! Now take me to bed." I smirked.

"Well fucking show me where it is!" Scooping me over his shoulder as he howled like a wolf. He was hungry like an animal in the wild, and so was I.

James practically ripped all of his clothes off and then mine. He was like a beast mounting me. Grabbing my ass with one hand and my hair in the other, as he pushed me into doggy position. I gladly complied. I wanted his large shiny and ever so fucking hard cock deep inside of me. I knew in this position he would hurt me, but I wanted that, and he knew it. We weren't making love, we were hardcore fucking. He was untameable at this point, nothing could stop him from taking whatever he wanted and I wanted him to be out of control. He spit on his hand and wiped it on his penis, then spit directly onto my ass crack, I could feel it running down to meet his hand which he smeared around my opening. He released my hair, dropping my head down slightly as I arched my back up to meet his strength. James held the sides of my ass like he was riding a bull, as he pounded away at my pussy. My whole body was being thrown around, but he kept going, over and over as he thrashed his pelvis into my ass. He howled.

"This is fucking mine… mine! Understand?! Mine! Oh my fucking god… I love this pussy so much!" His screaming made me wetter as I whimpered, *"Yes James, yes James."* I was his sub and he was my dom. This was just the beginning of his need to dominate me and mine to allow it. James began to smack my ass, at first hard, but then harder, and harder. I was screaming for him to stop, pleading over and over, *"Please James, you're hurting me, you're hurting me… please"*.

He finally stopped after a while and threw me onto my back, placing a pillow under my ass and legs on his shoulders. He told me to touch myself.

"I want you to cum with me Allie, so play with your little, sweet pussy. I can't hold on much longer, I want to fill you up. I need to see my cum dripping out of your cunt! Play with it now!" He commanded me as the sweat dripped from his face into my mouth. I did what he wanted, I was so fucking hot for him, and

all I wanted to do was please him. It was everything to me, I loved his control over me in bed.

"Yes my love, yes yes, I'm almost there... I'm there, I'm there baby, cum with me James!" I cried out. My entire body flooded with the most intricate tingles of pleasure and my pussy pulsated around his manhood, as my body convulsed from the multiple times I came. *"FUCK Allie, I want to cum, now open your mouth... open your fucking mouth, wide!"* James roared like a lion. I did what he said. Swiftly pulling his rock-hard cock out of me, he moved quickly up to my mouth, grabbing my face with one hand and his manhood in the other, stroking his unyielding snake furiously, then he boiled over and so did his cum. Directing the hot liquid into my mouth and down my throat, swallowing over and over, and still, the overflow hit my lips and ran down my neck. I smiled inside, loving what had happened. I didn't understand it yet, but I really loved it and I know he did. James moved from my body gently and left to get a towel for me. He became gentle after that. James loved to control me in bed, but he was so sweet after. At least for now.

We showered and didn't say anything about the sex, I think we were still trying to process and live in the moment of what we just experienced. So we did the alternative and talked about food. He begged me to not go back to work. No one was around to tell me otherwise, so I agreed to stay home with him and decide on where to go to dinner. In the meantime I thought a drink would be a good idea and so did he. I quickly poured myself a Tequila while he was showering and took an Adderall, then poured two more for us. He still didn't know I was ADD or as he would most likely think I was addicted to a drug the government is putting in kids' hands. He would most likely be right, considering that Tory had me on Adderall since I was ten years old.

James looked amazing as always. He was wearing some of his designs, all in black; a black blazer, shirt, and pants, and a cool LV leather belt finished it off. He always had a big watch on, this time wearing an *A. Lange & Söhne, Zeitwerk Minute Repeater.* This was no ordinary watch, anything but. I was wowed by it, and him, *so goddamn gorgeous I thought*. He resembled the watch in many ways, he was put together and brilliant, yet so fucking complicated. I loved him for a long time, until I didn't.

We decided on Park Chinois, one of my favorite very upscale Chinese restaurants, which in addition had one of the sexiest cabaret shows in the world. The maitre d' greeted us and especially James, because I might have been the face of James John, but he was James John. Everyone recognized him. He was flashy, yet classy, dangerous, yet boyish, but one thing that never changed is that he was hot as fuck and every girl wanted him. I like that they did, it made me gloat. I also knew that he liked to make me angry by flirting, but I don't think he knew that I wasn't really jealous, it was more of a disrespectful thing that I could never get used to. I had a slight temper, which I learned from my mother Tory and that still remains to this day.

We sat in the back in the center, far enough away to have privacy, yet could see everything, basically the best seats in the house. Tonight I chose one of his designs, and since he had not seen me in his new dress, I wore it. An eye-catching shiny gold-tone, v-neck, sequin dress that featured a fun fringe detailing with pink four-inch Prada pumps. My hair of course was down and rockstar sexy. He loved this glamorous look on me more than anything, even if I had jeans and a t-shirt, the hair had to be full of body and picture perfect. So, I wore the look for him most of the time. There were still those times when I would go full sunglasses, baggy jeans, and kicks to brunch, it would drive him crazy, but I loved doing that to him here and there, it kept him on his toes. The cocktail servers were sexier than ever tonight and James, as always, made sure they too enjoyed their own bottle of Champagne in the back. I didn't mind, it was booze, he wasn't offering sex. He just liked to showboat.

We caught up, and I told him about the job and how much I loved it. He, about the new line of clothes in all of the interviews and meetings he was taking in New York City. And then he flipped out.

"Where the *fuck* is your engagement ring Allie?" James demanded to know.

"Calm down mister, calm down, it's right here." I pulled my diamond out of my zipped clutch and put it on. "I took it off for work, I was putting my gloves in chemicals and I'm working around paint for christ's sake babe! I didn't want to lose it or damage it in any way, it means too much to me. Ok!" I jumped on him verbally. This would be my cover-up in order for him to believe me. Of course that wasn't the reason. I felt like saying, *fuck this ring, I'll wear it when I want to.* Of course, this thought stayed in my head.

"Ok… fuck! Calm the fuck down! Put your claws away little kitty," he poked at me. I rolled my eyes, shaking my head. Most of that was real and he did get under my skin completely, in more ways than one. This was us; dysfunctional, sexy, high tempered, and in love. James and Allie in a nutshell. I don't know if you've ever been in love or addicted to a person, or both. I have, and I wouldn't trade it for anything in the world. I love love love being addicted to love or the desire to be taken or the desire to take someone. If you mix it all up in the pot, it's pretty damn exciting. Trust me, I know firsthand. James and I were irrational, crazy in love, and highly functioning codependent lovers and everything in between. This love story is not going to end well, but I'll let you be the judge of that.

James grabbed my face with one hand pulling me into him. I followed his lead, knowing what he wanted to do to me, and closed my eyes. The kiss was deep and passionate. I felt him and his heart. James loved me like a lunatic would love the madness. He would forever crave me, want to own me and some part of me did too. People were watching us, but we didn't care, we were now the act and he loved it. Until he didn't love it, out of the corner of his eye my distracted boyfriend caught a guy snapping a photo of us and went ballistic.

"What do you think you're doing? Erase the photo now!" James stood up and demanded. Now standing directly over the stranger. The man smirked and showed him as he erased it. "Good boy," James scowled. But, it didn't end there. The guy thought James being famous wouldn't do anything to him, so when he turned away the man called him a jerk off. James turned back quickly and pushed the antagonizer off his chair and onto the ground. Then all hell broke loose, another guy snapped a photo and ran out. I knew at this moment it could look a lot worse because the man was on the floor. I think the smart ass wanted this to happen so that he, like every other person out there, could file a lovely little lawsuit.

I had learned a lot from my mother, so I grabbed the girl's hand that he was with and escorted her to the ladies' room while the manager and doorman handled what was going on. James was too busy talking to notice I had left. I walked her into the bathroom, she didn't know what was happening because she was slightly wasted. "Listen, your boyfriend started that. You know this, right?" I asked her. While holding her up in the largest stall I could find.

"Yeah, he's a real jerk. He always starts shit and he isn't my boyfriend," she slurred. I realized she was high on alcohol and so I did what every NYC girl would do for a friend at this time. I asked her if she needed a bump of coke, she smiled and said yes. I didn't have any, this wasn't my thing, but I knew where to get it and fast. I ordered her to stay put and she happily agreed. Walking swiftly I went to a guy working that I knew would be at a lounge two doors down. I told him what I needed and handed him three hundred pounds. I asked him to give me two hundred worth of coke and keep the rest for himself and *not to say a fucking word or else.* He was thrilled to get the money.

"No, never going to say shit. Come on lady, it's people like you that keep me in business." The dealer laughed as I walked away. I ran back to the bathroom where the girl was waiting, pushed back into the stall and pulled out the coke, threw a bunch of it on the back of the toilet, rolled up a bill, and told her to fucking snort. I had her do four or five lines and waited patiently for it to kick in, the entire time snapping photos of her hoovering it with her legs spread all over. I didn't think she would make too good of a witness. Ten minutes went by and the drunkard was now alive and smiling.

"Thank you, I needed that," she said while popping to her feet.

"You're welcome, but I'm going to need something from you. Don't speak, listen. Your dick boyfriend messed with mine and now it's a problem. I am going to record you here and now, you will say exactly what I tell you... nod your head if you understand." Pointing my finger in her face, as I held her to the wall. I don't know what came over me, I suddenly felt protective and resourceful. I definitely had a little Tory pulsing through my veins.

"Yes, ok, yes, but can I have the rest of the coke?" She asked.

"Of course, it's all yours sweetheart," I replied condescendingly while pushing her hair out of her face. Like a good addict, she did her confession.

The video was perfect, she did what I told her, explaining that her boyfriend had planned the entire scene to basically blackmail James into giving him money. I know what you're thinking, evil little genius. Well, that's exactly what I'm beginning to be an evil, fucking little genius.

I went back to the table and told the manager to get the girl a cab, and he did. James was cooling down while chatting with some fans from another table. Seemed that everyone had taken one side and that was James John. I said my hellos to all of them and invited them for Champagne. They joined us happily. James knew what I was doing, which was making everything subside. I looked over at him and we locked eyes, I mouthed the words I love you and he reciprocated. We stayed for another thirty minutes and politely left the club.

"Let's get a real drink now, what do you say tough guy?" I joked.

"I don't know, maybe we should make a few calls, I'm worried about the girl he was with," James said while pulling me towards the car.

"Wait a second, I want to show you something," I explained to him what happened in the bathroom, what I did exactly, and the recording I took. I also had her number, address, and a photo of her driver's license, if we needed to follow up with our people.

"You are fucking amazing. Who are you? Where's the shy little Allie? My baby's not a kitten, she's a lion!" James was in amazement, he couldn't stop talking about his badass girlfriend protecting him. He loved that I had his back. I gained even more trust and love now, this moment kind of sealed it. Loyalty was everything to James. I was his everything now.

It was instinctual, protecting what is mine. I guess that is what a mother is supposed to do, shame mine never did, or did she? I wondered how far I would go to protect someone I cared about. What was I capable of exactly? Who am I becoming? David was a faded thought with all of James's testosterone around. He was all I could see right now. We were like Bonnie and Clyde, but without the killing and with lots of sex.

"Ok little Miss Thing, let's go for that drink. Let's go to 5 Hertford." James said while smacking my ass into the car.

"Yes sir!" I saluted him.

Of course, we had a table waiting for us when we arrived and he had a perfectly placed bottle of my Clase Azul Reposado Tequila as well, with a bowl full of quartered blood oranges and small block cubes, everything was just so perfect, just the way I had become accustomed to. I smiled and kissed him, he knew what I liked, even the smallest of things mattered to him when it came to me, details were everything to our opulent lifestyle. Don't get me wrong there is a lot wrong with this picture, and more will unfold as the years go by, but in this moment I loved him, I needed him. We were a dreamy couple, people were in awe when they saw us. It made me feel really fucking special. People came to our table that he knew and said hi. He loved the attention, but started to ignore everyone, he wanted to focus on me. Turning his body towards me, he grabbed my hand in his, "I love you and no one will ever take you from me." He stared at me as if to study my reaction. I knew this little game, he did it often to fuck with me. "Babe, I love you too. I'm not going anywhere. After all, I'm your fiancé... Right!" I smirked, and gave him a soft kiss. I knew how to tame the beast, well at least some of the time. The response was perfect because he went into the inside pocket of his jacket and pulled out a small box from Boodles of London. Inside to my surprise were these mega-expensive earrings that I babbled on about one morning while we were cooking breakfast.

"*The Woodland Heart Platinum Diamond Drop Earrings!* You remembered babe. How could you have remembered? I don't know what to say. I love them, I love you… I love you so much James," I gushed, as the tears followed. I couldn't hold back the emotion. He would forever surprise me. It wasn't about the gift, it was about him caring enough to remember the small things I might have said throughout the days. Our driver was standing behind our table, James signaled for him to come over.

"I love you and these will look amazing on your beautiful little ears, but for now give them to me and I'll have Joseph keep them safe." Smiling, I agreed and handed the box to our driver.

"You are the *sweetest* future husband, and I am the *luckiest* girl in the entire world." Kissing him over and over again on his lips and around his face. Saved by the bell, a hot bottle girl leaned over and asked us how we would like our drinks. We laughed and simultaneously said, *"on the rocks, two-quarters of orange, squeezed."*

CHAPTER 17

The Angel and the Devil

The next morning I woke a little late for work, rushing to get a matcha from Jenny, who like every morning, was there waiting for me.

"Jenny! I'm late, why didn't you wake me?" I hollered.

"*Sorry*, Mr. John told me not to. He said you had a big night," she said shrugging her shoulders. Shaking my head with a half smile, I thought this was just so typical of James. Jenny explained to me that James had to leave for Milan because something went sideways with a deal he had made. She said he would text later. Knowing James, he didn't fly anywhere unless it was really necessary in business. I'd hoped that everything was ok, but chose to only send him a message, rather than asking him a million questions by phone, I knew I would only distract him.

I gulped down my tea, got dressed, and headed to the studio in Battersea. I didn't expect to see David, he seemed to be avoiding me or maybe that was my ego talking and he was just onto something with his work. We always think it's about us though.

Working all day was exactly what I needed. I finished all of David's work by 4 o'clock, then I started to finish my own art. I was painting with acrylics on a large raw canvas on the floor when Becca stormed in. Noticeably upset by the look on her face.

"Hello down there. Seems I've been seeing a lot of you laying around on your back. You and I little homewrecker need to talk!" She said angrily. I was speechless and stumbled while trying to bring myself to my feet. Struggling, I fell backward cracking my skull pretty hard. I don't think that was what either of us wanted and she immediately ran to help me. I was bleeding from the back of my head pretty hard when David walked in. "What the hell.. are you ok? What happened? What did you do Becca?" Losing his shit from the site of the blood, he demanded answers as he came to my aid with some towels. Becca stuttered, "I don't know, she just slipped on the paint. I, I, I never," then began beating her hands on her legs, *"fuck this, I didn't do anything, she fell!"* She screamed hysterically running out of the studio.

"I did fall, no one pushed me. Why would you say that David?" I questioned him, and then proceeded to throw up all over his shirt. Knowing that I wasn't ok he carried me to the sofa in his office and called a doctor friend of his. Dr. Frank immediately came over, he must have lived close by, because it seemed like only minutes had gone by. I began to feel tired and out of it from the hit. Dr. Frank smacked my face and told me not to fall asleep, stating that I had a concussion. He shot my head with something to numb it and gave me a few stitches, yes stitches right there in the office. I thought this was either really weird or really cool. I went along with it, I wasn't in any position to fight them. David paid him on the side and he reassured us that no one would hear of the incident. While he and the doctor were saying their goodbyes I popped an Adderall, I knew this would do the trick and keep me up. Then came the time to talk about what was really going on between them. I needed to know why Becca was so upset. David came clean, telling me that Becca had found all of the sketches and he had to tell her about our time together and what was going through his mind.

"What are you feeling David?" I questioned him.

"I don't know. I think I could fall in love with you." Confessing, I could see the man was desperate for me to say the same thing back to him. You could see he was hanging on by a thread. So I did. I don't know why, but when I was with him, it was the only time I actually felt completely good about myself, like I wasn't born from evil or something silly like that. I felt worthy. I felt like an artist. I felt like a woman that deserved happiness and most of all love from a really good-hearted man.

"I could fall in love with you too David. I might already be falling." I began to sob. David also got emotional and pulled me gently to his chest. It was one of the hardest moments of my life. To be vulnerable is one of the bravest things you can ever do and I was wide open for him to destroy. He murmured, "Now what are we going to do?" I had no words for that question. I was engaged to someone I loved passionately, laying here covered in blood with another man that I also had enormous feelings for. I didn't think it could get any more complicated, but it did.

I needed to be alone to think, so I asked him to drop me off. Walking to my door was dramatic, I felt like the loneliest human in the world as I watched him drive off. I could not keep myself together, dropping to the ground I began to cry. What was I doing? Why did I feel so hurt? I didn't know then, but I was breaking my own heart. David was special, very special. He wasn't like everyone else, he was an entirely different kind of man. A keeper, a man to love forever. I felt a hand on my back, it was Jenny. Relieved I asked her to help me to my flat, and she did.

Jenny was concerned, she tended to me like a good friend and held me while I cried. I needed her then, she was a rock for me at this moment. Hours passed and I told her to leave, she looked exhausted and I really wanted a glass of Tequila. I knew she would bitch about it, so I insisted she go. Two seconds after she was gone, I grabbed a bottle of Tequila, not looking for a glass, putting it to my lips, I chugged it for ten seconds. I stopped to take a breath and continued to drink from the bottle, then grabbed for a pill and sat down. Feeling high immediately, I sunk into a corner chair in my living room. I sent James a text and then one to Tory. Pausing to remember what I was doing I proceeded to send my besties text messages in New York as well. I was drunk and missed my girls, so I suggested a call next week. Why did I text Tory? My guess is that I was feeling completely exposed and part of me really wanted to talk to my mom.

The doorbell rang as I took another swig of my Tequila. It must be Jenny. *Why is she back here?* No, it was Dominique! *What the hell is he doing here?* This was the very last thing I expected or actually wanted. "*Hi*" is all I said. He on the other hand was full of questions and emotions, wanting to know why I looked like Carrie from that scary American movie and if I needed to see a doctor.

"Nope! The blood stopped," I slurred my words.

"You're drunk," he shook his head with a slighted smile, picking me up into his arms as he sat me down on the sofa.

"Yes Dominique I am, would you care to have some?" Shoving the bottle at him as it spilled all over his shirt. I apologized and straightened up a bit. I felt bad, *why take my shit out on him, right?*

"Angel… what are you doing to yourself? Let me take you upstairs and clean you up a bit, ok? Please, you need me right now. I can see it," he pleaded. I agreed to his help, I knew I couldn't do it without him. I shouldn't have been drinking and taking pills, I knew enough not to walk up the steps alone. He carefully pulled me to my feet and up to the master bathroom. Running a bath as he undressed me slowly, lightly brushing my nipples.

"My angel, what happened to you?" He asked sweetly.

"I hit my head at work, but I'm ok, the doctor stitched me up… see?" Pointing to the little blue stitches. I stood above him while he sat on the edge of the tub as he began to touch me all over. I liked it at first, but then I just began to feel sick over it. He put his hand on my vagina and began to rub it.

"Please, don't. I can't Dominique," I said quietly so as not to offend him.

He didn't listen. Scooping me up quickly, he marched with me in his arms and laid me abruptly on the bed.

"What are you doing?" I yelled. I tried to get up, but I was

dizzy, as he pushed me back down. I still continued to try and lift myself up, but he just kept forcing me back down as he unbuttoned his shirt, removing it and then his pants. I was spinning from the concussion and Tequila, so I wasn't able to fight with him. This was happening, he was going to take me and I wouldn't have a choice. Dominique told me to stop playing games as he held me down with his naked body. I didn't want to get hurt, so any resistance that I tried was over. All of the emotions of my past were in my mind right now and the man that I thought would never hurt me is now doing exactly that. I was shattered as I lay there crying. It didn't take much for him to hold my legs open, even though I was sobbing and pleading for him to stop. Pushing his hard penis into my vagina with might. He began to ram me like I wasn't even there.

"Angel, you feel so good. Do you like it? I was your first, remember?" Dominique howled while continuing to fuck me hard. I was whimpering for him to get off me, because I could no longer scream. *"Fuck angel, I'm going to cum! Oh your pussy is so tight! I want to fill you up... FUCK Allie, my sweet little angel... Ughhh, I'm cumming for you angel!"* He thrust hard, moaning loudly he collapsed onto my chest. I didn't say anything, but he did. Looking at me with a smile he told me, *"I love you angel, my sweet Allie. I always will love you, and you know you'll always remember your first,"* as he got up and dressed quickly. I didn't lift my head up, but I managed to ask him how he knew I'd be here alone. Dominique said to me that *a little bird told him that my fiancé was in Milan.* I cried softly into my hands as I watched him walk away. Turning back to me as he was leaving the room he muttered.

"Let's keep this between us, you know I have ears everywhere. Don't be any more reckless than you have been my little angel… oh and Allie clean yourself up." I could see pure evil in him. That scared the hell out of me. Feeling raw and empty, I struggled to even bathe.   I just wanted to try and bury it forever, but I don't know if this is possible. I was a girl when he had me, it made me sick to think about that now. I longed to feel safe again and there was only one person that could do that right now. Before I fell asleep I sent a text to Jenny: *Please book me a ticket for the early morning, I'm going to New York.*

CHAPTER 18

Hello Kitty

I didn't say goodbye to David in person, I chickened out, sent him an email, and left.

Dear David,

I don't know if I can even find the words to describe how beautiful and enlightened this time with you has been for me. One day in person I'll be able to, but right now I need space from this to see who I am. I'm sorry to just leave without talking, but it's for the best. You have to handle your life with Becca and I'd just be in the way. Please don't try to call me or email.

I meant every word I said to you. You had my heart.

Allie

The car ride back to my apartment in the rain seemed like the longest in the world. I was feeling down, and the weather wasn't helping much. It was such a relief to get back to my place, but then it wasn't, because I wasn't even sure why I was there. I sent James a text message explaining that I came back to the States for a week, and that I needed to heal my wounds and rest. He thought it was a lovely idea and planned on meeting me in just two days. I also received a text message from Serena, *Hi Al! You're back! We missed you to pieces, see you at 9 pm.. our spot, ok! Xoxo*. I was happy to see her funny emojis and also excited to see my girls, they're just what the doctor ordered for the pain that was ailing me.

I painted for a while to some tunes by Alexis Ffrench, his music was soulful and it paired well with my Tequila. Realizing it was 6 o'clock already, I decided to run out and get a blowout, since my head still had stitches, I didn't want to bleed all over the place again. When I returned there was someone in my apartment because I knew I didn't leave the music on.

"Hey! What did you really think we would wait till 9 o'clock to see you?" Serena and Beth were howling. I was so glad they had made it down earlier. I really needed to talk with them.

"This calls for a celebration!" Beth said as she popped a magnum of Billecart-Salmon Rosé Champagne.

"I've missed my sisters," I began to cry from happiness. They came to my aid, giving me the warmest hugs that I had ever felt. I needed them so desperately right now. Asking me over and over to tell them what was wrong, I had no choice, but to spill my guts about David. I left out what happened with Dominique, I didn't know what they would do and I didn't want them telling James anything. He would end up in jail if he found out what he did to me. They agreed that coming back to New York City was for the best. Beth, especially being the maternal one, had a strong opinion.

"Listen Al, you don't belong there with some eccentric artist, no offense to you as an artist, but he seems really kooky. You can't trust that for a partner, besides James lives and breathes you. Al, he loves you and you love him. Don't forget that over a crush, ok?" Beth pulled me to her and hugged me tightly.

"I know you're right, you're always right goddamn you!" I laughed. Immediately I felt better, Beth always said the right things.

"Okay bitches, now in the words of a historically awesome, purple-wearing man, let's fucking party like it's 1999!" Serena shouted. She was right, we were all together, I was feeling very sentimental and was so grateful to be with them. They were my sisters in arms.

We went off to my wardrobe to figure out my clothes and knowing Serena, her clothes as well. She had a habit of coming over and changing out of hers and into mine. Sometimes I never saw the items again, but I didn't care, she had great taste and whatever, she was my size. Serena was still up to all of her nasty little habits and pulled out her coke, laid it on a table in my dressing room, and ripped two lines. Beth and I just shook our heads and laughed. I guess I was a little better than she, for now. We joked, and decided to all wear white, as a rebirth of my return to NYC. So of course I found us all white dresses and we happily changed like teenagers. Serena in a short cross-strap bodycon Herve Leger dress, Beth in a Giorgio Armani mini wrap-dress, and I wore one of my favorites, a Tom Ford transparent ruched mini dress. After we finished and were pouring another bottle of Champagne, I glanced down at my ring and decided to keep it on. I wanted to feel his love, the ring made that a possibility as a reminder.

Beth, miss organized, decided on Le CouCou.

"I haven't been to Le CouCou since the opening for James's

line, five years ago today." Deeply in thought about that crazy night in which I saw Dominique kissing a woman, the memories rushed over me, it was surreal.

"Babe, I'm sorry, how fucking insensitive of me…. shit, I'll cancel it!" Beth insisted. I told her not to. This has to happen, besides this was once my favorite restaurant. Serena was lost, she didn't know what we were talking about, which made the situation funny. So we were off, and the band was back together again.

Oh how I missed the energy of New York City, my city, the city! I was feeling good as if a weight had been lifted. My thoughts turned to my Tory. I hadn't seen her yet, but she texted me and asked for lunch tomorrow. I agreed, but part of me really missed her. My only hope was that she didn't suspect anything was wrong with me.

"Hey, snap out of it babe, earth to Allie!" Beth clapped.

"Sorry ladies, yes let's get this party started with a bottle!" I knew a night of fun with my girls was exactly what all of us needed and were going to have. It was just like old times, we were laughing, drinking and Serena, our party director, was taking us to some cool soiree in Tribeca later. I was happy with that idea, considering I lived there and we were eating here. We dined on all of our favorites and said goodbye to our cheery maitre d' Michael. He always had the same special table for us, we loved people-watching and it was right in the center of the room where you could see everyone.

"Oh my god! Isn't that... oh what's his name? Shit, oh I know, Raph!" Serena said theatrically. And there he was, Raph, the only guy that I thought I could talk to after the shit went down with Dominique.

"He's on a date." Beth chimed in.

"He is," I replied. Everyone took a pause to see what I wanted to do. "Well, I'm not going to run away, I should say hello... no?" Referring to my friends. I got mixed reviews from them. Serena said, *no fuck him,* and Beth the opposite, *be an adult and say hello.* What I really wanted to do was bury my face in his beautiful brown skin and cry. Sounds weak, but this is what I was feeling. He was always there when I needed him, and he was such a good guy. Not to mention hot as fuck. I mean those green eyes could make a girl go insane. I ordered some doubles of Clase Azul and blood oranges and Serena made a toast. *Here's a toast to the man I love. He is rich, and he adds much to my life. He buys me everything I want... but, please don't tell his wife!*

"Yes, folks, she is so ridiculous." Beth poked fun at Serena.

"Alright, here I go! Save my seat ladies," and I was off to either *make a fool of myself or make a fool of myself.* I knew there were no other options, I was doing exactly what I would tell a girl not to do.

Approaching the table was the longest journey because he spotted me immediately and I had to walk toward him while looking directly into his mesmerizing eyes. If it isn't hard enough just looking at him.

"Allie baby! You're here. I heard you were in London?" Raph smiled from ear to ear. He didn't hide his excitement and I think the girl he was with could clearly see that.

"Raph, hi! No, I was in London and now I'm home." Smiling back. I could only see him in the room. The prince in shining armor, the man you only read about, was standing right in front of me. The girl he was with nudged him on the elbow, "Aren't you going to introduce your friend to me?" She insisted. He apologized and did the introduction. I, of course, asked how they knew one another, it turns out she worked for his firm and it was a business dinner. I don't know why it made me happy, knowing that it wasn't a date, but it did. We chatted for a few more minutes and I excused myself and pretended to have to use the ladies room. I walked into the bathroom and freshened up, also wondering if he would be outside waiting. He was.

"I kind of hoped you would be here," I said.

"You knew I wasn't going to let you leave without telling you how beautiful you look," Raph flirted.

"Really? You never called, or wrote to me." I don't know why I went there, so serious, I should not have acted upset, but I had to know.

"Allie, I did, I emailed you over and over again. I also called you." Raph defended himself. *How could that be?* I checked my phone contacts and found his number was blocked in my cell, my next thought was someone blocked him here, then most likely they did on my emails. *Who could have done this?* My immediate thought was James, but he wasn't like that. He never looked at my call logs or anything, so then who?

"I'm so dumbfounded right now, thank god I bumped into you. I would have never known that someone blocked you on my cell phone!" I apologized profusely and asked if I could call him later. He said yes. I knew he had more to say on the subject, but his guest was waiting and so were mine. But, not before he turned to me to say, "I missed you girl, you know that... right?" I couldn't help myself, I had to say something, I was feeling so many emotions.

"I missed you so much, you have no idea!" I blurted out exactly what I didn't want to say, but oh well, the cat's out of the bag, I have feelings for him and always have. How could I? I never even slept with him.

I went back to my table, we paid the check, and left. Serena was in charge, so we followed her to a cool party in Soho. It was small, but quite cool. Elizabeth Dittle was the host, she was a producer in Hollywood, a lot older than us, but really attractive and confident. Her friends were much younger like us, I found it intriguing. I asked Serena what she thought of it. She told me that *she likes to date younger guys and girls, that's why.* Ok, well then it all makes sense now to me. A woman that dates younger, why not? Men do it all the time, look at me, I'm a perfect example. Women should be able fuck younger or date or marry for that matter younger people. I wondered if I would, I was almost certain I would date whomever I wanted, and so far I have. Well, that is if I weren't engaged. Not that I acted like I was in London. I think Raph might be the only guy that is even close in age to me that I've liked.

"Elizabeth!" Serena squealed. She turned around to all of us with a smile and introduced herself politely.

"Who are your lovely friends, little miss Serena?" She inquired. All the while looking at me. Such a look she had, like she was eyeing me up. I suddenly felt warm. Was she looking at me like fresh meat? We all said our hellos and then followed Elizabeth to the bar. Serena disappeared after one minute to tend to her nose with her favorite white powder and Beth saw someone she knew. And there I was, alone with Elizabeth, well not alone, we were in a room full of people, but in this very moment, I felt alone with her.

"So, you must be Allie? Serena talks about you a lot. She absolutely adores you." Elizabeth went on about this and that, as if she knew me already. It was quite flattering. "Wow, she said all of that. This is why she should be my publicist! No, but really… I love her, she's family to me," I gushed. Elizabeth offered to show me the rooftop. I gladly agreed. We left the party on the first floor, and I followed her through her massive triplex. It was stunning, very modern, and very white. Her rooftop was also impressive, she had loads of exotic plants and trees, large white chaise longues everywhere, and a twelve-person dining table next to a small plunge pool.

"Is the pool heated?" I asked.

"It is this evening, why do you want to get in?" She asked. I felt like she wasn't asking, but possibly more so inviting me. I started to feel warm again. She was affecting me, like a man would do to me sexually. At least I thought so. Was it the alcohol? I wasn't sure, but I would soon find out.

"Without this sounding strange, I've been dying to meet the infamous Allie... you know I watched you in the last James John show. You really are stunning." She confessed. I was speechless for a moment, but strung the words together.

"Umm, thank you... thank you so much. Why did you want to meet me?" I was a bit hesitant, but I needed to know.

"Well, since you asked. I wanted to meet you because I wanted to see you close up. I found you sexy as hell, and I wanted to know if that was real or just an act." Getting closer Elizabeth leaned in. I felt her heat, she was like a panther ready to pounce on its prey. She was hot, any person could see that. I guessed around forty years old, 5'7". I examined her, my eyes reading her like a map; her breasts and lips were big, hair was short, silky brown. Her clothes were impeccable as well. As a matter of fact, she had the same Tom Ford dress that I wore just the other day. Sophisticated, powerful, and sexy I thought.

Did Elizabeth want to kiss me or am I reading into this? I did her. I wanted to feel her lips on mine. I had never kissed a girl, let alone a beautiful woman. What would it be like? Without thinking, I stepped closer to her, now almost touching noses. Then I leaned in, signaling to her that she could kiss me and she did. The softest pillowy lips. Oh how her tongue maneuvered in my mouth. She kissed me perfectly, deep and passionate like I'd imagined a kiss would be from a woman. I was fiercely bold, gently grabbing onto her waist, I pulled her into me. Our kisses got more feverish. I could feel my pussy pulsate and knew I was wet to touch. Elizabeth aggressively made her move. Sliding her hand up my dress and between my legs, she gently felt around my clit and then pushed a finger inside of me.

"You like me," she murmured while continuing to kiss me. I moaned lightly in her mouth. I loved it, I wanted more. I wanted her to lick me more than anything. I think that is exactly why she brought me here. Pulling her hand away from me I gasped, I didn't want her to stop, but she wouldn't for long. Bringing me to the lush chaise, she sat me down, and then politely asked me if she could lay me back. Then the words fell from her lips like a concert pianist hitting the notes.

"Can I lick you?" Elizabeth bit her lip waiting for my response.

"Yes, yes I want that," I replied affectionately. She proceeded to pull my dress up to expose my privates. Taking her time she began to kiss my legs, then my inner thighs, then softly on the outside of my mound. I gasped loudly as she got close to my wet slit. I tried to lay still, but it was so hard to do, I was fully charged and ready for her mouth. I desperately wanted to release it for her and for me. I knew she wanted to taste me, I could see the hunger in her eyes. She slowly slipped a few fingers into my hot box and began to fuck me with them. Her mouth lightly brushed over my clit over and over again, so soft, enough to drive me mad. She kept circling it like a shark. Elizabeth was pushing me to the edge. She knew exactly what a woman's body desired. I wanted more, but she only gave enough to keep me begging.

"Please Elizabeth, give me more. You are killing me," I whimpered as I stroked her hair softly while I held her close to me. Finally she put more pressure on my clitoris, licking it perfectly in circles and up and down, over and over as she pushed inside of me with her fingers on my G-spot.

"Elizabeth, please, ohhh please Elizabeth. Oh my god! Please don't stop, I am there Elizabeth!" I let go and the floodgates opened. I was cumming all over her gorgeous face and she absolutely loved it, as she looked up at me, but staying on my pussy. She wanted me to cum again. I would if she stayed and she did. "Oh my god!" I came again and again. I was in heaven, I had never experienced this before. I collapsed and she slowly pulled up from my quivering legs. Elizabeth looked at me like a cat that just swallowed a canary. She, so satisfied, but so was I. Elizabeth politely slid my dress back down and then pulled me into her arms.

"I've got to go back to my party. Go to the bathroom in my room, just over there, tidy up and I'll see you downstairs," she said as she kissed me tenderly. As she walked away, I couldn't help but think this might have been one of the hottest experiences I'd ever had. I liked that she kept my smell in her mouth as she went back to the party, that was another turn-on. The thought of her kissing people hello after eating my pussy made me want her more.

CHAPTER 19

Lunch is Never Just Lunch

I woke up the next morning still buzzing and bewildered from what had happened with Elizabeth. I had given her my cell, now wondering if she would call, or if I even wanted her to. I had never been with a woman, and I was feeling a bit all over the place. I liked what happened, It made me feel empowered. Could I be bisexual? I wasn't sure and at this point, my ADD was kicking in. I picked up my phone to check messages. There were two, one from Beth and the other from Raph. Hers read, *let's get a plan together, love you.* His read, *I'm drunk, where are you? I miss you Allie baby!* Two completely different messages that both put a smile on my face. I said yes to Beth and then wrote a message to Raph asking him if he wanted to grab drinks, but I erased it, changing it to brunch. I was a little scared to drink late at night with him, anything could happen. Besides, brunch is daytime and daytime means I'd be safe from myself and my illogical actions or so I thought. He responded with a hell yes.

I picked Locanda Verde at The Greenwich Hotel. My favorite celebrity spot, owned by the Hollywood actor Robert DeNiro. It scores high on my list, one it's in my neighborhood, and second I love their grits, shrimp, and tomato sauce, it's to die for. I can't lie, I was a bit nervous to see Raph again, but I knew that James would be back either tomorrow or the next day and I wouldn't have this opportunity again for who knows how long. *What opportunity did I want? Should I be doing this?* I didn't have all the answers, but hey a girl's gotta eat, right?

What to wear was my next thought. I love to dress, and so did he. I started throwing my clothes everywhere, thinking I had nothing. Then my phone rang, oh shit, it's Tory, I forgot I had lunch with her. I answered and to my relief, she rescheduled for next week. I went to the back of my massive wardrobe room, found a cute Helena denim jumpsuit, and paired it with a pair of yellow Manolo Blahnik Khan suede slingbacks. Did my makeup with a heavy black liner and no lipstick, with just a light amount of blush and bronzer. My hair was down, but messy, parted down the middle and tucked behind my ears. Added my yellow-gold Rolex Daytona, and rocked the look. New York is funny, we had different looks for different hoods. What you wore on the Upper East side didn't make sense anywhere downtown. I know I grew up most of my life in the UES.

I could have walked there but I took a car because of the heels, the streets in Tribeca can be brutal on a girl's shoes. Pulling up outside I spotted my charmer Raph, there he was chatting it up with an elderly lady, he had her laughing and blushing. He could make any woman smile. I think he lived for that. I was no different than anyone else, already beaming when I caught a glimpse of him. What was it about him? Maybe the fact that he was warm, considerate and may I say hot as fuck. Raph put his hand out to greet me, pulling me up to him on the sidewalk, and of course, I fell into him.

"Falling for me Allie?" He grinned.

"Good to see you." Leaning in, I kissed his cheek while

breathing in his delicious cologne.

"Same, it's been too long lady," as he returned my kiss. It gave me goosebumps and I shook my shoulders involuntarily. "Are you cold?" Raph teased.

"Funny, no, let's get inside, I'm starving," I said, giving him a shove in the door.

"Alright, alright, let me get this woman some food," he announced in the direction of the young hostess. She lit up when she saw him. I just rolled my eyes, he just couldn't help that he was beautiful. Raph made everyone melt, even some of the boys, if you know what I mean. Thick brown hair and green eyes, yum I thought. We got to a nice table near the windows in the far corner, right where I wanted to be with him, away from the center for once. James and I never came here, this was my local spot that I'd frequent with my friends. I absolutely loved it. I decided to pace my alcohol intake. We ordered some specialty Tequila cocktails that they made called a Tromba Tramonto, it was perfect as a starter to the day. We caught up on all of what he was up to and some of what I was. I explained to him that I had to come back to New York City for some family business, and made the story believable. We finished up our brunch and a few more drinks. We were riding high on our cocktails when he interrupted, explaining that he had a prior engagement, he had to attend some afternoon housewarming party.

"Oh? Really.. umm, I thought maybe... oh never mind." I stuttered. It made no sense, but I conveyed my disappointment. Why was he leaving? This wasn't like him to bail, actually he never did with me. I didn't know what else to say, I didn't want to be a needy little girl. "Well, I was just about to ask you to come with me!" He gloated. He knew I was feeling him, and relished in it. Tilting my head I flashed a cute flirtatious smile back at him, while biting down on my lower lip. I couldn't hide how happy I was with him and at this point, I didn't want to.

Walking outside I remembered I had left my Adderall at my loft, I made an excuse to stop by so I could get them. I didn't take a lot of them, just enough to keep me uptempo. He had only been in my loft once before when I was just sixteen when he stopped by to bring me a gift for my new place. I had to turn him away that day because James was inside. If James knew back then he would have destroyed Raph, but I wasn't too concerned at this point. Raph seemed like he could handle himself fine now and besides James was in Milan. I was free to do whatever I wanted, and there was only one thing I wanted.

"Do we have time to have a quick drink… since we're here?" I asked, while already pouring.

"Well, since you put it that way," he replied. The pour was a double of my favorite Tequila and without hesitation, we both threw them back and I poured another and then another. I played some music, took a pill, and before we knew it, we had been talking for hours and had missed his party. Oh well, I thought. I didn't want to go anywhere but here anyway. I had Raph right where I wanted him.

Would I kiss him now? Should I? I started compartmentalizing pretty well at this point, so my fear was non-existent. Now I was beginning to wonder if he would try a play on me. "Well, should we call it a night?" He asked. I didn't know if he was teasing or if he was serious, I couldn't chance it, I had to come clean. Without any more games, I grabbed him by his shirt and pulled him into me. He came willing.

"You're not going anywhere. I've wanted to do this for such a very, very long time… I know you feel it." Leaning in close enough to feel his breath on mine. Which was just what it took. Raph picked me up into his muscular arms, with my feet dangling, and kissed me. The kiss was mind-blowing, so intense, deep, and methodical. Like he'd been waiting to do it forever. I was dying to kiss him all day, barely containing myself. His Hermes cologne on his skin made me out of my head, my pheromones lit up. The arousal grew with every second I took in the smell of him, it was like a drug. I knew the kiss would be perfect again.

"I've wanted you for so long… I need you in my bed." I whispered under my breath between kisses.

"You know I have too Allie, now show me that bed," as he kissed me softly. I dragged him to my massive white love nest, pulling him on top of me. We were still fully clothed, but it wasn't going to be for long. I stayed calm, to let him lead, because if it were me I would have shredded his clothes with my teeth. This man was all I could see right now, he was like blood to a vampire. He had never penetrated me, and I felt desperate to feel him inside of me. Unzipping my jumpsuit, exposing my bare breasts, he pushed me slightly away from him, so that he could gaze at my body. He looked at me like I was the most beautiful thing he had ever laid eyes on. Amazed by what he saw, it was exciting to watch and even more so to feel. Raph then took off my shoes and kissed my feet, removing everything I had and again staring at me from above, just gazing like he just saw heaven. I don't why, but it caused an emotional reaction from me and my eyes filled with water. I loved how he saw me. No one ever looked at me with that much pureness, if that makes sense. He undressed his sexy swimmer frame, and began caressing me, as if to study my every curve. Taking his time was what he wanted, which made me want the same thing. I relaxed into a different type of sensuality, one that I had never experienced, it felt gentle and unrushed. Mesmerized by all of his glorious dark hair as I ran my fingers through it. I felt like I was in a period film, you know with the romantic classical piano taking you to new heights in the throws of passion. I longed for every moment we spent while it was happening. Touching him, I found a new way of loving a body, a man, a face. It was hedonistic. Something I wanted more of. I continued fondling him all over, positioning my hands on his shiny, hard eight-inch cock. I stroked it softly, like it was the most precious thing in the world. I could feel his precum in my fingers, I needed to taste it, so I slowly sucked it off my fingers while he watched. His eyes grew larger from excitement. We grew in our desire to do more. I stroked him, as he fingered my pussy. Lying on the bed facing one another's privates, we both began to simultaneously lick one another slowly and gently to learn each other's bodies. Stopping after it got extremely hot, he moved away from me. Standing above me I could see Raph's entire frame. His brown skin glistened as I gazed over his broad shoulders. Oh my fucking god. I thought he was going to enter me, but he didn't. Instead he ate my pussy like he was starving, he hummed into it making the vibration feel like a toy I had grown accustomed to. I loved his method, he played my box like an instrument. His large tongue circled my clit, while he had a finger in my ass. It was driving me insane, I wanted to cum for him so badly. I desperately needed to share myself with him and I would, all of me. There was no holding back, I needed to climax, as I felt my body fill with the most powerful heat. The ass fucking and tongue were taking me to the brink. *"Oh Raph, can I cum for you?"* I cried out. He didn't stop fucking my ass or my pussy, he just hummed yes while he savagely ate my wet flower. My body was totally and utterly charged as I begged to let go all over his beautiful face. My pulsating pussy made him go wild, he didn't stop, kept at me, licking and fucking my ass harder making it even more intense for my orgasm.

"Oh my fucking god, baby... oh baby, I'm going to cum... yes please fuck me, don't stop, don't stop, I'm cumming for you Raph!" Releasing a sweet smell of my sex. He pulled back just a little as my body jumped wildly. I couldn't believe what had happened, foreplay making it more intense than I had ever experienced. I was in utter bliss.

Now it was the moment we both had waited for five years to do and that was to have him inside of me, I could tell he was going to wait a second longer. I was dripping wet, so I knew I could take his huge rod. He slipped a pillow under my ass, so he could get better access to me. Pushing his massive cock in slowly he moaned deeply as I whimpered.

"Oh Allie, you're so fucking beautiful. I've waited for so long to be with you. Allie, this feels so right, so good." Raph cried out over and over again as he pumped my flower full of his manhood. Grabbing my hips, he pulled me into his cock over and over again furiously until he was losing his mind from the build-up. I knew he was at the top of his threshold. *"Allie, Allie, I love this, I love you… I want to cum inside, is it ok?"* Raph barely holding on. *"Yes baby, cum inside of me, I want you to,"* I whined.

"I will… I'm cumming inside of you now Allie! Now! I'm giving you all of my cum Allie, babe it feels so good, oh Allie!" He howled like a wild beast. Holding himself with one arm over me, so as not to crush me while he let go, filling my pussy to the rim with his hot sperm. Raph depleted, slid out of and fell next to me on the bed. We both began to laugh. I think we were in such a blissful state from what had just happened, that it surprised us both beyond our wildest dreams. It was the most beautiful, intense, deeply meaningful sex he and I had ever had. We kissed afterward for what seemed like an hour.

I was starving and so was he. We got up, not dressing, and went to the kitchen to make pancakes while chatting till the wee hours of the morning. Exhausted, we took a quick shower and made our way back to my bed. He had an early Monday morning, so I didn't get to see much of him while getting ready to leave. I let him do a few business calls and waited for him in the kitchen.

"Good morning lovely lady, how did you sleep?" Raph asked.

"Hi there. Good morning, I slept like a baby," I replied. Kissing me meaningfully, he explained that duty called and he had some fiercely important meetings that he wouldn't make if he didn't get back to his place and change now. I understood, he would have stayed if he could. We embraced for a few minutes and promised to chat later.

"I'll call you later Allie baby!" He winked, got into my elevator and was gone. Utopias would be something I would relive in my head all day.

I couldn't wait to spill it to the girls. I told them everything. I also knew they could help me understand what the hell I was doing. I didn't feel guilty, but I did feel scared. If James knew what had happened here, he would kill me and him, literally kill. I cheated once and got caught, if I did again, especially with Raph, all hell on earth would break loose. My thoughts turned to me, and what I was capable of. Completely conflicted now, I had this crazy, hot-blooded fiancé that loved me so much, that would die for me and I absolutely loved him for that. I loved the dysfunction, because it was so crazy and passionate. Yet there was Raph, this sexy, oh-so-GQ model, with charm, class, and kindness, the list could go on. Not to mention the sensuality, it was on a different level than anything I had ever experienced, it was mind-altering. Two completely, polar opposite men, and I loved them both, or at least I thought so.

CHAPTER 20

Mommy Dearest

I got a summons from Tory to meet her highness for lunch uptown or should I say Martinis at The St. Regis. Grabbing furiously in my closet at anything and everything, I needed to feel equal or at least look acceptable to her. *Fuck, fuck, I hate everything.* I thought to myself, but why did this always have to happen when I was getting ready to see her? I was in my beautiful walk-in closet or should I say room, and then all of the sudden I had zero to wear… I mean zero. The upside was that it was spring again, and I had more options to throw on the floor. *Finally!* Something spoke to me. It was a pair of off-white lambskin F mules, but what was I going to wear besides Fendi shoes? Just when I thought everything was going to shit. There it was, a dress, not a dress, the dress! My hidden gem; an Alessia Zamattio, Tropea Butterfly tiered pulled-sleeve mini dress. Running to the shower I was elated. My hair would get pulled back to make it an easier task, going light on my makeup, I could always add more for dinner, because this dress would work for any occasion. And just like that, I felt relief.

Walking into the hotel, like I did so many times over the years to meet my mother, brought back memories as I passed all of the doormen working the front door with their hellos. They all commented on how big I got or how beautiful I became. They were such nice people, I'd often stop and chat, but today I felt especially rushed with her text messages, she made our meeting seem urgent. I scouted the bar but didn't see her anywhere. I thought that was strange, because she only ever stood or sat in certain areas of the room.

"Hello young lady, you're late." Tory startled me, coming up from behind.

"Hi! What the hell was that about? You scared me half to death." I replied.

"Aren't we dramatic? I thought you saw me when you walked in. I was speaking with David Cohen, one of my bankers. He almost demolished a huge deal with my money, luckily for me his brother Jonathan is a bit brighter and fixed it within a nanosecond of his misfire." Tory explained with such passion. She really loved to make money.

"Well, Tory you always find your way through a disaster. Congrats." I condescendingly remarked.

"Don't be sarcastic. It's not becoming of a lady." She sneered, while grabbing my arm and abruptly pulled me into the bar. I didn't say anything, as she led me to our special little corner table.

"You look very nice Allie," Tory said as if she was surprised that I did.

"Thank you, so do you," rolling my eyes. I realized Tory always had the perfect clothes and hair. Today was no different in her Alexander McQueen neon pink single-breasted blazer and her matching straight-leg crepe trousers. Right down to her brown pillow-top, "It's Trippy" Tamara Mellon sandals, and her ever so gorgeous blonde mane. I studied her hair, so perfectly polished and straight down to her shoulders. It was always a fashion-worthy event when we got together, after all, like mother like daughter. You learn from the best, and you know the rest.

I remember as a little girl, wearing her heels around Tory's vast bedroom while applying her lipstick, like the many nights a week, she was getting ready to go out. I was only five or six then, she would demand that I walk with my shoulders back or tell me that if I didn't I was going to have a weak spine. I didn't understand what the hell she was talking about, but now I know it wasn't just about my posture, she meant walk in a room like you own it. Later she taught me that people either have presence or they don't, and that I must. So the walk was everything to the follow-up act. I guess that is why my modeling strut became pretty famous for the James Collection and others to follow. I had a real sense of confidence in my stride, and again I learned it from the best, Tory. I guess she did give me some of my gifts.

We sat and did our small talk, but I knew that was everything she wanted to speak to me about. I couldn't for the life of me ever read her completely, she was phenomenally great at hiding her emotions. I ordered her a Grey Goose, Dirty Martini, and myself a Clase Azul Tequila on the rocks. This should get us loosened up for whatever we were going to chat about.

"Please the suspense is killing me Tory. What is going on? I know you have something to tell me or blame me for. You're being extremely cryptic." I ranted a bit before realizing it. "Slow down, you sound like you did as a child," she half smiled. I would have liked to have wiped it off her face, but she was entirely right, I did sound exactly like a toddler. "Now listen closely, this is important… I wanted to discuss a conversation I had with James about your engagement," she explained. I was all ears at this point, what could they have been talking about? I specifically told him that I wanted to be in on all aspects of anything that had to do with our wedding. Tory went on to tell me that she asked James to postpone a wedding till at least next spring. I was listening and felt myself getting actually more relaxed. I was screaming inside my head, thank you god, thank you Tory.

"Why did you ask him that? And why wasn't I there?" I questioned her.

"He was in the same restaurant a short time ago with his Italian friends and I asked him to ring me the next day. The rest is history." She explained. I understood what she was telling me, but I didn't understand why James didn't share this with me. This dinner occurred over two weeks ago and for that matter why is she just now sharing this with me? I knew there was more to this sideways story.

I continued to probe, but Tory had nothing to say about the time gap, just that her company was merging with another and a wedding could really overshadow it and possibly make others think she didn't have her head in the game. I really thought this was the lamest tale I had ever heard, but pretended not to. I would get James in front of me tomorrow and get to the bottom of it.

We had a couple of drinks and then left to go to Marea on

Central Park South to eat. We dined on some of the best raw fish and had a decent conversation about real estate. Something that I was eager to learn about. Tory directed the conversation like a pro, and insisted I speak with her team about investing some of my grandmother's estate into some of Manhattan's prime up-and-coming areas, like the Lowest East Side. She explained it was rapidly changing and that this was the time to invest. I enjoyed hearing her speak with such knowledge and authority, she was a formidable woman. Promising that I would take a meeting, I wondered if she would be making money off of me now. Most likely, she always looked for opportunities.

I switched the subject back to James. "Do you like James and I together?" I asked.

"Well Allie, don't you think it's a bit late for my opinion on James now?" Tory laughed with sardonic amusement at the question. I ignored her sarcasm.

"I'm asking you now. I'd like to know how you feel about the two of us getting married?" I waited patiently.

"Oh you're serious, aren't you?" Tory paused to gather her thoughts. "Well, he loves you. I know that's important to you. He's very successful, and that's important to me. So… with all of that said, yes I do like him for you. I think if you can keep his dick in his pants, you'll be ok." That was as close as we could get as mother and daughter. This was Tory being crudely maternal. I don't know what I expected, a warmer response possibly, but that was never going to happen.

We finished our dinner quietly, she hugged me awkwardly, afterwards she went uptown and I went downtown. I had a nagging feeling in the pit of my stomach. I couldn't help but think to myself, she is up to something, but what?

James sent me a message at lunch that he would be home around 6 o'clock and would like for me to meet him at Balthazar restaurant in Soho, one of our favorite places to get oysters. I replied happily. So funny, how one second I could feel so many things for Raph, but when my fiancé texted, I could think of nothing else. I had not seen him for almost a week and it seemed like a lot longer. I had to run home and get my hair done and change into something wicked for his arrival. I still had this sick feeling in my stomach walking into my loft… what was my confusing lunch about and what were they hiding from me? I would get to the bottom of it.

CHAPTER 21

One Week in a Split Second

My phone rang and to my surprise, it was Serena and Beth, they were around the corner from my place, I just finished getting a blowout and had a few hours to spare. I invited them over. I missed both of them. We were supposed to do something over the weekend, but I was happy to see them sooner. They both had keys to my elevator, so they didn't have to ring. Entering my flat like a herd of buffalos was Serena holding a magnum of Rosé Champagne. "I'm a little bit tipsy!" She shouted.

"I see that!" I laughed.

"Hi Al," Beth said, giving me a hug.

"Hi love, how are you and our bestie… is she ok?" I said in a low voice, not that Serena could hear anything I was saying. She had a tendency of talking over everyone. Not in a bad way, she always made it quite a funny action. We could never be angry with her, she was just such a sweetheart. Beth said yes, and explained that they were celebrating hump day, basically Wednesday. I grabbed some glasses and asked the ladies to join me in the living room. Desperate for their opinions about my conversation with Tory, I told them how odd it was and what she requested. Beth was floored and rejected Tory's request. Serena on the other hand didn't see the rush and thought I was too young to marry James right now. Maybe they were both right? I asked Beth if she thought her father could find out anything for me, he was my attorney, and she agreed that we should have a conversation with him now, but just not today. Who could forget it's hump day?

We drank while listening to some of The Teskey Brothers' music, Serena loved to sing "Crying Shame." It was like listening to a cat dying, but we loved her just the same. She had this spark of light in her eyes, like no one I had ever met, I'd often wished for the same thing in mine. I wondered if people could see my darkness, it wasn't always there, but I know after growing up so damn close with Tory, it was. She had a way of bringing me into a place with no windows. I didn't know exactly what my mother was capable of, but I would slowly begin to figure it out. After all, our secrets can only stay hidden so long, eventually, karma will catch up and the walls of deception will shatter, even the best liars. Maybe these walls are just metaphors for people, but the fact remains you either walk through life cracked or just fucking broken. I was both.

"Hey, hey earth to Allie!" Serena yelled. Snapping her fingers in my face, I came back from my thoughts.

"Hi hi, sorry! What the hell ladies, let's make a drink, then you're both coming to my room to pick out my clothes." I insisted. I made myself my typical Tequila and orange, for them, I opened another bottle of Champagne and we went scurrying off to my room. Back to my massive closet, I felt like I lived for it, not in a bad way, I loved to dress. Beth would be doing the styling tonight, Serena was doing the jokes, and I was just loving my two friends, feeling grateful I had them.

"You know Al, I always loved this outfit from James'

collection on you, well at least that one time you wore it on the runway." She laughed, holding up a pair of leather, crystal leggings, and a micro-rhinestone encrusted bodysuit. The plunging overlap neckline went all the way to the stretch yarn bottom, which was right around my waist. Needless to say, we were going rocker chic.

"Oh, and don't forget these, the outfit wouldn't be complete without his skull-pointed-toe pumps." She signaled for me to get up and put it on.

"Yes indeed, I need some earrings and a watch too babe," pointing to my safe. Serena pulled out the mack daddy of all watches, which was one of my favorites and a twenty-first birthday from Tory, yes Tory bought me a birthday gift on my twenty-first, an Audemars Piguet, Royal Lady Diamond white gold watch. It was one of the only gifts she had given me, but this made up for all of them tenfold. The earrings Beth chose for me were an elegant pair of two-carat studs that I bought for myself from Graf. Lastly, I scooped up my engagement ring, the symbol of *I am not single* and slowly placed it on my finger. I was ready to see my betrothed. I felt hot, the excitement was building. I missed him again, and I liked this familiar feeling. No matter what I did with anyone, the one man that really stood by me was the man I pledged to marry, James.

It was getting late, my girls headed out to meet some cute guys they knew and were hooking up with. I called for a ride, and off I went to Balthazar. Walking in was always fun, I knew everyone and they always saved us a seat at the bar at the beginning, so we could see the whole entire restaurant and bar scene. There he was my devilishly handsome fiancé chatting with the owner Keith. He was wearing all black as well with a studded leather number he designed.

"Baby!" James waved me over wearing the most beautiful full smile. My sweetheart was happy to see me. I could only imagine how much. We had not been together for almost a week, but it seemed so much longer. It's funny how Raph and Elizabeth were suddenly a distant memory.

I knew that I had to just allow it to be a little secret and we could be happy together. Still madly in love with James, all it took was one look from him. His sex oozed from his pores and his desire to see me was written all over his gorgeous, chiseled face.

"Hi stranger, hi Keith." I leaned in and kissed James lightly on the cheek and then hugged our friend. Keith excused himself, he knew James had just returned and that the love birds needed their space.

"Hey, come here." James pointed to the space between us. I moved in. "Now a little closer." He pointed to his lips. I smiled while leaning in happily, kissing him softly with my tongue. "Fuck Allie! It's already hard, we'd better sit down." James pulled out my stool and directed my ass in it. "You look stunning, I love those on you... I love the entire outfit on you. Babe, thank you for wearing it tonight. You know I make these clothes with you in mind." Pulling me to him, he kissed my nose in admiration.

"Thank you baby, I love everything you make, and I love you." Holding James's face in my hands, I looked deeply into his eyes. "I don't want to wait to get married, let's do it next week." I waited for his answer. I either meant what I said, or I was trying to draw him out. I should have in hindsight waited, but the involuntary comment just rolled out without my knowing.

"You do? Really? I thought you were the one that said it was too soon. What changed your mind?" James questioned me with a confused look on his face. Now I was perplexed, that wasn't the reaction I was expecting.

"No... I mean yes, of course, I always wanted to marry you baby," I stuttered. "I've been thinking about us, and I don't want to be without you and I know you love me James. Let's do this! We could plan a party and not tell anyone we're actually getting married. I'm not sure what kind of party, something to bring our friends and family in. Besides it's better this way, then the press will leave us alone on this day... our day. What do you think?" I rambled on with excitement. I was even convincing myself that I really wanted this, but just maybe I did.

"You're serious," James said as he sat with his mouth wide open. I thought he was in shock, it was bizarre. "Allie, it's a lot to do in just a week," he paused. I waited patiently while he gathered his thoughts, I had said enough, now it was his turn. "But, hell yes, let's get fucking married baby!" He shouted.

"Shhh, shhh." I giggled under my breath. His response was surprising, but still, I liked it. He kissed my hands and then pulled me tight to his chest. Holding me close James whispered.

"Now, I'm starving, so let's eat or you'll be the main course." We enjoyed a laugh as it began to sink in. We are really doing this. We are getting married.

I looked at him that night with only pure love. He was so freaking happy and my heart was full. We chatted at the bar, entangled in ideas of what our magical day and night would look like. He, as a fashion designer, had such a beautiful eye for detail, and this was something we were going to need for our very special celebration.

"Babe, I just thought of this, I won't be able to design your dress. As much as I want to, I need to have someone else work with you." James looked disappointed. I reassured him that he could have the final word on who would be creating it, which seemed to give him some relief. James didn't love all of the designers I wore, so I wanted him to be happy seeing his bride walk toward him.

No one wants the groom running away. I questioned myself, but would I run away?

We celebrated with a couple of bottles of Louis Roederer Cristal Rosé Champagne. My head was buzzing from love and the bubbly. He decided it was too early and yanked me to a little speakeasy that had live music on Seventh Avenue called Little Branch. A hidden gem that we frequented, and a place where he knew his best friend Will would be after his dinner. Who was I to turn down a good party? Just as we suspected there was Will, I had only met him once before briefly in Los Angeles, where he lives in the Hollywood Hills. He was around my height, a round cute boyish face, brown moppy hair, and some nerdy, yet cool rims. I immediately liked him. He was smart, comical, and playful. He was in tech, came from a family of successful investors in Palo Alto, he too became an investor, but his money went to the questionable blockchain. Which in turn made him a very independently wealthy man at a very young age. Will was there with his girlfriend Antonia. She was a chatty, petite Latina girl with extremely big, beautiful boobs, and a smile that would go on forever. They were a cute couple.

James ran over to his bud and picked him up with a bear hug. My guy was super strong and sometimes forgot this.

"Hey dude! I see you've gotten bigger." Will pounded on James's chest.

"I think you've just gotten smaller my friend." James grabbed Will's head and rubbed it. We sat at a small table off to the side and chatted over a couple of drinks, the guys caught up and Antonia and I got to know one another. She was really cool, and with her own success, she started a chain of healthy fast-food restaurants in Los Angeles and was now up to five. Antonia gushed over my engagement ring and asked the big question, "When is the wedding?" James and Will overheard her. Smiling at one another, I told James to tell them.

"Well, that's why I wanted to make sure I made it over here to see you. It's in one week buddy!" James boasted.

"What the… you're serious aren't you?" Will asked.

"Yes we are and I'd like you to stand next to me, be my best man?" Grabbing Will in for another notorious hug. We explained a bit of what we were thinking, or should I say, James. I didn't really have too much to say about it, I was still a little shocked, happy, but shocked. He liked everything way over the top with bling, so I wasn't sure what my perfect day would be like. I felt as long as I was saying "I do" to him, it would all be beguiling.

We had one more drink, all lit up, and tired. We said our goodbyes and planned on speaking tomorrow about the details of our nuptials.

"Let me get you home wifey. Now this is going to sound funny… your place or mine?" James asked.

"Mine, we're closer." I replied, pulling him to our driver who was parked out front. We were only ten minutes away from my place, that was the good thing tonight. My thoughts were racing, there were a lot of details that needed to be sorted, but my mind quieted when I looked over at James. I had never seen him so content. This made me feel at peace for what was coming… a quicky marriage?

We rinsed off and got into bed, but sleeping was the last thing I had on my mind. All the excitement of the wedding had me restless, and there was only one thing that was going to tire me out, my sexy fiancé. James was laying on his back naked looking at some emails from his phone. I grabbed his phone from him.

"No phones in our sacred space young man." I teased.

"I apologize babe, I just wanted to shoot something to my assistant. Tomorrow is game time. We have a wedding to plan." My man said with such utter conviction. I knew this was real, but was I ready for it? I had to be now. But first, I had to get what I wanted and that was for him to be inside of me.

"I want you so badly husband," I whispered in his ear. James grinned as he sat up quickly pushing his body against the headboard and pulled my legs around his body to straddle him. Placing my hands around his neck I began to kiss him passionately. I felt his tongue moving softly around my mouth as we touched one another's naked bodies. I wanted to worship his strong, tattooed body and arms. The black ink he wore was like armor, it made me feel protected. He was such a sexy badass.

Slowly I moved my body down, I wanted his penis in my mouth. I wanted nothing more than to please my god. Keeping my ass held high while I positioned myself on all fours, licking and sucking away at his long, hard cock. His rod throbbed as it was pumping full of blood, I knew how to please him.

"Slow... slow down Allie, I don't want to cum yet," he moaned. I did as he asked, flickering his balls with my tongue while using my hand to stroke his shaft. I was skilled with this man's penis and I knew it. He asked me to stop, then ordered me to lie down on my back. I did as he commanded, I liked him being dominant.

"Now take that sweet little pussy and put it on my face," James groaned.

"Yes, husband, anything you desire." I moved to his smiling face. I would have given him anything he wanted. Wanting only to please him, I needed James, and I would show him this however he wanted. I felt submissive, and I liked it. He directed me to a 69 position, putting my ass facing his mouth, so that I could suck his cock while he sucked on my wet box. Grinding on him, I started to lose myself and went faster on his rod. He didn't want to explode yet, but I could taste some of his liquid, so sweet and warm. Moving me off him, he laid me down on my side and slowly slid it into my vagina from behind. *"Oh fuck, oh my god, fuck. You are so wet and tight. I want to cum, baby I can't hold it much longer. I want to fill that sweet little hole up with all of my cum."* He howled like a madman grabbing tightly onto my hips. Pushing his cock harder and deeper into me I screamed out with pain and delight. Longing for him to hurt me, I needed more. Quickly grabbing for a small vibrator in my nightstand, I placed it close to my clit. Rippling pleasure through both of us, it was time for us to relieve our suffering. We needed to cum together.

"James my love, please fuck me harder... hurt me James... I love your big cock. James fill me up with all of your love baby," I screamed out wildly.

"Yes! Fuck! I'm going to baby, fill the tiny cunt up with my cum. Hold on, I'm cumming baby, grrr... I'm cumming Allie!" James roared like a wild beast.

"Yes! Yes! Yes!" I moaned deeply as we shared the most intoxicating orgasm.

CHAPTER 22

50/50

The following morning James reassured me all would be fine, and not to stress over any of the wedding plans, he had already had his assistant looking for the best wedding planners. He also told me that he was having lunch with my mother today to talk about something to do with an investment. I couldn't for the life of me understand why he would be doing some sort of business with Tory.

"James, care to explain… what kind of business?" I questioned.

"Well, it's a real estate deal. She asked me to come in a while back. I didn't think you would mind Allie… so, do you mind?" He acted completely innocent about something that I found so shocking, but who was I to question the man I loved, the man I was going to marry.

"No… I guess not, but I wish you would have told me. It threw me off guard." Explaining to him, but why? He knew it would provoke me.

"I'm sorry babe, it's not that big of a deal, trust me. Can we talk more about it later? I've got to go, I love you." Kissing my head, and poof he was gone. But the thought of this so-called deal weighed heavy on my mind. Could they be keeping something else from me? Was this the only secret that he had? *He wouldn't lie to me, would he?* I tried to put the thought out of my head, but only time would tell if my fear was actually intuition.

I received calls from three of the top wedding planners in the city and made a plan to speak with all of them at the end of the day. In the meantime, I arranged my canvas and painted, but I was distracted and couldn't focus on the art, so I poured a small glass of Clase Azul on the rocks and downed it. I felt better, so I did what I thought was the right thing to do and that was, pour another and then another, followed up shortly by an Adderall. I was flying high around noon when I called Beth. I needed her opinion on the Tory and James deal. I also wanted her to help me with the wedding planners. She asked me if I was ok because I was a little uneasy when I called. I told her what I knew and she insisted on coming over after a lunch meeting. I needed her, like I did many times before, because Beth was always the level-headed one in the bunch. I knew she'd be an hour, so I jumped in the shower to primp and sober up a bit.

Beth arrived around 1:30 as I was walking out of my bedroom, I met her at the elevator. "Hey you... what is going on?" Concerned, she walked over to me and gave me a hug. "Beth, thank God you're here. I am not sure, but I'm scared. I have this sick feeling in my stomach," as I held on to her tightly.

"Don't worry Al, we'll get to the bottom of this shit," she reassured me today like she had done a thousand times. Beth and I have been best friends since we were 12 years old. We knew everything about one another. I explained what James and I discussed this morning and we both agreed that this was quite strange. Beth, just like the attorney she was, pulled out a pad and pen, "let's write everything down, including anything that might have happened financially to you in the past year. I have a feeling this has to do with your newfound money somehow, Allie." She was analytical even as a child. I think it came from her father also, he was a brilliant attorney.

"Umm, let's see, my contracts with the brands, including James's, also my grandmother's estate, which included property, stocks, horses, and part of a company in Europe," explaining as she took notes.

"Got it, ok. I need a second opinion, so I'm calling my dad, he'll know where to start." Picking her phone out of her purse, she excused herself to speak to him for a few minutes. After she returned, she explained what he proposed. The first step was to get their investigative team on it to check into anything that was floating around on public records and the second was to call Arnold who could hack into anything, off the record of course, and get him to find out anything he could. Her father agreed that it seemed suspicious, and as my attorney felt that we should be proactive in order to secure my inheritance or anything else that might be at risk. I was sick to my stomach after I heard his words.

"If James is in on something with your mother, I will kill him myself!" Beth shouted. She always kept her cool, but she was worried, which in turn made me a nervous fucking wreck.

"But what if our suspicions are wrong? What if James is not up to anything with Tory? I could be screwing up our wedding right now!" I cried out.

"Yes, ok you're right. This may just be nothing, so with that said, let's call the wedding planners and proceed as normal. I also don't want to cause suspicion. James isn't stupid." Beth suggested everything was done as normal, but with all the pieces of the puzzle in play.

Hours later after lunch and a couple of glasses of wine, Beth called each one of the experts, agreeing to come over, she allocated the time slots. Each one an hour; the first one at 2:30, the second at 3:45, and the last one at 5:00. We opened a bottle of Champagne to celebrate like nothing else was going on. We had such a nice time chatting with the first two, but the last woman was over the top amazing, so much so that we immediately forgot about the others. Her name was Rose, she was a tall, lanky, forty-something-year-old woman from Nigeria. Rose had a fascinating story about her father, he was a diplomat, but something had happened and they had to flee to London with just her sister and mother. She had a tough adjustment as a teenager and that I could relate to.

"You have to plan my wedding!" I insisted. Beth agreed and opened another bottle of Champagne. We were enjoying the ideas she presented when James walked in.

"So many beautiful women in one room, how did I get so lucky?" Grinning from ear to ear, like the devil he was. Oh how charming he is, and sexy. It was hard to imagine he would be sinister enough to hurt me somehow. My suspicions turned to doubts. He could never betray me, he loved me. James got heavily involved in our discussion for a while, he was very much a creative force, and he had to have input, unlike other men that wouldn't care for this sort of thing. After an hour he decided to take us all out to dinner to celebrate finding Rose; the perfect wedding planner.

James made a reservation at Il Mulino, a small high-end Italian restaurant that we frequented often. We loved it because the maître d' kept our outings there very private, so the paparazzi would never just show up "unexpectedly." It was a beautiful night filled with grandiose visions of our wedding, which by the way was in one short week, but with the money we had, anything was possible, right? My mind crept away for a minute during dinner, and the thought of us really getting married began to scare the hell out of me. Was I too young for all of this? This was basically my first real relationship. Not his, he had plenty of women. James was known as a "playboy" for many years, the press were taking bets on how long we would last. I felt cruel, but maybe they were right, they might have seen something I didn't, but now wasn't the time. I wiped the negativity out with a smile. I would just have to see, there was no sense in rocking the boat if there weren't any waves.

The night turned out well after all of my fleeting thoughts were drowned out with a shit ton of Champagne and liquor. It was getting late. Rose left first, she had a child at home and needed to tuck her in. Then there were three.

"Well, as much as I would like to stay out, I have an early morning meeting," Beth explained while gathering her things. James insisted on his driver taking her home. I got up to say my goodbyes to my friend with an embrace.

"I love you so much Bethie," I whispered in her ear.

"I love you too Al," she whispered back. James walked her out, returning quickly.

"Ah, now I have you all to myself, my pretty," smiling as he gave me a full-on French kiss.

"Someone's happy to see me after only a minute," I joked.

"I'm so fucking happy… we're getting hitched babe!" He shouted in the restaurant. The staff had to have overheard him.

"Oh shit, do you think they'll say anything?" I was concerned. The last thing we needed was for this to get out, we would be hounded by the reporters. I couldn't stand the idea of this. James got the magnitude of what could happen. He went over to the two waiters and the maître d', handed them a wad of cash, leaving them with engorged smiles on their faces.

"That should do it." I loved that James stayed in control, and handled everything. He was the man, and I was definitely his woman. What tomorrow would bring was another story, but at this very moment, I could only focus on this evening. Tonight I only wanted to make love to him. To believe in my man.

When we got back to my loft, we each prepared in the bathroom for bed. I remember looking at him time and time in this very spot, thinking to myself *"I am the luckiest girl in the world."* I even liked brushing my teeth with him. There was something almost sexy about being that comfortable with him. My body and heart would light up in moments like this as I stared at him in the mirror.

"What? Why are you looking at me with that goofy smile?" He joked.

"Because I love you silly boy," I smiled with toothpaste seeping out of the corners of my mouth. James came behind me, wrapping his arms around me, and kissed my neck.

"I love you too, meet you in bed," tapping me on the ass as he ran to jump in bed like a child. The smile left my face as quickly as it came, my body filling up with doubt. *What if he's lying to me?! What will I do? Fuck!* My mind shouted.

"Stop, enough!" I shouted at myself.

"Babe, who are you talking to?" James yelled from the bedroom.

"No one, be right there," I hollered back. I needed to quiet my thoughts, so I took one of James's pot gummies and relaxed at my makeup vanity. It seemed to do the trick, because within minutes I felt euphoric and I was back to just loving him.

James, my strong, tattooed man was laying on his back with just a sheet covering his penis. I crawled up on the bed from his feet and made my way to his lips. I needed to feel his tongue in my mouth first. His passionate kiss warmed our loins up quickly as the sheet began to rise. Grabbing for some coconut oil that I kept next to the bed, I scooped out some with my fingers, dripping all the way to his manhood. I stroked his cock while kissing him, on my knees leaning into his mouth I left myself exposed. He placed his fingers in the oil as well and began to play with me, rubbing softly but furiously I began to moan. I loved his touch, he knew my body as well as I did. He loved to please and needed me to love pleasing him. James pushed a couple of fingers in me and began to finger me, while I continued to stroke his cock.

"Oh fuck Allie, I am so turned on by this. I want to lay you down babe," he said while moving slowly to position me. Looking up at him and all of his glory, I moaned deeply as he entered me.

"Oh James, oh..oh...oh!" I cried out as he continued to make love to me. Kissing him passionately as he went deeper into my wet flower.

"Allie, it feels so fucking good. I love your pussy, it's so fucking tight! I need to fill it up soon." He moaned loudly, as I played with myself. I wanted us to cum together. Reaching for my egg vibrator, I placed it on my clit, while it stimulated his shaft. This took us to another level, we were dying to cum now.

"Baby, I love you. I love you! Cum for me James, cum inside of me, give me all of your sperm!" I screamed.

"I'll give you every drop... Allie, I can't hold it... here it comes baby, all for you, every drop... all for you! I'm cumming, I'm cumming Allie!" Howling as he pushed one last time as hard as he could while lifting my hips up as his sperm shot deep inside me.

"Yes! Yes! Yes James!" I came so hard that my body flailed. Out of breath, we lay in awe of what had just happened saying

nothing as I quickly fell fast asleep in his arms. I was so content with my lover.

CHAPTER 23

A Surprise Guest or Two

Waking to the sound of the water in the master bath, I glanced over at the clock. *Shit, it's already 8:45.* Panicking, I ran to the shower where I found my stud all soapy.

"Hi babe, are you ready for round two?" James smiled with his hard-on.

"I just walked in… how the hell can you be hard already?" I teased.

"It's called the Allie effect," he grinned.

"Behave, we're late, we *have* to meet Beth and Rose this morning, something about eating cake. Remember? We have a wedding to plan mister!" Pushing him away from me I began to wash quickly.

"Alright, alright, I get the point. I'm out of here." James left me in peace and went to get dressed.

"Don't forget to give me your list of designers for my dress, I have to make appointments asap!" I yelled from the shower. He mumbled something and left the room. Knowing James, he already had my appointments made. He was very serious about my wedding dress and his tuxedo, but especially the dress. This was not just about us, it was also about how the world saw us. The perfectly hot, sexy, wealthy couple that everyone wanted to be.

Making my way to my closet, I pulled out a button-down silk Versace shirt dress and a pair of slip-on, black Jimmy Choo heels. I knew there was a chance I would be naked while someone was fitting me today, so this was an easy number to take off. I wore a simple stainless steel, white-faced Daytona Rolex and a pair of small diamond hoops. I felt exhilarated for the new day our life would bring us. James was making my matcha latte when I walked into the kitchen. He had the New York Post sitting on the breakfast bar for me and the New York Times for him. Reading the papers together in the morning began to be something we really loved to do together.

"Awe, you know I adore you for always doing this. You'll make a fine husband," kissing his back as I wrapped my arms around his hard body.

"Yes I will," he replied. Turning to me. "Come on young lady, sit down and drink your matcha," placing my tea on the bar.

"Yes sir!" I leaned in and kissed his hand.

I sat looking at him, I was in awe of my life. I was beaming from the excitement of what our day would be like, I think he was equally as eager. The first stop was in Brooklyn at BcakeNY. A cake maker to the celebs, such as JayZ, Madonna, and Jennifer Lopez. I had met the owner Miriam once before, Serena had her make a cake for Beth's birthday one year. She really had a way of inventing the most amazing themes in her sweet, floury delights. People came from all over to try her pastries. I was famished from all of the sex, so I knew this was going to be a good morning already.

Upon our arrival, we first tried a butter cake with dark chocolate icing and a cherry glaze. Next it was a simple, yet the most moist Red Velvet that any one of us had ever tasted. Lastly, a pure berry cake; blueberries, strawberries, raspberries, and blackberries were all packed on the outside, and a strawberry cream center. They were all so decadent, but I think we all had one in particular in mind.

"Well, what do you think, Allie?" Miriam asked.

"I love all of them, but the last one… oh my heavens, it was something out of a berry dream!" I replied. Wearing a bit of the cake on my lips, James wiped it off while teasing me.

"I agree, I agree, yes same." James, Beth, and Rose concurred. We spent another half hour chatting and enjoying more sweets. We decided on a five-tier cake that would stand five feet tall on a table, adorned with hundreds of white and pink sugar flowers. I could see it in my head. It was magnificent. High on sugar, we said our goodbyes and jumped into James's Escalade.

"Peter, you know where to go next please," James said to his driver.

"Where are we going?" I asked curiously.

"Now now, just wait, I want it to be a surprise," James grinned. Even Beth didn't have a clue where we were going, but one thing rang true, we were heading out of the city towards the Hamptons. I hadn't been out there since my grandmother passed away, so I was freaking out a little from it all.

Just as I had suspected, we were pulling up to my dead grandmother's, now my inherited house in Bridgehampton.

"James, what are we doing here?" Beth asked sternly.

"You'll both understand soon. Please, it's a positive thing," he explained politely. Confused and physically upset I tried to hold my composure because I knew James would always have me, that he would never intentionally mess with my mind, at least I didn't think so. There were multiple cars in the wrap-around driveway; one was a gold Bentley Continental GT coupe, and also another black Escalade. My dread was now turned to curiosity and so was Beth's. He was visibly happy as we approached my house. *It couldn't be her, could it?* I thought to myself. My mother happened to have a gold GT.

We walked through the magnificent entrance and into the Great Room, this was a grand space that Eve called The Parlor. The room was filled with an abundance of light from the fourteen-foot-high windows. They were adorned with pale blue, silk, and velvet drapes. The furniture was all tones of off-white with various blue pillows lining the two long sofas that faced one another in front of a beautiful marble fireplace. Above the fireplace was a portrait of me that Eve had done when I was just a girl. I looked innocent and frozen in time, but she loved it. Would I have it taken down was the question? I glanced over at Beth who was almost visibly crying from laughter at the painting, I couldn't help but laugh too. I was up there in the room just staring down at everyone, quite odd I thought, but why didn't it bother me before?

I opted for a quick sip of liquid courage, so I made myself a small glass of Tequila that I kept there. I could hear voices coming towards us. Walking in, to my surprise was Tory, her newest assistant Bobbie and the global designer; Ralph Lauren. I couldn't believe my eyes!

"James is that who I think it is?" Covering my mouth in disbelief.

"Yes Allie, that is exactly who it is…. *surprise*!" James squeezed me from behind. Beth was beaming as she approached Mr. Lauren with a handshake. Ralph Lauren was one of my favorite designers, I had walked for him a few times and admired his work. James and Ralph embraced in a bro hug, but I opted for gushing over the sight of him. I was even thrilled to see Tory, she could tell I was in awe over the situation.

"Hi little girl," Tory said with a half smile.

"Hi! You're here too, this has got to be good!" I don't know why but I pulled her in for an enthusiastic hug. She was stiff and I felt awkward doing it, but I had a feeling it was the right thing to do. Instead of returning my affection she lightly dusted off her jacket as if my embrace wrinkled her. *This now I am accustomed to*. As a child when I needed her hugs and kisses she wasn't there, and if she was there, she would just say, *please no touching… you'll mess up my makeup and clothes.* I knew now that Eve did the same thing to her, and that's why she was so fucked up. I was determined to break this pattern with my children… someday,

I'd hoped.

Everyone stood around chatting and getting acquainted. James turned to me, "Ok love. So, you're probably curious to know what's going on here," he beamed with delight. He loved making a scene, but more so he loved making me smile.

"Yes, yes, of course I am!" Still in shock from all of it, I let James continue.

"Mr. Ralph Lauren, who I consider a good friend, and your beautiful mother, a woman of impeccable style, and who is also a good friend of Ralphs, got together in the city and had a sit-down," James explained slowly as Mr. Lauren kindly interrupted while he cleared his throat.

"Please allow me to explain, folks. I am going to design your damn wedding dress," he said as a matter of fact.

"You're what! Oh my God! Is this true?!" Jumping up, I couldn't contain myself and leaped into Ralph's arms. It was quite funny, as he loved the reaction, my mother on the other hand gasped at the sight of it. So it was worth it seeing Tory squirm in embarrassment. James was tickled pink as he watched me go on about Ralph's work and how much I'd always admired it. It was beyond my wildest dreams and this was just the beginning. James had the staff break open some rosé Champagne as we toasted to the wedding. It was one of the most beautiful days of my life, but would it last? My happiness slowly turned to dread. I felt like something could go wrong now. I carried on as if I didn't have this pain in my stomach from the sick feeling that

overcame me. So much so that I had to excuse myself. I exited quickly, finding myself in my bedroom where I had some more of my trusted friend; Clase Azul Reposado. I poured it in whatever I could find, in this instance, it was a red wine goblet, and drank it down, like a camel finding water in the desert.

"Are you really that scared?" Tory barked, startling me.

"What? You're like a cat sneaking up on me. Why are you here? Did you follow me?" Accusing her only made her love it more.

"No Allie, I just thought you might want to talk to someone, you're clearly upset, but my question to you is why? Why are you running off, during what is supposed to be one of the most brilliant moments of your life?" She stated the obvious.

"I....I.... um, I am not sure why actually," sitting down I slumped as I crossed my arms while still holding my drink.

"Well, there we have it, you're not sure about him, are you?" How dare she state this, as if it were true. Like a light bulb went off in my head, something resonated and I knew she might actually be right. I was just about to reject her comment to save face and Beth walked in and interrupted, what could have been a bad or should I say worse conversation.

"Hey, everything ok here? Everyone is asking about you two." Beth is clearly concerned. She always had perfect timing. Even as a child she looked after me like a mother hen.

"Beth, so nice to see you. Looking good as always. Well, this is my cue, I will see you downstairs ladies." Tory exited as fast as she came.

"I see nothing has changed with her, still the same as she ever was. Is she the reason, ugh, you look like you've seen a ghost?" Walking over to me, Beth sat and put her arm around my shoulder. I began to cry softly as I leaned into her.

"Hey you, I don't know what's happening here, but you're going to be fine. I'm here now. I love you Al," Beth comforted me like the best friend that she always was.

"Thanks Bethie. I've got this, I'm just overwhelmed. We should go back down." Wiping off my face, I pulled Beth up to her feet as I embraced her. Forcing a big, goofy smile, she laughed and we went back down to the festivities. The rest of the day I chose to be present and not think about Tory's words and my insane thoughts. I was in love, or so I thought, and nothing was going to ruin this wedding, *or was it?*

Beth got a ride with Tory's assistant, and Ralph went with Tory in her car, so it was just James and me at the house. My dead grandmother's house, and now mine. James excused himself to change and I hung back to look around. The memories that filled that house were mostly wonderful. How could I even think to sell it? I love this place, it actually made me very happy. I walked to the back of the sprawling house where the music room was. Eve had a baby grand piano sitting in the middle of the room, where I loved to watch her play. She was much better than I was, I only played for a few years before I opted to play the cello or as Eve would say, *it chose me.* Off to the right of her bench was my instrument just polished, looking rich as the day I got it. I had been playing the cello since I was seven and mastered it by the age of twelve. I still played from time to time, but most people didn't even know I could, even James. Sitting down my mind wandered back to the days when I played with Eve. I started to join in on her social gatherings with her adult friends when I was just eleven. She played with the best classically trained musicians for years, until most of them died, including her, except for one, Thomas O'Reilly who championed the violin. Thomas was still very much alive, and was now my neighbor here in the Hamptons. He always had a crush on my grandmother, it was obvious to me, but for some reason, he never told her and she never really caught on. I thought it was a bit sad. I had every intention of seeing him before I left. He was such a sweetheart, originally from Ireland. Thomas had been briefly married to a nice woman named Rose, but she and their son Deckland died in a horrible car accident when he was just 39 years old. Thomas never remarried, sold off his businesses, and apartment in the city, and stayed in the Hamptons. He must have been reaching his mid-eighties by now, but it didn't seem like the case the last time I saw him, which was at Eve's funeral.

I sat down and scooted to the front of the chair, and placed my left foot slightly forward. Adjusting the cello endpin so the body of the cello gently rested against my chest, and balanced it between my knees. It brought me back fast to the beautiful music I used to make with Eve. I didn't know what I wanted to play, it just spilled out of me involuntarily, Sergei Rachmaninoff's Sonata in G minor for cello and piano, Op.19. My other half of this was missing, the piano and the pianist; Eve. I strummed hard, smiling, recalling the first time I sat to play with her. For as many ugly things that had happened in my young life, this made up for most of it; music. It would become my partner in my paintings.

James had come in to watch, unknown to me. I continued through the piece till the end. He clapped, startling me. "I didn't know you played. Why didn't you tell me?" Clearly confused and also pleasantly surprised by what he had witnessed.

"Hey you, um I guess I never thought I would start playing again. It was something I loved to do with my grandmother… I thought it would make me sad to play again," I replied. My tears filled my eyes, but I was determined not to cry, so I pushed them back as I had done for many years.

"And does it… make you sad?" He asked.

"Actually, to the contrary." I surprised myself.

"I'm in awe of you right now Allie. I don't know what else to say, I love you. Just when I think I know you… I find out something else that just blows me away," James said walking over to me. If I had any doubts about him and I, they went out the window in this instance. I loved him too, so fucking much.

"You're going to make me cry James." And he did. The tears weren't going to stay inside any longer, as they broke onto my cheeks he pulled me to my feet and I buried my head into his chest.

"Come here, babe. I got you. You sensitive little thing."

Wrapping his strong arms around my back he squeezed me softly. James was such a bad boy in public, yet he could be this massively compassionate man in private. He wasn't at all what I initially expected.

"Kiss me," I whispered as I looked up at him. Picking me up into his arms so that my lips met his, he began to kiss me passionately. I could feel his intense love and heat. It made me feel wanted. Gently he put me onto the ground and began unbuttoning my dress, I followed his lead and began undressing him. Our clothes were off, the room was dark. Pulling me up to straddle his waist, he walked us to a small leather sofa that was sitting against the wall. Laying me down, he towered over my body.

"You are so fucking beautiful," James said, as he inched down to my stomach, and began kissing it lightly. He then made his way to my thighs, kissing around my wet flower, getting close to it, enough to make my head spin with anticipation.

"James, please, I need you to lick me," I whimpered in desperation for my orgasm. Looking up at me one last time, he engulfed my pussy. Licking around in circles and flicking my clitoris, the man was a master at this. I moaned deeply, *"James, oh my god, don't stop."* Keeping at it, I was in ecstasy as he put two fingers inside of me and began to push in and out fucking my tight box. It was sliding with ease as my flower began to get even wetter. He hummed as he continued and the vibration was pushing me to the edge. My entire body filled up with the most exhilarating rush of pure joy. *"Ohhh, oh baby, I'm going to cum for you. Please don't stop!"* I screamed out in pleasure. Pushing hard and flicking faster, my pussy began to fill with blood as my clit throbbed in delight. My involuntary release was coming full force all over my beautiful James's face. My whole body filled with tingles as the largest orgasm began unfolding in his full mouth. *"I'm cumming my love."* I whimpered quietly with the most divine pleasure I had ever had, as my body collapsed.

James arose from my limp body with a sexy grin on his face, he knew just how good it was.

"I'm not finished with you yet," he said while stroking his engorged cock. Slipping it in slowly at first and then he thrust while screaming out. "Fuck Allie! You feel so good, so hot and wet." James grabbed a hold of my legs and began pushing deeper into my pussy. His cock was so hard, and his balls were so tight as I softly caressed them from underneath him. "Oh babe, you're going to make me cum too fast if you play down there. Fuck! I mean it," he wailed. I pulled back slightly. I wanted him to fuck me for a while.

"I love your cock honey," whispering in his ear, as he pushed even deeper into me.

"Do you? Tell me how much you like it. I'll give you more if you do… Fuck that feels so amazing!" He cried out. I grabbed his face, I wanted his tongue in my mouth when he came. I needed all of him.

"Kiss me deeply James," I begged. He did, but that was all my man could take. Pulling away from my mouth while looking savagely at me, *"Your tight pussy is killing me Allie… I'm going to*

cum, I can't hold it! It feels so fucking good babe! Here it comes, FUCK I'm cumming... I'm filling your little pussy up with my hot cum!" He howled like a wild animal as James fell onto my body. Laying on me for a few minutes to catch his breath, James then moved off me and put my body in the crook of his arm as he pulled me towards his chest. I nested in awe of what happened between us. It was powerful like the music I played, and was not to be taken for granted. I knew he was the one at that moment. I was finally with someone I trusted and who adored me. I could let my walls down and be with him completely. *Couldn't I?*

The next morning when I came down to breakfast, to my surprise it was Thomas.

"I was just thinking about you Mr. O'Reilly," approaching him with a big hug.

"Oh my, look at you! You are the prettiest thing I've seen in ages," greeting me with an embrace and saying his thank you's to James.

"I see you two met," I said. I knew James must have gone over to his house and invited him after I shared stories about Eve and Thomas.

"Yes we did, I thought it would be a fun little surprise in the morning. We should all have breakfast together." Turning to Mr. Reilly, "Please stay with us, I happen to make the best coffee," James said as he grabbed my hand to squeeze it. I fell more in love with him once again.

"I would absolutely love to, and yes to a coffee James," Mr.

Reilly replied. We sat down and spoke for hours about Eve and his life, me as a child and we also invited him to the wedding. It was special for me, and James made it all happen. He wasn't exactly who I knew him to be, he was completely morphing into this man one could only dream of. Would this last? One thing Tory taught me was that everything wasn't always as it seemed.

CHAPTER 24

What's Hidden Will Never Stay Hidden

That same day I had an appointment to speak with Beth's father who also happened to be my attorney, Charles Hollingsworth. We had to go over my prenup and also my grandmother's estate. I didn't know what was in store for me that day, but I did know that it would take many hours to sift through all of the logistics. I had a plan to paint that evening, but that got squashed by our meeting. I was on a deadline for sharing some paintings with a gallery that was interested in my work. Little did I know that something bigger than the curator was behind it.

I walked into Mr. Hollingsworth's office. All dark wood with a big red leather bound chair that he sat in. "Well, there you are. Oh Allie, it is so very nice to see you again. How long has it been five or six months now?" Charles said with a big smile as he moved out from his desk to greet me.

"Hi, Mr. Hollingsworth. It's been too long, that's for sure!" Giving him a quick hug as he directed me to sit in the small living area he had in his office. We spoke for another thirty minutes as we caught up on life. Then the business side of Charles rang through. He was a very intelligent and aggressive lawyer and felt he had an obligation to take good care of me. He looked at me like I was one of his kids.

"I've been going through your grandmother's papers quite thoroughly. There was a lot to read. Eve had multiple overseas accounts and also many charitable organizations we had to work through," he continued. "Your inheritance was like reading a book that had a lot of useless wording. Damn attorneys!" Joking, Charles made light of it all. I knew this wasn't going to be an easy day, but the one man I trusted with my money was Mr. Hollingsworth.

"So, is there anything that stands out that might alarm us?" I asked.

"Well at first, there was nothing out of the ordinary, but then there was this agreement with an external shell company that came to my attention. It wasn't your grandmother's company, but there was an agreement, it looks like she signed something that had to do with you." Explaining to the best of his knowledge.

"I don't understand. It had to do with me?" I was confused by his statement. What agreement? This all had a Tory feeling to it. "Let me guess, my mother?" I replied.

"I'm not sure it's her, but I will find out. Rest assured, I have the best people working on this. I am personally overseeing it. You're like my daughter, I won't let anyone take advantage of you. I think you've seen enough of that for such a young life." Charles empathized. Beth had his DNA and always stuck by me, protected me. I knew he meant what he said.

"I don't know what to say, I…I really appreciate it, Mr. Hollingsworth." Looking down, I had feared the worst, that Tory was up to something and god knows who else. Walking over to my chair, Charles lifted my chin.

"Hey kiddo, look at me. Nothing bad is going to happen, trust me." But could Charles protect me from what was happening, if my grandmother couldn't any longer, what was this company doing? Mr. Hollingsworth didn't know right away, so it must be something serious. I felt like he was holding back as well, I don't think he wanted me to spin out before my wedding.

Charles changed the subject to my nuptials. "I'm looking forward to your wedding Allie, Beth hasn't stopped talking about it." I decided to follow his lead and change my attitude and fear into something positive.

"Well you know, she has actually taken over the wedding planner's position." I joked. "Yes, that sounds like my Beth." We both laughed. Beth was always the one getting everything done efficiently. She never missed a beat. It had to be right or nothing at all. "I'm happy you and Helen will be there. Can you tell her that I said so?" Asking nicely. "Of course. She's quite excited to be attending, she hasn't stopped looking for a dress since the moment you announced it, but please don't tell her I said that." He smiled, extending his hand.

"Deal, my lips are sealed." I shook his hand. Still, I couldn't shake the fear that Tory had something to do with what was going on. I just felt it in every bone of my body. Something inside of me hoped I was wrong, only time would tell.

Switching back to business Mr. Hollingsworth turned to me, "I have one last thing we must go over now. It's your prenuptial agreement." This was the last thing I wanted to talk about, but I knew we both needed to finalize it. There was an abundance of money and neither of us wanted to get screwed at the end, if there was an end. James had an empire and his net worth publicly was around 400 million. Mine before my grandmother was a mere five million, now after Eve's passing rose to 100 million.

"Is this as complicated as I think it is?" Asking, but I already knew the answer.

"Yes, but complicated is my specialty. I will break it down for you like this. It's fair to say that you don't need James's money or support, but you are now the face of his company. I feel that warrants stocks in his company. I also believe if you divorce, every year that you are married you receive a set amount," Mr. Hollingsworth explained in detail. Not only did he want me to be protected, but well paid if we divorced. He also suggested a set amount for me for every child I produced, two of his houses would be mine, and alimony with or without children for a set amount, depending on the length of the marriage. It was a bonafide business deal. I didn't know what to say, I certainly didn't want to come off as a money-hungry bitch, but this seemed quite normal in our world. So I agreed to it and hoped that James wouldn't be upset with me.

"Well, I have to be going now… you know, the dress and blah blah. James has my head spinning because of this damn dress, it has to be perfect in his designer eyes," I joked, but in all fairness, this was more than true. We said our goodbyes and Charles promised to reach out as soon as he found out more. I couldn't help but wonder what the hell was going on, but I needed to try and focus on my wedding, I couldn't let it all fall on James and Beth. I needed to be present, after all, it's not every day a girl gets married… *is it?*

Still, that nagging feeling stayed with me, haunting me like a ghost. I had to know what the fuck was happening here that I wasn't getting? My intuition is definitely sending me a loud and clear message. *Question everything you see.* I dialed Beth and Serena and asked them to meet me for a girls' lunch. Beth declined because of meetings, but Serena was always up for a cocktail during the day and she was the fun I needed right now. We met downtown at Balthazar, the bar was half empty, and she was waiting in our favorite seats at the head of the bar, so we could see the room. The bartenders were all people that I had known for a while, so my drink was brought to me without asking. "Thank you, Robert," I smiled.

I carried on with Serena. "Hey my girl, how are you?" Hugging me in my seat, Serena almost fell on me. "You had a couple of drinks before I got here didn't you?" I joked.

"No, I only had one," she grinned. I knew she had a few, but who was I to judge? I loved her regardless of her flaws and she of mine. "Hey, do you have some Adderall on you? I don't have any coke and I need something now," she asked desperately.

"Sure, anything for you sis." Digging in my purse I found my small Altoids mint box.

"I said Adderall," Serena whispered.

"I know, this is where I keep them, silly girl," I smiled as I handed her two of them. I would normally take one, but I knew what she required at this time to get sorted out a bit. "Awe I see, thanks Al, you're the best. I have my dealer coming, but he won't be here for like thirty minutes." Popping the pills with some wine, she seemed to instantly feel at ease.

"So, what is this all about? You haven't called me for day drinking in months," she teased. I explained what had happened at Mr. Hollingsworth's office and she, like myself, thought something seemed off. So we played a few scenarios out and all of them seemed quite paranoid to me, but then something hit me in the gut. "What if James were involved somehow?" Serena explained a theory that had to do with Tory. I must have had a worrisome look on my face because she put her arm around my shoulder. "Hey Al, I was only joking! James loves you too much to be sneaking around doing shit behind your back!" I knew what she was saying was true, but why did I feel otherwise? My mind was telling me one thing and my heart another. I brushed it off and ordered another drink, pulled out my Adderall, and put one down.

"One for me!" Serena held out her hand.

"Yes, my friend." I handed her another one.

"Oh look just in time! Snap! It's my guy, I'll be right back." Jumping to her feet Serena followed a normal-looking guy outside. So funny in New York City, you would never have guessed in a million years that that little, white, clean-cut, twenty-something-year-old was a dealer. I guess it takes all kinds. Serena returned to only excuse herself to the bathroom. I looked at my phone at a couple of photos of James and me, and I began to feel saddened. *Was I jumping to conclusions? Was I as paranoid at Tory?* I needed to stop what I was feeling and change it up, so I called him. He answered, "How's my girl?" I could hear a bunch of people around him.

"Hi babe, I'm good. I'm just having a drink with Serena," I replied.

"Uh oh, don't be too bad today," he joked.

"Hah, you know us don't you?" I returned the banter.

"Babe, I have this dinner tonight uptown, I can't get out of it. I would ask you to come, but believe me, you would be as fucking bored as I will be," he explained.

"Oh yes I remember, don't worry I'm good, I'll eat with Serena and then go to my place. I'll see you tomorrow after work for dinner... love you." I did mean it, I do love him.

"Love you too." The phone was dead. Ok, that was a brief and abrupt call, but I knew he had a lot on his plate with work now and our wedding, I couldn't fault him. He was trying so hard to make everything perfect for us.

Sitting with Serena we got caught up. It's so funny how cocaine just seemed to get her straight again. This would go on for a long time, till the very same drug stopped her in her tracks. It's a dirty and dangerous habit. We talked about the wedding of course and also the guy she was seeing. Turns out he was the lead in a pretty up-and-coming band in the U.S. Serena loved to get into relationships fast and get out equally as fast, so I wasn't sure if the "new guy" would even make it to the wedding. I told her that she had to come to the dress fitting and explained she couldn't be late or Beth would have her head on a platter. She agreed at the time, my hope was that she would.

"Hey I know I said I could stay for an early dinner, but my new guy's in town for one night and I *really* want to see him." She pleaded for me to let her off the hook.

"Of course, you did your friend duties, you listened to me for hours. I love you… go have fun." We kissed and hugged goodbye, I thanked her for coming and she was gone as fast as she was here. I loved Serena, she was unapologetic. She liked to have fun and didn't ask permission. I think most of us hold back a little, but not her. I only hoped that she wouldn't run out of steam one day. With the fun, sometimes came the consequences. My phone buzzed, it was a text from Serena. *"I love you. Don't be afraid, it'll all be ok."* I'd hoped she was right, but again that feeling that something wasn't right crept back in. I couldn't stand the doubt, so I did what I had to, ordered another drink and gulped it down, paid my check, and opted for something closer to my apartment. So I went to this tiny bar across the street from Locanda Verde called Smith and Wills.

I sat sipping my Clase Azul when I heard a familiar voice chatting behind me, then it was beside me. "Allie… hi… how are you? It's been too long." Raph was standing over me with his piercing green eyes and a wide smile.

"Hi, I'm really great, I can't complain," I replied with my

mouth wide open.

"You're obviously upset I'm here, should I pick another bar?" He asked.

"No, don't be ridiculous," I said while closing my big mouth. What was it about Raph, he would come into a room and the world would disappear. He was just so damn sexy and sweet.

"Can I sit down next to you? It seems to be the only seat at the bar," he teased me. I insisted that he did. We picked up naturally like old friends, enjoying conversations about what we were up to for work.

"I heard you and Amber broke up. I'm sorry." I wasn't sorry, and I don't know why. Maybe I wanted him to remain single just in case I ever needed him.

"Oh yea, thanks. And I heard you were getting married any day now, at least that's what the New York Post is saying," he joked.

"Yes, soon-to-be Mrs." Replying with a half smile. I wasn't happy telling him it was true. I wanted it all; James and Raph. That wasn't going to happen. It's a weird feeling when you feel so much for two men at the same time. We continued our conversation for hours when Raph suggested dinner. I happily said yes.

CHAPTER 25

A Test of Faith

We left the bar. I was a little nervous, if the paparazzi saw us out, James would lose his mind. "Allie, I know I shouldn't say this, but I don't give a fuck, you are visibly nervous, so… let's have dinner at my place. I'll give you the key, let yourself in and I'll go get us some Indian from your favorite spot around the corner. I felt relieved as I agreed and grabbed his keys.

"Yes, that sounds like a good idea, thank you for understanding." I jumped into a car and went to his loft. Walking in, I could smell his cologne everywhere, so masculine, musky, yet sweet. It got me a little excited, knowing that we would be alone in his place soon and no one would know except for us. I played some soft chill music and made myself a drink. My head was spinning a bit from not eating, so I took another Adderall.

"Allie baby, I'm back with the food!" Raph yelled from the front door.

"My hero… smells yummy, I'm starving!" Excitedly grabbing one of the bags to help him to the kitchen. We unpacked the food and began eating immediately while talking about this and that. Raph was trustworthy, so I had to get his take on what I was going through and my suspicions.

"Can I ask your opinion on something important?" I asked.

"Of course Allie. You can ask me anything, I'll always tell you what I honestly think." Explaining that he would always be here to listen, it put me at ease and I began to open up.

"Ok, please keep it between us, never talk about it to anyone. My attorney found something in my grandmother's papers. It appears there is an agreement and it has something to do with me. I have a weird, sinking feeling, like someone close to me is involved," I explained desperately. Raph could feel my pain, so he instinctively came to my rescue. Sitting next to me he put an arm around me, I rested my head on his shoulder.

"I don't think you should worry, at least not until you know anything for sure. You might just be nervous about the wedding. You have a lot going on," Raph comforted me like he had done before. He was a rock of a man, loyal and always so patient. I realized I was a little drunk at this point, so I shouldn't have looked up at him in such close proximity. It was like I was asking to be kissed as I stared into his eyes. He gently put his hand on my chin lifting it up to his lips and I didn't resist.

What came next, shouldn't have, but I couldn't stop this connection between us. I didn't even think for a second about my fiancé. I just knew I could get away with it, and it felt good. There was no future with Raph or so I thought, I was just going on pure sexual energy and wanted more.

"I can't do this," I murmured as he continued to kiss me even deeper. I felt myself falling into his arms a little bit more. *What was I doing?* I would be married in less than a month, yet I wanted to bed down this hot stallion?

"Come with me," Raph said while standing up. Pulling me

behind him, I willingly followed closely behind as he led me to his bedroom.

He unbuttoned my shirt and I his, as we continued to kiss.

"I want you, I haven't stopped wanting you," he said as he put one of my breasts into his mouth. I wanted him too, and how could you ever stop thinking about someone so beautiful inside and out. I knew he was special from the moment I laid eyes on him in St. Tropez five years ago. He was funny, cheeky, sexy, dark, and handsome and those eyes, were so unforgettable. I wanted him to make love to me, even if it was wrong. I was in a trance, not thinking of anyone, but myself when the fatal call came and my phone rang out with a hideous buzz.

"I better look, it could be important." Slowly pushing Raph away from me. I saw the name, James. For me, this was the biggest of buzz kills and also a dose of reality.

"It's him isn't it?" Raph asked, but already knew from my face the answer.

"Yes. I'm sorry… I can't do this. I have to go." I quickly got up and ran to my shoes and bag. Raph caught me before I hit the door.

"Allie, stop for a second, please. I'm just going to say it, fuck it. I don't care if you're thinking of marrying him or what. I have to tell you that I fucking love you! I have since the first moment I laid eyes on you. I don't think he's right for you," Raph was desperate to tell me all of what he had bottled up. I wasn't kind, I had to stop him from what he was saying.

"Oh really? You're in love with me! You don't really know me Raph. Just stop! Don't you understand, I love him… I…I…I… don't know what the hell I'm doing here!" Yelling at him felt wrong, but I had to make sure he didn't pursue me. I paused, "I'm sorry Raph, but this was a mistake." I felt like a knife was going into my heart seeing how broken he looked. I didn't know he felt this way, how could I not know? I wasn't sure what I was feeling for him, but I knew it hurt so goddamn bad. He was the last person I ever wanted to hurt.

I went back to my place, where low and behold James was sitting in the kitchen with a Scotch. "Hey there you are, I tried calling you," he said, wearing a big smile.

"I didn't expect you tonight… you said you had a business thing." Walking over to him, I joined him at the breakfast bar.

"Well, I missed you, so I decided to come down after dinner," he said sweetly. I was only too happy he did call me. What if I would have stayed and not come back to my place? This was no accident, the universe was telling me something or so I thought at the time. I made myself a drink and James asked me to sit with him in the living room. Cuddling up to him, I felt relieved to be home.

"I have a surprise for my wife-to-be!" Excited James jumped up and pulled me to my feet.

"What?! A surprise! I love surprises," I squealed. He was an amazingly generous man, so I could only imagine what it could be. He explained that it was in the music room, where I had a mixing board and my record player. Walking over to the room, my thoughts briefly went to Raph and his words… he loves me, why tell me now?

"Close your eyes babe," James insisted as he covered them with his manly hands. Laughing as he guided me to the room, he pulled away his hands, then to my surprise was a cello, but not just any cello, an Alessandro Gagliano cello.

"Is this what I think it is? I can't believe my eyes! James, what have you done, this is too much! This is a four hundred thousand dollar instrument!" Screaming from delight and pure shock. I couldn't believe I was looking at an Alessandro Gagliano cello.

"I wanted you to be able to play here in the city as well and only the best for you babe." James meant every word. He wanted me to have the best of everything but also wanted to push me to play again. I knew he thought I was wasting my talent by not playing. So, I happily sat down on the edge of my chair and began to play for him. I chose Saint Saëns, The Swan. A beautiful piece that I once saw Yo-Yo Ma play with Kathryn Scott. It wasn't an easy task, but I picked it up quickly. I loved the sound and the feeling of it. James looked on, I could feel his happiness as I glanced over at him for a second. I finished, and as he applauded I stood up and took a bow.

"Bravo!" Scooping me up into his arms.

"Thank you, James. I love it, I love you." Suddenly a romantic gesture and James in front of me made me forget all about my almost deception with Raph. How easily I could compartmentalize. Was I becoming more like Tory, or was it just a DNA thing, either way, I was fine. I could compartmentalize, I was changing quickly.

I played for another twenty minutes and then let him know I was tired. He agreed and went to the shower. Telling him I'd join him shortly, I went to my laptop and checked my emails. There was one that stood out. *'Please come to my office first thing in the morning Allie. I found something, we need to discuss as soon as possible.'* It was from Charles Hollingsworth. He found something, my heart was racing, my natural instinct was to call him now, but it was going on 11 pm, and I couldn't. I would have to wrestle the demons and wait to speak to him in person. *Shake it off Allie,* I said to myself over and over.

I did my best and got into the hot shower with my hot man. He needed to be appreciated and I needed sex badly. I kissed him passionately as his cock rose to hit my leg.

"Oh, someone's excited," I teased.

"Yes, I am going to marry this beautiful, fucking talented woman in less than a week." He said in a low sexy voice.

"Mrs. James John has a nice ring to it," I replied. James looked into my eyes, grabbed my ass, and picked me up to straddle him. Pushing me to the shower wall, he slid the tip of his manhood in, gently maneuvering in all the way.

"Ohhh… that's my girl, so wet for me," he moaned.

"Yes my love, it's all for you," whimpering as he lifted me up

and down on his beautiful cock.

"Fuck Allie, I love how tight you are. It makes me want to cum. I'm going to stop, let me take care of you in bed." Placing me down, he guided me out of the shower. I dried off quickly and leaped into the bed.

"Come take care of me or should I?" I teasingly bit my lip.

"You know that makes me crazy. I'm definitely going to take care of that sweet, little box. Spread them, woman," James pushed my legs open and began to devour me. Working my pussy like an expert as he pushed three fingers inside of me. He began finger fucking me, while he gently flicked my clit.

"Oh my love, that feels so good," I whimpered. He continued applying a little more pressure to my blood-filled hood. I pulled at my nipples as the sensation shot down my body as he continued to push me to the edge. I couldn't speak, only moan because I was so close. I wanted to cum all over his face, I knew he would go mad and I would be in pure bliss. He kept at it, listening to my sounds as a guide, making me crazy as he circled around my sensitive clit.

"Oh James, I am ready to cum for you. I'm ready, baby. Ohhhh, ohhhh babe... oh my god!" I released over and over. Gently I moved his head away, I couldn't take the pressure on my vagina, it was all too sensitive for the moment.

"Did that feel good babe?" He asked sarcastically.

"Yes, beyond good," I said in a euphoric tone. James waited

patiently for me to regain my wits so that he could be taken care of. I lay for a few minutes as he caressed me. I felt his hunger, I had to give him what he needed as well. Leaning over him I said, *"Can I lick you now?"*

He grabbed his rod. *"Please babe, suck me."* I gave him a devilish grin and crawled my way to his hard cock. Licking and sucking, as I stroked him with one hand, using the other to play with his balls, as I balanced myself on my knees. He was going nuts, *"Fuck Allie, that feels so fucking good. I want you to suck my cum down. Take it all,"* he growled. I knew he wouldn't be long and I would drink him dry. *"Yea babe, that's it, suck it... I want to cum so hard soon babe. I love your mouth."* Placing his hand on the back of my head he roared. I worked his tip softly, sliding my mouth down to my hand at the base, over and over again. Quickly picking up pace as he held the back of my head gently, while he rocked his hips. I could taste a bit of his precum, I knew it was because his explosion was very close. *"Ohh babe, fuck...I'm going to cum in your mouth. Fuck Allie... I'm cumming... Fuck babe, I'm cumming!"* Bucking wildly as he let loose in my mouth, filling it up, I swallowed.

CHAPTER 26

The Final Countdown

Part I

The next morning I was having a matcha, debating on my clothes, knowing that I had my appointment with Mr. Hollingsworth at his office in a couple of hours. This time I was ready for whatever he was going to tell me. Charles however called and left a message, I must have been sleeping when he left it. It read;

Good morning Allie,

Apologies I spoke prematurely and I don't have all of the facts yet, please give me a bit more time and I'll let you know when to come to the office. Enjoy the wedding planning and let me worry about the rest.

Warmest regards,

Charles.

I got physically sick, which was probably a good thing, because I felt better afterward. My nerves subsided. I realized I needed to keep moving, I was getting married. Since there was zero I could do about Charles and his cryptic messes, I took his advice and was determined to enjoy the final plans of my wedding.

We were going to have a quiet ceremony at Justice of the

Peace in New York City, then have the biggest soiree at my home in Bridgehampton, but I was feeling very uneasy about my wedding memories being that of a courthouse. I phoned James and he agreed that we needed to change the plan. We had just days to go. He suggested keeping the wedding small with just close friends and family, then as planned a massive, theatrical reception, I agreed happily.

I had my first dress fitting with Ralph today as well, so I called Beth and Serena to join me, I knew they would want to be there. I was beyond excited about the dress now, I didn't know what it would look like at this point, but knew it would be fantastic. I only shared with the brilliant designer what I didn't like, he being the best already, seemed confident of what would look amazing on me. After all, that is what he does. Ralph Lauren was one of the most respected and talented designers in the world. I knew I was in good hands. My girlfriends graciously accepted my invitation. I thought it only right to also ask Tory, after all, she did give birth to me. Whether she would be as gracious and come, well that was another story. I didn't reach her on the phone, so I left her a voice text telling her where and when. I secretly wanted her there more than I care to admit.

I arrived at Ralph's showroom at 11:30 am. His assistant Valerie greeted me with a smile, walking me through the massive space to a luxurious fitting and lounging area. There was a pedestal, like in films where the bride stands with the three mirrors, two lovely long sofas facing the mirrors, as to look on, and several small tables filled with Beluga Caviar and Ruinart Rose Champagne. There was also a very high rack with two dresses that were covered in custom silk wardrobe bags. I was dying to know why there were two, and what they looked like. I turned to hear the clamor of a few people walking in shortly after I arrived. It was Tory, Ralph, Serena, and Beth. I was completely surprised to see my mother, because she never responded to my message. I said my hellos to my excitable friends, and then to my mother and Ralph. I wanted to speak to Tory for a moment alone, so I excused the two of us, pulling her off to the side of the room.

"Did you get my voice text?" I asked.

"No, I'm sorry, I did get Ralph's call, so I came right over." She replied.

"I'm happy to have you here," I explained my gratitude. Then I tried to find a place to touch her, so I awkwardly placed my hand on her shoulder.

"Let's not get sentimental Allie, you know better, we aren't like that," Tory said, as she pulled away from my hand.

"Of course, we aren't. What was I thinking?" I slapped my hand away from her to show how ridiculous I could be in return.

"Oh Allie, you've always been so damn sensitive. I think it best to join the rest of the room now, don't you?" As she walked away I could hear her giving my friends praise for looking good as she explained to them how pleased she was that they had come. *Why couldn't she be happy for me, or even be nice to me? Why does she hate me so fucking much? It always felt like she never wanted me.*

Turning to Beth, she could see the look on my face, and knowing me so well she signaled for me to come over to her. She told me that she loved me and handed me a fresh glass of Champagne. She always knew what to do. We drank some Champagne while we chatted it up for twenty minutes, then it was time for Ralph to unveil the two dresses. He explained that I needed one dress to be married in and then another to change into so I could dance without constriction at the reception. The first one he had his staff take to a private dressing room and asked for me to follow them. They would put me into the first one and then he would enter the room and do his discussion about the dress between just the two of us. I liked this part, it felt personal, and I felt special. Like clockwork, the dress was slipped on by the pack of women in my fitting room and for the most part, it fit perfectly, except for the waist, where it needed to be taken in, which in a girl's world was not a bad thing. It was a stunning sequin-embellished strapless dress. Not just a strapless dress, but a strapless column gown made of over one million pearlescent sequins that brought a sense of shimmery dimension to the gown. To finish up the look Ralph had made a 25-foot tulle veil completing the magnificent wedding dress.

I walked out of the room minutes after Ralph. He was there to greet and escort me to my pedestal. The girls were howling with joy, and even Tory looked floored by how special this dress was and just how jaw-dropping I looked. It was surreal, the dress, the designer, the best guy in the world, my friends, and also her; Tory.

"I have no words for you, well maybe a few, you look so so

so beautiful Al!" Beth stood by me looking up.

"I couldn't agree more, you are a vision, my dear. You might very well be the most gorgeous bride I have ever seen," Ralph gushed.

"I could not agree more," Tory said. Serena, Beth, and I just giggled, we couldn't believe she chimed in with a compliment. I think she was finally proud of her daughter. I think. It was everything I could have dreamt of, a perfect wedding dress, a pretend mother, and of course my best friends.

The second look for the wedding was completely different. It was a short white dress with a cape built into it. I really found it to be an elegant yet fun number. I could move around in it, dance and eat, yet still be couture and fashion-forward. Everyone agreed with Ralph's choice and I wholeheartedly loved both looks. I knew James was someone involved a little, at least I suspected. I removed the second look and said my goodbyes to Ralph. Tory told Ralph they could drive together and grab lunch. Before she left she pulled me aside.

"I wanted to tell you that I'm really happy for you. I think you're making a solid choice in your life. James will be good for you," Tory stated as she quickly made her exit. That was as close as she could get to me these days. I was all too happy to pick up any breadcrumbs she was throwing today.

To my surprise, Serena brought a change of shirts for the three of us. "Let's make a toast and put these on." Serena threw one at each of us and then grabbed another open bottle of

Champagne and poured it into our glasses to the top. Beth was smiling, so she had to have been in on it. She had handed us a white, very fitted, short-sleeved t-shirt. It had pink fluorescent letters on the front that read, *bachelorette party bitches*.

"Oh my god! You didn't!" I squealed. It was obvious I was being led to a party for me. I had wondered if it were strictly girls or would James and his friends be joining us to make it a double party.

"I'll be right back, I'm going to do a bump," Serena whispered and quickly left the room. "Do you think she'll ever outgrow that shit?" Beth said sarcastically.

"Maybe if she gets pregnant," I joked. We both laughed and agreed that it would be a while before our friend stopped partying like a rockstar and decided to quickly change the subject.

"So, what did she want...Tory?" Seemingly concerned Beth asked.

"I'm not sure, she said I was good with James and that she was happy for me. Bizarre no? I'll take it, if that is her way of being supportive." Smiling, I could remember times when I was just a kid when she would be nice to me, then the next day she ignored me like I was the plague. My grandmother used to say she was just sick, that she couldn't help it. It still hurt me, even now when she didn't acknowledge me, so for me, this was progress.

"I hate to say this, but that woman is as cold as fucking ice, I don't believe a word she says. Be careful, you always get hurt when it comes to your mother." Beth abruptly reminded me of my life. I snapped out of la la land.

"You're so right, what the hell am I thinking? She doesn't have a material bone in her body." Coming to the realization that this was most likely an act for my friends and Mr. Lauren, and that she was a good actor. It wasn't easy, I still wanted her to desperately be a mother. At least I was getting that, sort of, for my wedding.

Serena popped her head out of her bag of coke just in time to join us on our exit.

"Hey ladies! Are…you…ready…for some fun?!" Serena howled.

"Hell yes!" I went up for a high five with my hands.

"Hell fucking yes!" Beth hollered, as she met her hand with mine. We left like the three musketeers, just like we did thousands of other times. I loved them. We would be friends until we died, or at least at the time, I thought so. I didn't know when we left that they had a pack of other girls we went to school with waiting at my neighborhood haunt called Smith and Mills. Again I thought, *what are the odds?* I had just left there the other night with Raph, so I could only pray I wouldn't see him again.

Walking into the bar was like walking into high school, with so many of the same faces, just slightly older with more makeup, and also more designer clothes. Everyone yelled out their different funny comments about this being my last time to party with the ladies, or that I was going to be old and married soon.

It was hysterically funny. I was also handed a sash that said *Getting Married* and a drink with a penis straw.

"Oh no, you didn't!" Serena said, while grabbing the penis straw.

"She probably needs the straw," Beth whispered to me.

"You're terrible Beth Hollingsworth," I winked and then started my hellos to all the gossip girls that attended Sacred Heart Private School for Young Ladies with us in the Upper Eastside. A blonde girl named Charlize handed me a crown that said, *Getting Married to a Rockstar* on it. I thought that was strange, actually, Beth did too.

"Who is she Al, and what's with the rockstar thing?" Beth snickered. I shrugged my shoulders, I had zero idea of who Charlize was and I didn't want to ask the embarrassing question, so I just gave her a hug and thanked her. What else could I do, right?

The party was a blast, all the ladies caught up about their lives after high school. Some of them I knew through college, but most of them faded out like the rumors in the halls of Sacred Heart. My driver used to drop me off there in our Bentley, like all of the other kids with absentee parents they would line up on the long street. It was almost like a who's who when you got there. Even Lady Gaga went to our school, so it was kind of a big deal to be here. One of the positive things about going there was that we had to wear a uniform, which meant everyone in the same outfit, not very fashion forward, well not completely accurate, some like Serena modified the length, but not too much because you would have gotten expelled. I happen to be tall, so naturally, my skirt looked shorter. Nevertheless, it was kind of fun to see all of the girls.

We had a few rounds and it was time for the party to go somewhere else, so they planned a party at a speakeasy in the West Village called Employees Only. This was a spot where you could catch a celebrity partying or some young tech finance guys spending all of their hard-earned Blockchain money. I happened to like it because I knew the owner Kate, and she absolutely adored me. So needless to say, I always got a special table in a corner overlooking the entire scene. Well, everyone kind of had a view, because there were only ten tables that fit six people. The place was dark and red, with high ceilings, opulent chandeliers, velvet banquets, and a hot female DJ called Sky, she was around thirty, and was a former model, she made the place even sexier. Kata, the owner, was forty, half Chinese and half African American, with long braided hair past her ass, and always had a long red dress of some kind. I never saw her with the same dress on, so the girl must have had a lot of red in her closet. Kata would always have a different, younger man with her, sometimes Latino, sometimes black. She was expecting us and had two tables waiting for us, only half the girls joined the second part of the party.

"Miss Allie Hart, one of my favorite people. I'm so thrilled to have all of you gorgeous women here to celebrate." Kata said, pulling me to her with a warm hug and two kisses on my cheeks. I thanked her for her graciousness and waved the girls in to meet accurate, some like Serena modified the length, but not too much because you would have gotten expelled. I happen to be tall, so naturally, my skirt looked shorter. Nevertheless, it was kind of fun to see all of the girls.

We had a few rounds and it was time for the party to go somewhere else, so they planned a party at a speakeasy in the West Village called Employees Only. This was a spot where you could catch a celebrity partying or some young tech finance guys spending all of their hard-earned Blockchain money. I happened to like it because I knew the owner Kate, and she absolutely adored me. So needless to say, I always got a special table in a corner overlooking the entire scene. Well, everyone kind of had a view, because there were only ten tables that fit six people. The place was dark and red, with high ceilings, opulent chandeliers, velvet banquets, and a hot female DJ called Sky, she was around thirty, and was a former model, she made the place even sexier. Kata, the owner, was forty, half Chinese and half African American, with long braided hair past her ass, and always had a long red dress of some kind. I never saw her with the same dress on, so the girl must have had a lot of red in her closet. Kata would always have a different, younger man with her, sometimes Latino, sometimes black. She was expecting us and had two tables waiting for us, only half the girls joined the second part of the party.

"Miss Allie Hart, one of my favorite people. I'm so thrilled to have all of you gorgeous women here to celebrate." Kata said, pulling me to her with a warm hug and two kisses on my cheeks. I thanked her for her graciousness and waved the girls in to meet her. This was going to be a night to remember. I couldn't help but wonder why James hadn't answered my text from earlier. *Hi babe, where are you? Did your friends plan a bachelor party for you, let me know, because I happen to be in the middle of my bachelorette party.* Was he ambushed for his party? Soon the night would unfold, and James would reappear, and damn was it ever going to be a shocking surprise. One that I never forgot, even now it's like it happened yesterday, so fresh in my mind.

We ordered a few bottles of my favorite Tequila, and of course tons of Champagne. The girls rotated so that I got to chat with all of them, and that was fun for a while, till it wasn't. You're probably wondering why it suddenly changed. One word, frenemy. This was a frenemy from high school and her name was Jules. She always had an agenda and today it wasn't any different. My first thought when she got to sit next to me was who invited this bitch to the party. My second thought was to be kind and don't let her get under your skin.

"Hey, wow, Jules… so glad you could make it," I said, barely able to crack a smile.

"Cut the shit Allie, we all know you're not a fan of mine and I'm certainly not a fan of yours!" She said, while basically spitting on me with her words.

"Alrighty then, so why are you here?" Laughing my words out. I poured a big glass of Tequila and drank it down, not affected by her.

"I just came to deliver this address to you. I don't like you, but I don't want this fuck to get away with what he is doing." Jules handed me a piece of paper. How cryptic I thought. *What the hell is this address and why is she the "deliverer" of what appeared to be bad news?*

"Care to elaborate? I'm not actually asking, I'm telling you," staring at her with disdain. "That's why I'm here. As you know I dated James for a minute, so I know that he has secrets. One of them is at that address. No, not just a secret, he'll be there tonight. The rest is on you Allie, whether you choose to believe me or not," she said as a matter of fact and stormed off like the wicked witch. I wanted so badly to pull on her hair as she left, not that I would, but she was just so despicable. She had balls coming here and dumping on my party.

I knew the only person in the room that might have an idea of what this address meant and that was Kata, she was in the now, and knew everything and everyone. I interrupted her conversation and asked her for somewhere we could talk in private. Kata brought me to a small room behind the bar wall where she would sit in her private booth and look at everyone partying through a one-way mirror. She was a voyeur, but also this was her way to get dirty little secrets on paper. I don't think Kata used the secrets she got, but how is anyone ever to really know? I told her about Jules and she instantly perked up. "What is it, Kata, do you know this address?" I questioned her with anticipation.

"Oh yes, I know the place. I used to go there with my ex all the time, but have not been there in over five years," she replied. I begged her to tell me what it was all about, but sometimes I

wish I didn't. Kata described it as a sex den for the elitist of New York City and around the globe. It was a members-only sex party, that took place six times a year in different parts of the world and tonight the party was being held here in a penthouse on Park and 57th. She continued telling me more about it. The clientele had to fit a certain mold, one you had to be extremely wealthy, and two you had to be very beautiful. *"Only the best of the best fuck here."* I'll always remember those words. What to do next was a question that was stirring in my head. I left her when we were interrupted by her flavor of the week.

I returned to the tables and at this point, it was filled up with hot guys as well, no doubt Serena's doing. I loved her energy and was thankful because she was bigger than life, which meant she could make everyone smile, even me.

"Hey why the long face? I got exactly what you need! Take this!" Pushing a small pill into my mouth, I didn't fight her on it. I wanted to feel good.

"What was that you naughty girl?" I asked.

Beth chimed in to answer, "It's fucking Molly… and I did it too Al!" She was clearly euphoric and letting loose. For Beth, this was a rarity, and the drugs part, for me too, other than my daily Adderall.

"This is exactly what I need ladies!" I yelled out. Which made the whole table scream out like they were at a rock concert. Now the party was getting turned up. I forgot about James for the time being and danced with my girls. I wasn't even sure at this point if I could believe a person like Jules anyway.

"I have a little gift for you!" Serena boasted as she handed me a small gift bag.

"Ok hand it over!" Grabbing the bag I laughed. Inside was a little black, Pulp Fiction sort of wig, a paddle, a small masquerade mask, and a full outfit; corset, stockings, leather boy shorts, and way-high hooker heels with a long black silk jacket that went to the floor. Serena begged me to try it on. I felt sexy from the Ecstasy, so I decided to do exactly that. I asked Serena to help me and she was all too excited to do so. Explaining in the bathroom what had happened with Jules, I showed her the address. I also told her about my conversation with Kata. Before I knew it, I was in the bathroom and in front of the mirror with Serena encouraging me to go to the uptown party. My first thought was to go, but why? I was high as fuck, and I was engaged. *But what if he's really there? I have to know.*

Returning to the room, everyone howled at my new look. I was told I didn't look like me, so I fantasy-played and became someone else. I explained in a British accent that my new name for the night would be Victoria. I then turned to Kata once again. At first, she didn't recognize me, which was a good thing. I didn't know the logistics, but I wanted to go to this party, and I was sure Kata could make it happen.

"Let me guess, the party," Kata grinned.

"Yes, please help me get in," I begged.

"But of course my little sex kitten. After all, you're all

dressed up and you definitely have somewhere to go." She agreed to call and quickly got on the phone. I could hear her speaking to a man, but I wasn't sure what he was saying on the other end. I just heard her saying yes and no. Kata hung up after what seemed like forever, in real time it was probably all of ten minutes. At this point my body was vibrating, the drug was making me horny.

She explained a bit about the procedure at the door and said to ask for Jamie.

"Please don't share this with anyone." I pleaded.

"No, I would never. I'm a girl you can trust with a baby," Kata devilishly laughed. I knew that was a lie, but I also knew she would only use this against me if she had to, and I would never give her a reason to do that. I told my besties where I was going and they were completely supportive, I think mostly because both of them were high and lip locked with some smokin' hot boys.

CHAPTER 27

The Final Countdown

Part II

I jumped into a black Escalade and headed uptown. Looking back I should have been nervous, but I wasn't. I also should have been hesitant, but I wasn't either. Instead, I laid my head back and fantasized about what it would be like. My head was buzzing from the drinks and Molly, but just enough to be aware of myself and what I was doing. I didn't know what I wanted entirely, but I think seeing James would give me my answers. The address was 452 Park Avenue. This was the tallest and one of the most exclusive residential buildings in Manhattan. I didn't know the floor because Kata didn't tell me, she just said to talk to Jamie at the door. I did just that, I asked for Jamie.

"You're speaking to him. You must be here for the Penthouse?" He asked.

"What gave it away?" I asked.

"The mask madam," he smiled.

"Yes, of course," I laughed. He explained to me that it was on the 85th floor, *"the top floor"* and that there was a private elevator that he would take me up in, but only after he checked out my credentials. This Penthouse was owned by a prince that I knew, but I couldn't recall who he was and from what country. I handed him my license, you would have thought he saw a ghost.

I guess he knew who I was, but I thought that was odd because he must come across all sorts of famous people or recognizable names in this line of work. I didn't know at the time, but he knew something I didn't.

I entered the elevator suddenly, a bit nervous. I was walking into a place full of powerful, rich, and globally influential people. When I stepped off, I couldn't help it, my mouth was wide open. I closed it immediately and walked out. A tall woman with just a small yellow feather covering her vagina greeted me, she was also wearing a feather mask that matched. I see why they said wealthy and beautiful because all of the women were stunning and only half the men were, which meant all of the men were wealthy. I had wondered how many of us girls actually had money here. I was getting the feeling this was a party that catered to the boys. I half smiled while I strolled through with the woman. She brought me to a small bar where she muddled two orange slices, and poured me a double of Clase Azul Tequila over one ice ball. *How did she know what or how to make my drink?* I didn't ask, I just enjoyed it.

I strutted around the room slowly to check out all of the players. It was a very ostentatious room, full of blingy chandeliers and gold everywhere, even the walls had gold. The rugs on the white marble floor were of "almost" extinct animals. The furniture looked like something you would see in a Sultan's Palace. The room was extremely big, I was guessing around 4,000 square feet. I could barely see people in the room, the lighting was low and there were candelabras everywhere. There were approximately one hundred people in the room. The men dressed in tuxedos and the women in lingerie, or gowns. There were naked ladies that appeared to be hosts of some sort, as they walked around with diamond-encrusted briefcases tantalizing the guests with interiors filled with pills and cocaine. It was wildly perfect with the French lounge music in the background. I had never seen anything so luxurious, so rich, so everything. My heart raced in excitement and fear.

I brushed a man's arm as I passed him, which caused a reaction.

"Hello, my dear. Please if you are going to flirt with me, you should at least talk for a minute, no? A handsome face, or what I could see of it, I imagined he was around fifty, full head of black hair, well built, a beautiful smile, and approximately 6'1".

"Hello to you, kind sir. It would be my pleasure to talk to you," I said with my fake British accent.

"Please sit with me, you're so sexy." The man grabbed my hand, and I let him pull me to a black velvet sofa.

"I can see you are very handsome, even with the mask on," I flirted back with him. He took liberties and placed his hand on my shoulder. I didn't know until she was in front of me. A young, blonde, naked girl stood at my feet.

"Please, I will store your outer layer." I knew right away she was talking about the silk jacket I had on. I gave it to her.

"You had her come over, didn't you?" I shyly asked.

"Yes I did." He paused and continued, "You've never been to

this party have you?" The stranger knew, but how I thought.

"What makes you think that?" I naively asked.

"I would have never forgotten those lips and that tiny, ever so little scar… your mouth is absolutely divine," he said with deep hunger in his voice. It made my privates tingle. I was getting turned on by just his voice.

It was dark, but not dark enough that you couldn't see the room and some of what was taking place. I could clearly see a woman practicing fellatio on a man only ten feet away from me. I have to say, it was marvelous. The stranger's hand never left my thigh as he explained the party in detail. He told me that there were many bedrooms, some for watching one couple at a time and others where there were many joining in.

"Shall we make up names?" He asked.

"Yes, my name is Victoria. What is your name, handsome devil?" I asked.

"You can call me Lion," he said, as he moved his hand to the outside of my panties. He could clearly feel my wetness as he brushed the outside. Lion moved away from my box, I think he just wanted to know if I was moist to touch. I didn't stop him, I enjoyed it for the time being, but I thought I needed to explore on my own, after all, why not see what else the room has to offer? I decided to be brave and get up.

"Well Lion, I will see you around. I'm going to take a stroll. Goodbye." I twirled around to see what was in the opposite direction. As I left I could hear him say that I was breaking his heart. It made me smile.

Walking around the vast room I got the front row to some sexy shit. There was a beautiful playboy look-alike in front of me with a woman in a gown kissing while a man licked the playboy's breasts. I assumed the playboy was alone and the couple were together enjoying their meal. I looked to the right and saw two men kissing and then turning their mouths to a woman. I also loved this, so avant-garde I thought. My mind wandered back to James, *what would I do if I saw him here?* When I arrived at the other side I realized I was in a massive hall with doors along it. I could see there were more of these women that worked the room with the feathers, one approached me.

"Victoria, please follow me. I'll guide you through." As the beauty handed me a fresh drink. I realized it wasn't a question, it was more of the way things went. The people throwing this soiree were very powerful, you could sense it.

The first room I walked into was full of sex, an orgy was happening. There was a double, King size bed in the middle of the room, half moon, bar top tables surrounding it on both sides. It was clearly for voyeurs to watch their spectacles and a place for their drinks. There were multiple girls standing around waiting for a sign that you wanted to join. They were there to hang your clothes. I opted for a peek. I threw back my drink and before I sat it down the blonde was back to hand me another. I was beyond tipsy and feeling uninhibited. I stood there with the three-inch barrier between me and that bed feeling vulnerable. I didn't move though, I just watched. I was hot and bothered, I wanted it, not this, but something called to me. I knew I wanted to move on to the next room.

Escorted again to the second door. There I found a room with a stage inside, this one had two women together using strap-ons on one another and a man kneeling on the floor, licking whatever he could. He was dressed in leather from head to toe and his mask covered his entire face except for his mouth and nostrils. The women were naked except for their tiny leather, Catwoman headpieces. There was a man sitting in the corner jerking off as a woman licked his balls and on the other side there was a very young man licking an older woman's box. Scattered were others touching and kissing. I again got hot while watching. I remembered my girl experience and now wanted more. I imagined that girl on the stage fucking and sucking me. But there was one last door, I had to see inside.

Entering this room was different. It was a no-noise room, which meant zero talking or moaning. The room was entirely black, only very faint, small lights guided you on the floor to move around the space. The girl handling me explained this was "the" game room.

"What do you mean? What is the game room about?" I whispered in her ear.

"It is where the host of the party gets to pick two people and place them in the center of the room. They must participate in this game or never return." She stated it like she had done it a thousand times. I wasn't thinking, I was only anticipating the live show of two strangers fucking. Why did I care who would "never" return, as if it were so detrimental to their existence or mine for that matter.

I waited quietly with the full room of spectators, something like the people of the Roman days waiting for the slaughter of two men willing to kill. Someone tapped me on the shoulder, breaking the verbal rule, and whispered to me, "You are it... this is a gift from me to you," the stranger said. I knew the voice from somewhere or at least my drunk self thought she recognized it. But maybe I was delusional, she could have been a character from a movie for all I know. I whispered back, "What... why me? I don't understand." I felt like I was walking in someone else's body as she guided me to an unknown place to wait. The beautiful stranger kept my mask on, but also covered it with another. I couldn't see, my blood was racing through my veins, and I was frightened, yet I didn't make it stop. I wanted to know who was going to be in the arena with me. I couldn't fight my desire, I needed to stay.

I felt sets of hands helping me walk to the center. Someone in the group told me not to remove my mask until I heard music. I waited in silence, for what seemed like an eternity, my heart ready to pounce out of my chest, yet I knew in my mind it was only twenty minutes. Every few minutes someone came in to take another piece of my clothing off. First, it was my shoes, then my thigh highs, next my skirt, then my corset, and lastly my thong. I stood in the room not knowing anything, except for the fact that people were looking at me naked and I was absolutely turned on by this overwhelming desire to be watched and to be taken.

A person came from behind me and removed the black covering and now I only had a mask and my wig on. I could not see any of their faces, as it was completely dark except for the tiny lights outside of the circle I was in that illuminated me just enough. I felt a body push against mine. It was a man. I naturally put my hands on him and worked my way around to feel him face-to-face, but didn't want to open my eyes just yet. This was taking me to another level, I just wanted to do more, to feel things I had never felt. The molly had electricity shooting through my body, heightening the touch and experience a million times fold. The stranger placed his hand on my wet privates and rubbed ever so lightly, the sensation was beyond ecstasy. I still couldn't see him, but I wanted my lips on his regardless. I kissed him, he turned one back roughly. I didn't like it, but yet I did. I opened my eyes and backed away. I couldn't see all of him, but I did see his familiar body art. It was James. I felt relieved for some reason, possibly because I was about to be with him here, but then a wave of fear and sickness rushed through my body. I was confused. I heard people surrounding me, moving me again to what felt like a narrow table. They laid me down and then he was on top of me. He was so hard, so big, as he pushed my weak thighs apart. I lay there not fighting it, not denying my desire to let him take me. Did he know it was with his fiancé?

He entered me slowly as if to feel every inch of the way. I wanted to scream out, but I could not. Just as gently as he went in, he thrust hard and deep. Again I wanted to call out in agony from the pleasure, but I did not. Then there were hands everywhere pushing us into one another, falling to the ground, while the others touched us furiously until they were gone. We had found our way back to one another. It was a relief. I needed him to save me from their hands, we were in this sexual dream together and now we were in a strange, volatile way connected. The lights around the two of us went up slightly. At first, I didn't know my way around the small space we were in, but then my eyes quickly got adjusted. I could see the spectators taking off what appeared to be night goggles. We were the act all along.

Next was exhilarating. I needed him, I went for his lips and he kissed me, kissed me like he had done a million times. I pulled back and fell to the ground, I needed a second to compose myself. I looked up at his hard cock and beautiful body. *Full of tattoos, full of tattoos....* it couldn't be. It's my man. My fiancé. The light confirmed my delusion. I was confused, high on Molly, and drunk, yet still able to know that I loved this, all of it, including the shock of James, being the man I am fucking. It seemed wrong and so right if I could do this and not think. Something inside of me liked the possibility of him not knowing that it was me, yet the other part was completely and utterly disgusted. I wanted to feel just sickened, yet another side was intoxicated by what was happening and that was the side that had control over me. I pulled him to the ground and laid him on his back. Mounting him as I slid down his beautiful rod. He put his hands on my ass lifting me up and down onto his glistening cock. I loved it so fucking much as every fiber in my body tingled with pleasure, I desperately wanted to scream at the top of my lungs, but words were forbidden and something in me loved the torturous silence. Riding him over and over, bucking like I was on a horse, while my juices dripped down his balls. I could feel his cock pulsating, and I knew this man, he wanted to cum. So instead he stopped me abruptly. This was my exit, I pulled myself off of him, but he was seemingly hungry for more. Grabbing my arm harshly as if he owned me, he threw me on my back, as I tried to sit up he pushed me down by my stomach and made his way down to my pussy. He ate me without even knowing it was his future wife. I just let him go at it. He used his fingers just like he did to me in our bed. I loved it and I hated it, but I never stopped it, I couldn't. He kept at it, fingering me and flicking my hard, swollen clit till I couldn't hold on. I didn't make a sound the entire time and this wasn't going to change. I just held his head tight so as not to move far from my orgasm. I came and came over and over again. He knew it because my body convulsed and my clit was engorged. I lay limp as he mounted me. Thrusting hard, there was no love in this. Pounding away he desperately wanted to cum and he did, ripping a condom off he released all over my tits and face.

I was disgusted only minutes after what happened. I was confused and drunk, in a haze, I gathered my clothes and I scurried away to find a bathroom. I was once again greeted not seconds after I got up by the beautiful blonde. She guided me to a private bathroom away from it all. I thanked her for her assistance, and she told me not to worry, you aren't here.

"What do you mean, I'm not here?" I asked.

"Everyone here is not really here, privacy is sworn by members, you have nothing to be concerned about," she explained. "I will wait just outside for you, here are your clothes." The blonde exited. I felt relief in her words, but not from my actions. I, at least knew that I might find him here, I wasn't a member of this secret society, until now that is. My mind was racing with madness, I began to cry and fell to the floor. *Is this over between us?* I didn't know him, hell I didn't even know myself. *How the fuck could I continue with a wedding? How could I go on with this charade?* I left with an escort putting me into a blacked-out Mercedes outside of the building. Before the door closed, the man said that I was welcome back anytime and that a representative would be in touch. I was numb now, I didn't feel anything, I just wanted to shower and go to bed. James was supposed to stay at his place, so I could have a night to sleep and then wake to examine everything I did in the morning. *On second thought.* I asked the driver to turn around and drop me at James's address. I knew he wasn't there yet, because I left him at the party.

I walked in, and the first thing I saw was an engagement photo of us from the New York Times framed, I smiled and then began to cry. *What have I done? Why did I go to the event?* I should have stayed away, then I wouldn't be in this situation. I loved him, and I wanted to be married to him, but now? How? *How could I be with him?* I knew what I had to do. I wrote him a note.

James,

I love you, but I won't marry you. I know where you were last night, I know. My heart is breaking for us. Please don't try to contact me. Goodbye.

Allie

I placed my engagement ring on the paper and left it on his laptop. I knew he would see it in the morning while he had his coffee. I went home, took a shower, packed a bag, and called a car. I took one long look at my apartment, knowing that I may not be back for a while, it made me sad, but I had to get out of here and now. I got into a blacked-out Escalade and rang my concierge service. *I need a one-way ticket to London.*

Acknowledgements

This may seem unorthodox to do, but I've been known to go against the grain, so why change now? I would like to express my deepest appreciation to myself for being even stronger than I thought I could be. 2023 was a colossal mental and physical challenge to me. I had a lot of twists and hard turns to contend with in order to get myself back to who I am; healthy and worthy. I went through some of the hardest moments in my personal life, but I wouldn't change a thing, because I truly believe everything happens for a reason, and everything that we have to endure, in the end, can make us courageous and triumphant. I'm going into 2024 in the vortex, feeling amazing and whole. My zest for life and pure light surrounds me and is going to serve me well in my phenomenally celebrated life. I've come to the realisation, once again, that I have a purpose in my wondrous existence and feel a massive shift driving me towards the next chapter, so to speak. For that I am so very abundantly grateful. I am an empowered woman with purpose once again.

I would also like to express my heartfelt gratitude to my friends Caroline Alexa McBride, Steven Lyon, Rupal Vanmali, Daniela London, and Lee Tal. Thank you for listening to me without judgement when I didn't even want to hear myself talk. Every one of you has such beauty, talent, and hardships, yet you take moments out of your life to stop and offer me uplifting words of encouragement. My true confidants when I was confused and hurting. You've helped me through 2023 with some extremely pivotal decisions in my work and personal life. For that I will forever be in your debt. My only hope is that I do the same for you throughout our lives.

Who would I be if I didn't include the clan? Thank you to my siblings; Jenny, Julie, and Brady. Also, to my Mom, you may be perfectly flawed, but I am grateful for the strength that you bestowed upon me. Growing up fast wasn't easy, but nothing is … is it?

One thing I remember my mom Rory saying was, "Don't be boring." No one could ever accuse me of that.

About the Author

Hallie Hart is a prominent international artist, writer, and documentary film maker from New York City. She has exhibited her paintings in over twelve countries and is a part of the permanent collection in the prestigious Museo del Parco museum in Portofino, Italy. Hart opened her US Flag retrospect titled 'Unity' in her House of Hart gallery in Aspen during the pandemic to share a humanitarian message. Catching national news, 'Unity' became a public art event in May 2021, touring the United States, displaying her flags for all Americans.

Hart graduated from the University of Pennsylvania with a MA in English Literature. Her passion for creative writing spans decades, yet was never revealed until now. Hart currently finds herself deeply engaged in the canon of Erotic romance. In her second novel *Unzipped Twenty-One*, she brings the reader on a journey of a young women's newfound feminine power and the freedom that comes with it. . A literary joyride filled with lust, love, opulence, celebrity, and fashion. Hart describes *Unzipped* as 'half-fiction' and says the books are based around her life.

Hart currently resides between the United States and Belgium.

Follow Hallie for *Unzipped* updates:

Instagram: @unzipped_official
Twitter: @unzipped_book
TikTok: @unzipped_official

"The *Unzipped* series by Hallie Hart is an absolute must-read for any discerning female. Juicy, seductive, and completely compelling, you can't put them down. Hart shows insight into her incredible international life through her modeling career, and the lusty males barking at her door. Learning through her alcoholic and drug-addled mother and her life growing up in Manhattan, and on the French Riviera. Prepare to learn a few things!"

Lucia Gillot, Staff Writer SPIN, European Editor WONDERLUST, New York Metropolitan Magazine, Yahoo, AOL